Fortune's Favors

Fortune's Favors

Nyx Fortuna: Book Three

MARLENE PEREZ

www.orbitbooks.net

Copyright © 2014 by Marlene Perez
Excerpt from *Charming* copyright © 2013 by Elliott James
Cover design by Wendy Chan, cover illustration © Shutterstock.
Cover copyright © 2014 by Hachette Book Group, Inc.

Orbit
Hachette Book Group
237 Park Avenue
New York, NY 10017
www.orbitbooks.net
www.orbitshortfiction.com

Originally published as an e-book by Orbit Books
First print on demand edition: August 2014

Orbit is an imprint of Hachette Book Group.
The Orbit name and logo are trademarks of Little, Brown Book Group Limited.

The publisher is not responsible for websites (or their content) that are not owned by the publisher.

ISBN: 978-0-316-33469-3

Printed in the United States of America

With much love to the big and little Ms

Acknowledgments

Thanks to Lindsey, Laura, Alex, Ellen, Susan, and Devi at Orbit and to everyone at Foundry Literary + Media, especially my agent Stephen Barbara.

Contents

Contents

I shall seize Fate by the throat.

—Beethoven

Chapter One

Mortality was overrated. I'd wanted to be able to die for over two hundred years, but when I finally did, someone had brought me back. Instead of facing death, I was tucked into bed in my apartment above the Eternity Road Pawn Shop. I wanted to know who and why, but first I had to stop throwing up.

I leaned over and heaved into a conveniently placed bucket.

"You're awake," Talbot observed. My best friend had dragged a chair from the living room and had apparently slept in it. Talbot didn't look like his usual immaculate self. His auburn hair, normally tortured into submission with high-end hair products, was a jungle of tangled curls. There was a pungent odor in the room, a hint of unwashed body, but that was probably me. I resisted the urge to sniff my armpits.

"How long have I been out?" I felt like someone had beaten me with a bag of rusty nails. I was shivering, sweaty. The blue walls of my bedroom reassured me that I was safe, at least for the time being.

"Two days," he answered flatly.

"Where's my jacket?" The events of the past few days came flooding back. I'd made a deal with Hecate and she'd screwed me over, which was why I was in my current condition. It felt worse than any hangover I'd experienced.

I'd strangle Wren with my bare hands if she'd taken the jacket. Or my mother's charms. My hand went to my neck, but the silver chain was still there. She'd taken what she needed, Hecate's Eye, right before she stabbed me.

I felt more like myself once Talbot helped me slip on my World War II fighter pilot jacket.

"Any word on where Hecate is?"

He shook his head. "It's been quiet. Too quiet."

It had been forty-eight hours since I'd set Hecate free and she'd double-crossed me. In my defense, I had been desperate to save Willow.

"Willow?" I managed to ask. She'd been possessed by Hecate. Danvers had sacrificed his own wife as a vessel for the goddess he served. I was praying that she still needed her or the naiad would already be dead.

He shrugged helplessly.

"What about Naomi?" My cousin was the only person in the Wyrd family I cared about.

"She was safe, last I heard," Talbot said. He was trying and failing to sound casual. He'd been in love with my cousin practically since they met. I'd thought she felt the same way.

To avoid my eyes, he crossed to the window and opened the shades. Late afternoon sunlight flooded the room and I put up my hand to shield my eyes.

He adjusted the shades so only a trickle of light shone through.

2

"Last you heard? What does that mean?" Dating a Fate couldn't have been easy, but Talbot was devoted to my cousin. If they'd broken up, it was probably my fault.

Before Talbot could reply, Ambrose appeared in the doorway. He was a big man, with a wolfish grin that was noticeably absent. He looked grimmer than I'd ever seen him. "It's started. We have to go."

I nabbed a flask and filled it with a little of the green fairy. Ambrose and Talbot exchanged looks, but didn't say anything. Strangers often didn't realize the two of them were father and son, but their exasperated expressions were identical.

We headed out of downtown Minneapolis in the Eternity Road van. Ambrose gripped the steering wheel tightly as he drove.

He turned suddenly and a sign caught my eye.

"We're going to a park?" I asked, but Ambrose didn't comment.

Ambrose turned into a long driveway and parked in front of a sign that read PAN CONFERENCE CENTER.

"That means we're here," Ambrose announced, but he didn't sound particularly happy about it.

"Emergency pawnshop retreat?" I joked, but it still hurt to breathe, so I avoided any more smart-assed comments.

He gave me a grave look. "Be prepared."

Black flies buzzed above our heads as we walked. Another sign, this one reading ASPEN ROOM. I flinched when I remembered the naiad Hecate had killed in her attempt to escape the underworld.

The door to the Aspen room was ajar, letting out the putrid odors of decaying flesh, something like rotten eggs, congealed blood, and sour milk.

There was a long table in the center of the room and a fire burned in the stone fireplace. The rotten-egg smell was identified by the picnic lunch slowly spoiling in the summer heat. Against one wall, piled high like logs for a fire, were bodies. So many bodies.

There was a strange plonking noise. "Is it raining?" But the source of the sound was the large galvanized tub in one corner of the room. Something was hanging directly above the tub, fastened to the oak beam by a rope.

It was a forest nymph and blood and honey dripped from her body in equal parts. There was a low hum in my ears and I thought I might faint, but I realized it was the mournful sound of honeybees that had gathered around her broken body.

The walls dripped with blood and vomit and other substances I couldn't identify. I tried not to gag as I surveyed the scene. It was something out of the nightmares I'd had as a child, stealing into my sleep. The sight of blood could bring me back to that time like nothing else. I battled the urge to flee.

Ambrose was stoic, but Talbot's skin had a green cast. He rushed outside and then we heard the unmistakable sounds of his retching.

Tria Prima symbols were smeared onto the once white walls. Hecate's own brand of graffiti.

"It looks like she took a bath in their blood," I commented. I had set a monster loose upon the world.

"Bathing in the blood of her enemies was her trademark in the old days," Ambrose replied. "Hecate draws power from it."

"So she chose these people from the House of Zeus randomly?"

He shook his head. "Never randomly. She's sending us a message."

"I got the message when Wren stabbed me."

"That was just a love tap compared to what Hecate has planned," Talbot said from the doorway.

"What message, anyway?" I asked. "I don't know any of these people. I'm not from this House." Why had Hecate started here instead of attacking the House of Fates?

She thought she'd killed me, the sole member of the House of Fortune, but my aunts were still alive. At least I thought they were. The Fates had defeated Hecate once before, but they'd been at full-strength then. Long ago, the Fates took Hecate's items of power and imprisoned her in the underworld. Hecate had never forgiven them.

We'd managed to determine that the victims were all members of the House of Zeus. Three brothers, the gods Poseidon, Hades, and Zeus, had divided the world into three. Poseidon had taken the sea, Zeus the sky, and Hades got stuck with the underworld. Eventually, the magical world divided into four Houses: the House of Zeus, the House of Poseidon, the House of Hades, and the one that everyone feared, the House of Fates, which was my family House.

"She's declaring war on the world," Ambrose said. "These are her first casualties."

"Yeah, but why all the fuss?" I asked.

Talbot winced and then shot me a dirty look. "Show a little respect for the dead."

"I meant, why hasn't she let loose the full force of her power?"

Ambrose stared at me. "I think this is quite bad enough without asking for trouble," he said.

"I think Hecate doesn't have all her power back," I explained.

"But she has the bead," Talbot said.

The bead of power I'd practically handed to her on a fucking platter, because I'd been thinking with the wrong part of my anatomy.

"Then why hasn't she released Willow?" I didn't want to think about what Danvers would do to her once he'd recovered.

Ambrose looked at his shoes. He didn't want to tell me Willow was most likely dead.

"She's not dead," I said. "She can't be."

Ambrose put a hand on my shoulder. "Let's hope you're right."

"What should we do with the bodies?" Talbot asked.

"I'll make a call," Ambrose said. "The House will send someone to identify the victims."

"The sooner we get out of here, the better," Talbot said.

I agreed. It wasn't a night to linger among the dead.

"Shh!" Ambrose put a finger to his lips. "I hear something."

Silence. And then, a small moan.

"Someone's alive," Talbot said. "Over there."

We ran toward the faint sound. A satyr lay on the ground, almost obscured beneath a pile of dead bodies. We pulled him out of his grisly prison. He had been blinded and blood still dripped from his mutilated eyes, but he was alive.

"Jesus," Talbot exhaled.

"We should have checked," I said.

"There were so many victims," Ambrose replied.

I tried to do a healing spell, but the satyr shook his head. "First I must deliver a message to the son of Fortuna," he said.

The message had already been received. Hecate had just declared war.

"I'm here," I said.

"The world will burn and you will not be able to stop her," he said before he passed out.

"Is he still breathing?" Talbot asked.

I checked. "Yes, but he needs more help than I can give him. We need Doc."

"Doc won't come," Ambrose said, "but Trey is on his way."

"Trey Marin?" I stiffened. Willow's uncle had let her marry that psycho Danvers.

"I know you don't like him," Ambrose said. "But we have to get the Houses to unite if we have any chance of defeating Hecate."

Trey was the head of the House of Poseidon, which meant I'd have to tolerate him.

I had assumed that getting the Houses to unite against Hecate would be the easy part. Apparently, I was wrong.

"There's something else," Talbot said. "Something's missing."

"Like what?"

"That satyr is missing a limb," he pointed out. "And half the bodies looked like something gnawed on them."

"Or some*one*," I said.

"Baxter?" Talbot suggested. "You think Hecate kidnapped him for this?"

"Baxter Lamos hasn't harmed a living thing in over five hundred years," Ambrose said.

"He may not have had a choice. Hecate can be very persuasive," I said.

The blinded satyr died before Trey arrived. Willow's uncle brought two assistants, who carried shovels. Trey's sun-bleached hair held more gray than the last time I'd seen him. He still held himself with the precise posture of a soldier, but his blue eyes were weary.

"Still no sign of Baxter?" I asked him. The flesh eater had been Trey's go-to guy for cleanups like this one.

He shook his head. "He's probably dead by now," he said flatly. "If Hecate took him, she did it for a reason."

There was a copse of trees about a hundred yards from the conference center. We dragged the bodies there and started to work.

"Nyx, you should rest," Ambrose said. "You're bleeding again."

Despite the warm summer night, I was shivering, but I refused to stop. "No rest until they're all buried."

"At least use a healing amulet," Talbot said. "Here, try this." He handed me a tiny blue crystal and watched me until I'd said the words.

"Can we get back to work now?"

He nodded and returned to digging.

When we finished burying the bodies, the sky was the color of clay. I stretched and yawned.

Trey held out a hand. "Good work tonight, Nyx."

I didn't take his hand. "My hands are bloody."

"Mine, too," he said. His hands were immaculate, but I understood his meaning. We both had blood on our hands.

"Ambrose, I'll be in touch with the heads of the other Houses," Trey said. "I am hoping we can work together to defeat the goddess."

Funny, he didn't sound very hopeful.

I fell asleep on the way back to Minneapolis, but my slumber was full of dark dreams, shadowy figures, and the sound of baying hounds.

I woke to catch the last bit of news on the radio. Dogs in animal shelters all over the county had chewed or clawed their paws bloody to get out of their pens.

"Hecate," Ambrose said before he reached over and turned off the radio. Nobody said anything else the rest of the way home.

Chapter Two

By the time we reached Eternity Road, I could barely hold my head up and the bandage at my throat was spotted with blood.

Talbot and his father lived in the other apartment above the pawnshop. Instead of going to his place across the hall, Talbot followed me home.

"I don't need a babysitter," I said.

But he was stubborn. "I'm not leaving you alone," he said. "You almost died."

I reached into the fridge for a couple of beers. "Suit yourself."

I tried to hand him a bottle, but he waved it away. "One of us should stay sober."

I was halfway through my first beer when there was a knock at the door. I reached for my athame.

"Who is it?" Talbot called out.

"It's Doc."

Talbot and I stared at each other. Doc, the mysterious man with the scarred face. He was the last person I expected. Talbot let him in and Doc skittered his way into my apartment.

It was summer, but he still wore his ratty trench coat. Doc spent a lot of time on the streets and the coat looked like he often used it as a blanket.

"How's the patient?" Doc asked.

"As much of a pain in the ass as always," Talbot said, but there was affection in his voice.

"He should be in bed," Doc scolded.

"Will you two quit talking about me like I'm not even here?"

"You'll never heal if you drink yourself silly," he scolded.

I studied him. There was a little more salt and less pepper to his graying hair than when I first met him. The left side of his face was scarred, but he was still handsome. I didn't see a resemblance. Deci had told me Doc was my father, right before I killed her, but it was possible she had lied. It was also possible she'd told me the truth.

"Doc, we need to talk." I had a few hundred questions for him, but I'd settle for learning the most important one.

Talbot took a look at my face. "I just remembered, I need to ask my dad...something." He left, but I was sure he'd be back to check on me.

Doc shifted uneasily, but stayed put.

"Are you a necromancer?"

Long pause. "Yes."

"Are you the one who called me back from death?"

Another one. "Yes."

"Are you my father?" I asked.

Long, *uncomfortable* pause this time. He looked at the door like he wanted to leap through it, but settled for the jittery tapping of his foot that was his constant habit.

"If you have to think about it, then I guess the answer is no." Silence. "It *isn't* a no?"

"Not much of a father, am I?"

"Honestly, no. At first, I thought Ambrose might be my father, but then I realized he was too decent to abandon us." My mother's words rang in my brain: "Please do not have any illusions about that man. Believe me, he would kill us as soon as help us."

"You hoped it was Ambrose," Doc said softly.

He was right. "Yes."

"You had no suspicion I was your father?"

"Hell, no," I answered him.

"I had no intention of ever telling you," he replied.

"What changed your mind?"

"Your eyes," he said. "They're just like hers."

"I know."

"I had Fortune's favor," Doc said. "And I threw it away." His habitual agitation grew worse. He touched his scarred cheek repeatedly as he stared at the door. He was going to bolt.

It was hard to believe we shared the same blood. The thought reminded me of something. Wren had taken some of my blood after she cut my throat.

"Any reason Hecate would want my blood?"

His gaze sharpened. "Why do you ask?"

"I just remembered that she had Danvers collect my blood after Wren…after Wren slit my throat."

He frowned. "There is magic in your blood," he said. "Stronger than most. You need to be careful."

"You missed my childhood by a few hundred years," I snapped. "So quit treating me like a child."

"Then quit acting like one."

Something in his face made me take a deep breath. My father was skittish at the best of times, and this was definitely not one of those times. He'd clam up if I pushed too hard. "I'm sorry. I spent the night burying Hecate's latest victims," I said.

"Death takes a toll on your soul," he replied.

"Isn't that what being a necromancer is all about? Death?"

"Exactly," he said.

I went to the fridge and grabbed another beer. When I turned around, he was gone.

"I wish he'd quit doing that," I muttered.

Talbot opened my front door a few minutes after Doc left. "Is it safe to come in?" he asked from the doorway.

"He's gone," I said.

"That's not what I meant."

"I know," I said. "Want a beer?"

"Nyx, it's breakfast time."

"Breakfast of champions." At his prissy look, I added, "I could use the company."

We sat in the living room in silence for a few minutes, until the entire conversation I'd had with Doc poured out of me.

"That's rough," Talbot said when I finished. "Do you think Dad knew that Doc is your dad?"

"Yes." Ambrose was Doc's only friend.

"He is just chock-full of secrets," Talbot said, but he didn't elaborate and I didn't ask.

I didn't want to talk about my deadbeat dad any longer. "The Book of Fates is missing."

"Maybe the Fates took it," he said.

"It's a possibility," I replied. "They weren't thrilled with the idea of me being the keeper of all the secrets, anyway."

My head ached. Talbot was bug-eyed from lack of sleep. We were both too tired to think clearly.

"We should try to catch a few hours of sleep," I said. I tossed him a blanket and retreated to my room.

I looked for the Book of Fates. It was supposed to hold all my aunts' secrets, but it was gone.

The Book of Fates was the Custos's responsibility. Deci had passed the title on to me when she died, but what happened when I died? I'd only been dead for a little while and I hadn't transferred the book like Deci had transferred it to me.

Had Wren taken the Book of Fates, too? Or did Morta take it back into her icy bosom? I hadn't wanted to be the Custos, but a peek at how they'd trapped Hecate would have been useful right now. She'd kill more people, unless I found a way to stop her.

I couldn't sleep. The faces of the people I'd buried wouldn't let me.

Chapter Three

I awoke to the sound of Talbot banging on my bedroom door. "Nyx, I know you're in there," he yelled.

"I'm coming," I said. I opened the door with a theatrical flourish. "Give me a minute."

"Someone has to make sure you don't drink yourself into a coma."

I ignored him. I'd cut down on my drinking. Mostly.

"Let's go to Hell's Belles. There's no food in my apartment and I'm starving," I said.

"What you really mean is you're out of absinthe." There was a definite tone in his voice.

"I just want some food. And to check in on Bernie." Bernie ran Hell's Belles for the aunties, but she was also a demon who had contacts in the underworld. If she didn't know where Hecate was, nobody would.

"Okay," he replied. "If you can manage to hold off on drinking. At least until after lunch."

"Quit with the lectures," I said. I'd stock up on liquor later, without him. I grabbed my athame and jacket and we walked to Hell's Belles.

Before we made it more than two blocks, a mage blocked my path. "Son of Fortuna?"

"Yes?"

He spit in my face. "I wish you'd never come to Minneapolis," he said, before crossing the street.

"Hey, buddy, wait a minute," Talbot said. He started after the guy, but I shook my head. I couldn't speak because shame clogged my throat.

At the restaurant, I grabbed a napkin from the dispenser and wiped the spit from my face.

Normally, people fought hard to get a seat at Hell's Belles. They made the best food in town. Today, it was empty, except for a couple of mortal kids who'd obviously pulled an all-nighter and a Korrigan from the House of Hades. The Korrigan's short stature drew snickers from the drunken college students.

We grabbed a booth near them and I gave them my best menacing stare. The snickering subsided. I was doing the mortals a favor. Korrigans were usually slow to anger, but once they got riled up, somebody usually ended up missing body parts. Other than the Korrigan, we were the only magical customers in the restaurant.

"Guess the news is out that I let the Hecate out of the bag," I said. "Could be worse. There could be villagers with pitchforks."

"It's still early," Talbot replied wryly. "What are we going to do?"

I was touched by the way he'd said we. Like there wasn't any doubt that he was standing by me, despite the fact that I'd screwed up. The prophecy foretold, *He, born of Fortune, shall let loose the barking dogs as the Fates fall and Hecate shall rise.*

I'd fought the prophecy my whole life, but I fulfilled it anyway. No wonder my aunts wanted to kill me. And now half of Minneapolis felt the same way.

"You mean because there's a big red target on my back and I'm not immortal now? Nothing."

"Maybe I could ask Naomi for a bottle of ambrosia?" Talbot suggested. Ambrosia, aka nectar of the gods, was the orange soda–like drink my aunts manufactured at Parsi Enterprises. It was also the secret to eternal life, at least for mortals.

"I don't know if that's a good idea," I said.

"You want to die before we put Hecate back in the underworld?"

I shook my head. "We should figure a few things out first. Am I dead? Am I undead? Am I a true mortal now or something else?"

I was voting on the something else.

"I should ask about the ambrosia. Just in case."

I shrugged. "Do what you want, but I already know her answer." Naomi was all soft and gooey around Talbot, but the girl had a spine of steel.

Talbot changed the subject. "What did Doc say?"

"Besides the fact that he's my father? Not much."

Bernie walked up to our booth and set two cups of coffee down. "What'll you have?" Bernie was barrel-chested with sad droopy eyes, and today, her eyes looked sadder than usual.

"Bernie, do you have time to talk?"

She raised a sardonic eyebrow before pointedly looking around the almost-empty diner. "I think I can spare a few minutes."

"What happened to all your customers, Bernie?" I asked. "Rumor of a health code violation?"

"You happened, Nyx Fortuna," she said. "You are bad for business."

I started to get up, but she waved me back down. "Don't get excited," she said. "It's not my business anyway, and the owners can afford a few slow days."

We both knew the owners were my aunts.

"Have you heard anything about Hecate? Where she might be? " I asked. Bernie had been my aunts' spy in the underworld and I'm sure Bernie was on Hecate's list. Maybe not as close to the top as I was, but I had no doubt that Hecate hadn't forgotten about her.

"I don't know where she is exactly," Bernie said. "But I did hear she and a bunch of demons forcibly moved out the owners of a riverfront house. Somewhere near the Warehouse District."

I sipped my coffee while I thought about Bernie's news. "Did the owners live?"

Bernie gave a slow shake of her head. "That's not the worse part. The goddess gave the Houses an ultimatum. Join her or else."

"Or else what?"

"Die." Bernie was nothing if not succinct.

I pushed my coffee aside. I needed something stronger to deal with the news that I'd started a magical war.

"I see." That was the real reason for the lack of customers. Hecate was forcing the magical in Minneapolis to choose sides.

Even Bernie's peach cobbler couldn't cheer me up.

When we left the diner, I was busying thinking about how

badly I'd screwed up that I almost missed Wren, but a flash of red caught my eye. She was weaving her way through the pedestrians, straight toward us.

Before I could even think about a spell, she was right next to me. Two demons trailed her, bigger and meaner than the ones who came after me.

She made a hand gesture like someone telling a dog to sit, and her personal lapdogs folded the tree trunks that passed as their arms and waited.

"You are looking well, Nyx," she said. Her glittering eyes met mine. She no longer looked like the small sweet bird of her name. Now she resembled a bird of prey, a hawk, or a vulture, feeding on others.

"No thanks to you," I snarled.

"Sometimes we must do things we don't want to do."

I didn't move, but she shook her head. "I wouldn't do that."

"Do what?"

"Whatever you are thinking of doing," she said. "I didn't come here to fight."

I didn't bother to ask why she was here. She'd get to it eventually, if I could refrain from killing her that long. But I was curious so I let her talk.

"Hecate wants to offer you a deal." Wren had ditched the Tria Prima robes as soon as she came topside, but she was still under her mother's thumb.

I rubbed my neck. "That didn't turn out so well last time."

"As a gesture of good faith, she told me I could let you in on a secret." Her bright smile reminded me I'd once thought of her fondly. But any lingering feelings disappeared when I remembered the slaughter at the conference center.

"And you always do what your mommy tells you."

Her bright smile disappeared. "Yes."

"Even if it means slaughtering innocent people?"

"Yes."

There was nothing left to say, except "No."

"You haven't even heard what I have to say."

"Doesn't matter. My answer is no."

She frowned. "You'll change your mind. I'm sure of that."

"I won't." Pedestrians made a wide berth around us. Most of them didn't even look up.

"You don't know everything about your family, do you?"

It gave me great satisfaction to say, "I do. It's Doc."

"You mean Hades, don't you?"

"Hades?" The name slipped out before I could conceal my ignorance. The god of the dead? There was no way Doc could be Hades, although he had brought me back, a difficult feat even for a necromancer.

"He didn't tell you, did he?"

"Doesn't matter. Why should I believe a liar like you?"

"Ask him," she said. "Ask him how he tracked my mother when she was pregnant with me. How he left her to die. Left me to die."

Wren's words had a ring of truth. It explained everything—his ruined face, his abilities that were above those of a normal necromancer, even his absence in my life. My father was the god of hell.

Doc was Hades, a powerful god. I couldn't get my head around it. How could my mother have loved Hades? How could he have stood by and watched while my aunts hunted and killed my mother? I wanted answers.

Chapter Four

Wren left and I didn't try to stop her. She was just her mother's puppet. It made me sick that even though I hadn't trusted her, she'd wormed her way into my life, into my bed. And it was all because Hecate had told her to. Maybe her mother had told her to lie about Doc, too.

"Shouldn't we go after her?" Talbot asked.

"Probably," I admitted. "But she's Naomi's sister."

"And your ex," he pointed out.

"An ex who tried to kill me."

"Still, an ex."

"Drop it, Talbot." The real reason I wasn't chasing after Wren is that I wasn't relishing the idea that I might have to kill her. The rest of the Wyrd family was pretty free and easy with murder. I wasn't.

"Are you okay?" Talbot asked. "Hecate is just trying to mess with your head."

"Doesn't mean it's not true."

"Hades is the god of necromancy," Talbot said, "but I

have a hard time picturing Doc as some powerful lord of the underworld."

My fists clenched. "I believe her. Doc brought me back from the dead. Do you think any old necromancer could do that?"

"No," Talbot replied. "But I'm glad he did."

"Doc is one of the most powerful gods there is and he let my mother die," I said. "It's always felt personal with Hecate and now I know why."

"She strikes me as a goddess who takes everything personally," he replied.

"I take it personally when someone tries to murder me. I always thought Hecate held a grudge against me because of my aunts, but it turns out it's my father she really hates."

"He's fragile," Talbot said. "And we don't even know if it's true."

"Bullshit," I said. "We find out that my father is a Greek god and all you can worry about is hurting his feelings?"

"I'm worried about you," Talbot said quietly, but I knew I'd hurt his feelings.

Doc had been the one to give me my mother's emerald frog, the one to heal the damage done to Elizabeth's face when she fell victim to Deci's pyromania, and the one to bring me back from the dead. He'd saved my ass more than once.

"I always wondered what his story was, but I never dreamed he might be my father."

"What did your mother tell you about him?" Talbot asked.

"Nothing good." I replied. The vision of my mother as she lay dying reminded me of how my father had failed her, had failed me.

I gritted my teeth and went looking for him. Minneapolis was a big city, but I'd figured out a few of Doc's hiding places. It took me a couple of hours of combing the streets, but I found him. He was waiting in line at the shelter on Third Street.

I pulled him aside. This was not a conversation for mortals' ears. "Come with me."

He followed me into an alley that smelled so bad that not even the junkies would use it. "How can I help you, Nyx?"

"Who are you?"

"You know who I am," he replied.

"That's not what I'm asking," I replied. "Hecate's daughter says you're someone else. A god. Don't lie to me."

He gave a longing glance at the exit, but returned his attention back to me.

"I'm Doc. I am your father," he said. "But that's not who I used to be."

"Who did you used to be?" I already knew the answer, but I wanted him to admit it.

"Who have you been talking to?" he asked.

"Hecate's daughter paid me a visit," I said. "Now are you going to tell me or not? What's your real name?"

"Hades." The one word changed everything. I knew it was true. Maybe I'd always known. "Nyx, I wanted to tell you, but I never found the right time."

I snorted. "You had plenty of opportunities."

"Who would you rather have as a father? Doc or Hades?"

"I would have rather had someone who was around," I said. "Like when my mother and I were running for our lives."

"I failed you," he said softly. "I failed her."

The skittish, scarred man before me bore no resemblance to the great god of the underworld. "I still find it hard to believe, even though part of me knows it's true."

"How else do you think I called you back from the dead? A mere necromancer couldn't do that."

"Everyone thinks Hades is dead."

"He is," he said. "All that's left is me. A broken god."

I stared at him. Despite his nervous tics, his scarred face, and his attachment to a somewhat ripe trench coat, which he wore even in summer, I believed him.

"What happened to you?"

"Power corrupts, Nyx," he said. "I loved your mother, but I wanted her sister. I did what I wanted, regardless of other people's feelings. It didn't end well. Not even Hades should mess with the Fates."

"All this time…" I stared at him, unable to reconcile the broken man in front of me with a powerful god.

"What do you want, Nyx?" he said. "If I don't go in soon, I'll lose my bed."

"You can stop her, stop Hecate."

He shook his head. "I no longer interfere in the magical affairs."

"You interfered with me," I pointed out. "I would have died."

"That was different."

"Why?"

"Because you are my son and I couldn't watch you die," he replied.

"If you don't help me defeat Hecate, everyone will die."

He shrugged. "Death isn't always the worst thing. Sometimes living is."

I ignored the fact that I'd felt exactly like that not so long ago.

"You don't have a choice," he said. "Hecate needs to be contained."

"You're not going to do anything?"

His shoulders lifted again, a helpless gesture. I wanted to smack him.

"You knew the Fates were hunting us all those years, but you did nothing."

He nodded. "Yes."

"You let her die."

"It was my fault," he said. "Deci…"

"The mighty god Hades is nothing but a fucking coward," I said.

He bowed his head. "Yes. Your choices make you or break you."

Doc, my father, refused to answer any other questions. He didn't look back as he trudged into the shelter.

After he left, I cruised the Warehouse District. I couldn't tell which house Bernie had been talking about, but houses on entire streets had gone quiet and dark. No kids played in the street or in the front yards and the few people I did see hurried about their business, heads down. I didn't see any demons and besides, the neighborhood was too big of an area to canvass all at once, so I turned back and headed for Eternity Road.

Chapter Five

Talbot and I arrived back at Eternity Road at the same time.
Ambrose was locking the door.

"Everything okay, Dad?" Talbot asked.

"It was quiet, so I thought I would make an early night of
it," he replied.

Talbot and I exchanged glances. It was barely 4 p.m.

Ambrose caught our concerned looks and snorted. "I'm
tired, that's all," he said bluntly. "I opened the store at nine
a.m., while you two were getting your beauty rest."

Ambrose was a big man, but there were deep circles under
his eyes and his skin had a gray cast.

We offered to work, but Ambrose waved us away. Instead, we
followed him up the three flights of stairs to their apartment.

"I'll make you a cup of tea," Talbot offered his father.

Ambrose snorted. "I'll see you in the morning."

After he went to bed, Talbot and I settled on the couch
with a couple of beers to brainstorm.

"So who is running the underworld while Hecate is
upstairs possessing Willow's body?"

"What are you looking for anyway?"

"A way to get that particular genie out of the bottle," I replied.

At his blank look, I elaborated, "Find a way to get Hecate out of Willow's body."

"Why is she still possessing her anyway?" he asked. "Wren took the bead."

"I know," I said. "She's either keeping Willow just to piss me off or…"

"Or what?"

"The bead didn't work for some reason." Maybe I'd brought back the wrong bead when Wren had sent me through time and space, to India, where the simple red bead had been hidden.

"Like what?" Talbot asked.

"I'm going to go to the underworld and do some snooping."

"Pretty risky. She probably left a legion of demons behind to guard the place," Talbot commented. "I'll go with you."

"No," I said. "I have to go alone."

Too many people I cared about had already been in danger because of me.

I'd originally come to Minneapolis to avenge my mother's death and then end my life, but things had gotten complicated. Hope, however fragile, like me, was hard to kill once it had bloomed, and a tiny part of me still thought a happily ever after might still be possible.

That was, until Wren slit my throat and left me to die in a pool of my own blood. I'd thought my aunts were the worst thing around, but they were girl scouts, although rabid ones, compared to Hecate. And I'd unleashed her on Minneapolis.

I remembered Bernie's little trick and had stopped by the butchers for three slabs of meat for Hecate's hounds, which I laced with some horse tranquilizers and a hidden command spell. It wasn't as fancy as Talbot's had been, but it did the trick.

There was a gate to the underworld directly under Hell's Belles, the restaurant my aunts owned. It was located near a three-way crossroads.

I didn't want anyone to know I was coming, so I skipped the express route through Hell's Belles' basement and took the long way at it, through the tunnels. The tunnels were as disgusting as ever, and there were signs that someone else had been there recently. It was probably just kids looking for somewhere to party, but it set me on edge.

I'd been to the underworld before, to rescue my cousin Claire from Hecate. Not that Claire had been particularly grateful, but the aunts had been holding something over my head to get me to do it.

Now I was going back of my own free will. The trip downstairs was just as cold, nasty, and smelly as I remembered it. The road to the underworld smelled like the devil's armpit.

The hounds were guarding the gate. From a safe distance, I tossed the steaks at the hounds and then waited. There was a thud and then another, and finally the third dog went down. I tiptoed past them to reach the gate to Hecate's realm.

The road to Hecate's castle was strewn with false paths, traps for the unwary, and poisonous plants that would make a rattlesnake's venom taste like mother's milk.

"Stop that and take me where I want to go," I muttered, when I passed the same patch of wolfsbane for the third time. The path immediately formed a straight line.

I yawned. There was something I was supposed to be doing, something important. My lids started to droop. I was drifting off into a comfortable fog when I realized dark magic was lulling me to sleep.

"Wake up," I told myself. Then, when that didn't seem to be working, "*Excitare.*"

I fought off the urge to doze, but had to slap myself every few miles to stay alert.

Hecate's castle was in view, but I didn't seem to be getting any closer. There was rustling in the underbrush, and I froze, but the noise was not repeated.

Still, the hair on the back of my neck prickled. I was being followed. I bent down and pretended to tie the laces of my beat-up Docs. I scanned the horizon, but no demons appeared.

I decided I needed to be more specific with my requests to the enchanted pathway.

"Take me to where I want to go *quickly*," I clarified.

I walked along the path for no more than twenty minutes before I entered the palace. It was abandoned, and not even the lowest demon of the realm had stayed.

I wandered from room to room looking for clues as to Hecate's current whereabouts, the location of Hecate's physical body, which I was sure was still in the underworld somewhere, or a sign of a possessed Willow, but came up with nothing. The castle had been stripped bare.

I'd lost all sense of time during my search, but my growling stomach made me realize I'd been there some time. "This is a bust," I muttered to myself, but I went down one last hallway anyway. I was sure Hecate's body was still stuck in the underworld.

I came to a room I'd never seen before. The door was carved yew, the handle crystal. It was locked.

Before I could pick the lock, a roar sounded. There was a creature standing at the end of the hallway, blocking my escape. It had the head of lion, followed by the head of a goat. Its tail was the head of a deadly serpent. I was facing down a chimera.

The chimera charged me. I was trapped. I muttered, "*Obscura*," before it reached me and the chimera stopped, confused by my disappearance from its vision. It skidded comically as it tried to correct its trajectory, but came close enough to touch. The nostrils on the lion flared. I didn't wait to find out if it picked up my scent. I ran.

I made my way back through the same treacherous forest. I looked over my shoulder constantly, still worried about the chimera tracking me, but there was no sign of the beast.

I crossed back using through the same gate I'd entered, but someone was waiting. Danvers appeared to be looking for a way in, his wheelchair moving quickly over the uneven path. The movement rattled his teeth and his composure, but when he stopped in front of me, his usual snarl was in place.

Hecate hadn't needed Danvers any longer and thrown him away, but why was she still hanging on to Baxter? The flesh eater had vanished, but the harpy feather I'd found at the scene convinced me that Hecate was behind his disappearance.

Willow's husband. Danvers had stuck with his golf shirts, but his tan had faded. The curse I'd lobbed at him right before I died had taken care of his golf swing. His hands shook with palsy so much he could barely grip his wheelchair.

I probably should have felt sorry for him, but I didn't. He'd killed at least a baker's dozen of naiads to break Hecate out of the underworld. And he'd hurt Willow. In my book, that meant the bastard deserved every agonizing second.

The hounds still snored.

"You need to get a new trick," Danvers said. "Why not just kill them?"

"I'd never kill an animal," I replied. "Unless it was disguised as a human. But calling you an animal is an insult to the poor beast."

"What are you doing here?" he asked.

"None of your business."

"She was only playing before," Danvers said. "Hecate doesn't like to lose."

"Neither do I."

He smirked at me. "Just you wait, Nyx Fortuna. A whole lot of trouble is coming your way."

I smirked back. My life had been full of trouble.

I waited, but Danvers didn't make a move to cross over into the underworld.

"Been taken off the guest list, have you?"

"She left me in charge. I can go into Hecate's realm whenever I want," he blustered, but he stayed where he was.

I was torn. I needed to get back home, but I had an overwhelming desire to wrap my hands around his neck and squeeze until he told me where Willow was or he stopped breathing. "You don't have enough magic left in you to call up and order pizza, let alone control the dead."

"You're dead already," he replied. "You just don't know it yet."

I'd always known I wasn't destined for a paint-by-numbers happy ending, but I wasn't going to let a monster like Danvers be the one to kill me. He didn't make a move, though, and we stood there, locking eyes.

A single roar was the only warning I had before the chimera appeared.

Danvers's bloodshot eyes opened wide. "I didn't think they existed anymore," he said.

I was going to have to kill it. Hecate could do infinite damage with a chimera on her side. The chimera made its cousin Cerberus look like a teacup poodle.

The snake struck my arm. A sharp pang and then my vision blurred as the venom hit my bloodstream. Even if I managed to extract the poison, the lion would tear me to shreds. Or the goat's pungent odor would kill me. Fortunately, I wore my World War II fighter pilot jacket, which had healing charms sewn into the lining. It would slow the poison.

"Freeze," I commanded. The chimera froze. I took out my athame and cut two small slits into the wound and sucked out the poison. It tasted as bad as the chimera smelled, like rancid goat meat, and moldy fur, and dog barf. I spit it on the ground and then repeated the process until most of the venom was out.

When my vision cleared, Danvers was gone. The chimera was still frozen, but I could see its multiple eyes furiously working. What should I do with it? It didn't seem sporting to lop off its heads while it couldn't defend itself, but if I left it there, Hecate would use the chimera to wreak havoc topside later.

I weighed my options. The spell would hold the chimera for a few hours. If I got lucky, I'd have just enough time to figure out where to stash it before the magic wore off. If I wasn't lucky, the chimera would probably kill me.

I hated to wake him, but I was in a bind. I picked up the phone and dialed Ambrose's number. "Know anywhere I can stash a chimera in cold storage for a few days?"

"I do, but you're not going to like it," he replied. He was right.

Chapter Six

I went back through the tunnels and waited for Ambrose near Hell's Belles. He pulled up in the Eternity Road van thirty minutes later. He'd brought Talbot, which made it easier. Ambrose was a big man with a wolfish grin, and I honestly wasn't sure if he would have fit in the tunnels.

"Got any rope?" I asked. We needed something to keep its deadliest parts on lockdown while we brought it up.

"Take the dollies, too," Ambrose told Talbot.

Ambrose waited in the van while Talbot and I went to retrieve the chimera.

"I can't believe I'm actually going to get to see a chimera," Talbot said as we walked.

I stepped around a heap of broken bottles. "It's not as fun as it sounds," I warned. "It bit me once already. The spell may have worn off and it moves fast."

The chimera was where I'd left it, but the furious look in its eyes hadn't dimmed. We loaded the chimera into the back and then Ambrose drove straight to Parsi Enterprises. Parsi

Enterprises was housed in an old converted warehouse building in the North Loop neighborhood.

I missed my job there, but killing Deci had served as my official termination. I couldn't really blame them.

"You're serious about giving my aunts a chimera?"

"It's safer with them than with Hecate."

He backed into the loading dock, which was in the rear of the building, on the manufacturing side of Parsi, and flashed his lights three times. Nothing happened.

Eventually, there was a shine of silver and Morta appeared, her hair gleaming in the darkness.

My aunt's habitual chilly expression thawed when she saw the chimera. She snapped her fingers and a silent factory worker helped us load the still-frozen chimera onto a flatbed cart.

We stopped at a freight elevator and the factory worker went back to the plant.

Morta punched a code into the keypad and the elevator descended. The doors opened into a huge space that spanned the entire Parsi Enterprise building and then some.

"Thank you for bringing the chimera to me, Mr. Bardoff," she said.

"Don't thank me," Ambrose replied. "Nyx is the one who caught it."

"Son of Fortuna, you managed to trap the beast?"

"Don't sound so surprised," I told her.

I counted twelve occupied cages. They were state-of-the-art, large spaces that mimicked the occupant's natural habitat. Instead of iron bars, there were wards crisscrossing the cages. Additional wards ran along the hallway where we stood.

Deep in the bowels of the building, the Fates had amassed a magical menagerie. Lerna, a giant crab known for its fighting ability, scuttled among the rocks and water of one habitat. A lone Phoenix sat on a perch in another cage. In a darkened cage containing a miniforest, three pixies, naked and toilet paper white, sat waiting, their little yellow eyes gleaming through the darkness.

Ambrose didn't seem very surprised, but I was reeling.

"Did you know about this?" I asked him.

"I'd heard rumors," he replied. "But I never thought I'd see it."

"It's like a friggin' mythological zoo in the middle of Minneapolis," I said.

"It's not a zoo," Morta said. "Or a prison."

"Then why are you keeping them here?"

"Use your head for something other than decorating your shoulders," Morta snapped. "What do you think would happen if these creatures were released upon the mortal world?"

"They'd be hunted." The thought of trapping such wondrous creatures made me ill.

"Exactly," she said. "These are the last of their kind. They are safe and happy here."

Safe, maybe, but her "guests" didn't seem happy.

There was a lamia's dirt mound in the far cage, but no sign of the lamia. "What do you feed that one?" I asked curiously. Lamias fed on the blood of children. I couldn't imagine even my aunts being that heartless.

"Adult virgin donors," she said crisply. "She doesn't like it as much as the blood of the innocent, but it keeps her full. She eats innocents for food, but will kill for fun, so stay away."

"What's in that one?" I pointed to the cage. Behind the wards, there was a round wooden door barely three feet wide. The door had a thick iron dead bolt on it, and salt encircled the door. White chrysanthemum hung in garlands and runes written in an old language decorated one wall.

"Don't go near that cage" was my aunt's succinct reply. So I didn't.

Something about all those trapped creatures reminded me of the Fates' late lamented Tracker. He'd been too busy harassing me to have rounded up all the creatures before us.

"Morta, do you have other Trackers on your payroll?" I asked.

She gave me a sour look. "You killed our Tracker," she said.

"I killed Gaston," I said. "But it's not like you not to have a backup plan. Do you have others or not?"

"A few," she admitted. "But none as talented as Gaston was."

"Do you think he could track a flesh eater?"

"Yes," she said. "But he is a she."

"Can I meet her?"

"Perhaps," my aunt said. "This Tracker is unpredictable."

"Your last Tracker wasn't exactly working with a complete deck of cards," I said.

"You took care of that, didn't you?" she glared.

I glared back. "I did. Gladly."

Ambrose cleared his throat. "Nyx, it's time we got back to the store."

He said good-bye to my aunt, but I didn't bother.

On the way home, I stared out the window as Ambrose drove through the city streets. What were my aunts doing to do with so many mythical animals? Whatever it was, it wouldn't be good.

Chapter Seven

I was reading the headlines as I sat at the stool near the register at Eternity Road. I looked for clues about Hecate's and Doc's whereabouts, but there was nothing in the paper, except a brief mention of Baxter's disappearance. Hecate was out there, but it had been quiet since the slaughter.

Talbot leaned against a display case next to me. He was watching the customers with a bemused look on his face.

To the mortals, Eternity Road looked like an average pawnshop, but to the magical community, it was a treasure trove. Business at Eternity Road had more than doubled, but it was mostly low-powered magicians looking for protection charms. The store was filled to the brim with exotic and mundane items. There was an amazing selection of amulets and other treasures in a locked case next to the old-fashioned register.

"Too bad Zora's closed," I said. "We could send them there." Jenny, my ex-girlfriend's roommate, had died at the magic shop. After her death, the magic shop hadn't reopened.

Talbot gave me a sideways glance. "Have you heard from Elizabeth?"

"No, but I didn't expect to," I said. "She and Alex are safe and that's all that matters."

A shifty-looking wizard in a suit and tie tried to pocket a star amulet. I threw a receipt pad at his head. "Get out."

He tried to give me an innocent look. "Out," I said. "And leave the amulet."

The wizard scowled at me, but did as I asked.

Talbot grabbed a bunch of stuff and went over to Harvey, the enormous stuffed bear we never seemed to sell. Or maybe we didn't *want* to sell him. We amused ourselves by dressing Harvey up in a variety of outfits. Talbot draped a white silk scarf around Harvey's neck and then added a monocle.

I handed him a black silk top hat. "Try this."

Even dressing Harvey didn't warrant a smile from Talbot. He was still down about my cousin.

"Any luck with Naomi?" I asked Talbot.

"She won't talk to you, Nyx," he replied. "Hell, she's barely talking to me. Says she's sleeping with the enemy. Or was."

"I need to talk to the Fates before anybody else gets killed."

"Talking to the Fates might be what will get you killed," he replied. "Again," he added wryly.

When I first arrived in Minneapolis, I wanted to find my thread and end things on my own terms. Now I wasn't so sure.

"I'll have to take that chance," I said. "Besides, I'm not sure, but I think I'm already dead."

"Maybe you should look at it like you've been reborn," he replied.

"Have you gone all religious on me?"

"I just mean that it's a fresh start," he said.

"Bygones," I said sarcastically.

"Exactly," he said. "Bygones."

"And don't roll your eyes," he added.

"I'm not rolling my eyes."

"Yes, you were," he said. "Mentally."

"Are you going to talk to Naomi for me or not?"

"I'll talk to her," he said.

Talbot was my best friend, but he got a little holier-than-thou sometimes. I blamed his membership in the House of Zeus.

It was almost closing time when a group of demons came in. They were trying to act like friends out for a day of shopping, but there was a terrified mortal in their midst. A drunken woman in her early twenties, probably a coed, was sobering rapidly. She lost her buzz enough to know she had stepped in shit.

The clientele, who knew demons when they smelled them, went silent.

"Can I help you?" I asked.

"I've come for you, Nyx Fortuna," one of them replied. He looked like a professional wrestler and had a neck almost as wide as the door.

His fangs distended and his claws came out.

"Come and get me." I gripped my athame, which I carried with me at all times.

"Try to get the customers out of the store," I told Talbot in a low voice.

I threw it and it hit the short male demon in the neck. I had to dodge as black demon blood spurted everywhere. Hecate had sent the B team. What were they doing? Snatching mortals, but why? I muttered a quick boomerang spell and the athame returned to my hand.

"This is getting old," I told the taller male demon. "Tell Hecate if she wants to talk to me, she can do it in person."

"You don't want the boss making house calls," he growled. "I can handle a punk like you."

I sent a spell his way, but he kept coming. "Those dime-store spells won't work with me," he said.

His partner, a female with a Botoxed face and inflated lips, went for Talbot. His eyes went silverlight before he sent a spell her way. It stopped her, but she managed to rake her nails across his arm before it took effect.

Her buddy took advantage of my distraction and wrapped me in a headlock. I tried to break his hold, but he held tight. Until I drove my athame into his thigh.

The mortal's screaming distracted me and the other female demon, who wore Daisy Dukes and a snarl, drove her claws into my chest.

"Hear you're mortal now." She sniffed. "This is going to be easy."

The other demon advanced again. Demons were hard to kill.

It wasn't going to be enough to immobilize the demon. I'd have to kill all of them. Before I could make my move, the demon coming for me burst into flames. I jumped out of the way. Behind the demon, Talbot held a lighter and the bottle of absinthe I kept under the register.

"Thanks," I said. "You owe me a bottle."

He laughed.

"What should we do with her?"

The spell he'd cast was wearing off. The female demon had regained some of her ability to move.

When she reached for Talbot, claws extended, I reacted. My athame hit the chest of the woman, splitting it like an overripe pomegranate.

"Problem solved," I said. I pulled the athame out of the dead demon's chest.

A couple of college-aged mortals looked on with interest. "Are they filming this? I know my rights. I didn't sign a waiver," one of them said.

"Shut up," Talbot said. "Now."

The mortal subsided into an offended silence, but it was better than him getting killed.

The mages inched their way out of the store, but one of them got too close to the remaining demon. It reached out with one meaty paw and squeezed his neck until the mage gasped for breath.

"Let him go," I said.

The last demon grinned. "Make me."

Even the smaller demons tended to be cocky in a fight, and this guy looked like he'd eaten twenty or so of his friends. He also looked like he killed people as a hobby. The poor mage was turning purple.

I threw my athame at the same time I muttered the spell. *"Incendium."*

The knife went straight for his heart, but the demon blocked it with his hand. He held up the hand, which had been skewered through with the athame. A trickle of thick black blood seeped out of the wound, but the demon only smiled.

"This is going to be fun," he said. He dropped the mage, who stayed down and gasped for breath for breath.

"Not much fun for you," I said.

The demon laughed and a puff of smoke escaped. A flame escaped from his nose and then his body was encased in flame. The heat was intense. We shielded our eyes, but the smell of demon flesh permeated the store.

He burned until there was nothing left but a pile of greasy, noxious-smelling ashes. And the athame.

"Not so spontaneous combustion," Talbot said.

The rest of the customers had already left, but the mage the demon had almost strangled waited until the end.

"Thank you, son of Fortuna," he said. His voice was hoarse, and he rubbed his throat. "You saved my life. If you need anything, anything at all, just call."

"And who should I call?" I asked.

"Emmett Greenfellow, at your service," he replied.

"Emmett, it was probably my fault you were injured in the first place."

"The demon was the one who squeezed me like a grape," he replied.

"The demon was here because of me." I don't know why I was standing there arguing with him, but I couldn't seem to stop. I couldn't figure out why Hecate hadn't made an appearance. Maybe I'd hit her on the head harder than I'd thought. Or maybe she was busy pursuing my father.

"Others in Minneapolis do not speak well of you," he continued.

I bet.

"They're wrong about you. You're a hero. They just don't know it yet." He shook my hand and left.

I was the farthest thing from a hero. I stared after him, astonished that someone I'd never met before had such a high opinion of me.

I stayed that way until Talbot nudged me. "It's your turn to clean up the demon blood."

"Hero," he added.

I got out the mop and bucket. Some hero.

Chapter Eight

Talbot had managed to set up a meeting with my aunts, but only because they'd heard about the slaughter. Morta probably wanted to spit at me, too.

"Will Naomi be there?"

"She's still pretty pissed," he replied.

"Deci was evil, working with Danvers, and possibly even Hecate, and Naomi's mad that I killed her?"

"Evil or not, she was still her aunt." Couldn't argue with that.

The meeting was set to take place at Hell's Belles at midnight. Not exactly neutral territory, since I'd found out that the Fates owned it. But they owned half of Minneapolis, so I couldn't really complain. And the food was fantastic.

"Are you coming with me?" I asked.

"Nope," Talbot replied. "Family only or no meeting. Fates' orders."

I snorted. "Some family."

"It's the only one you have."

"I miss her, you know." Naomi was the only member of my family I wanted to claim.

"I miss her, too," Talbot replied.

"She's talking to you at least," I replied glumly. "And she didn't break up with you." The "yet" hung unspoken in the air.

"Nyx," Talbot said, "you know they might try to kill you."

"And now they can," I said. After over two hundred years, I was no longer immortal, which took some getting used to. You'd think my aunts would stop snipping threads of fate, since we were trying to save the world, but you'd be wrong. Morta's scissors were busier than ever.

He was right. I could be walking into a trap, but I needed to convince my aunts we should join forces, at least long enough to stop Hecate.

I decided to get there early. The restaurant was empty, except for Bernie and a stranger who sat at my favorite booth. Her back was to the entrance, and she didn't even look up when I entered.

She had long dark hair, which she'd shoved up into a messy bun and secured with a pair of takeout chopsticks. She wore jeans and a tee and a pile of textbooks were spread out in front of her. I dismissed her as a grad student looking for a quiet place to study.

I sat in the booth next to her, but facing the door. Bernie took my order, the blue plate special, and then stood there like she wanted to say something. The grad student held up an empty mug and Bernie left to fill it.

I waited, but the Fates didn't show up. They were probably still too angry to talk to me, Or it was a setup.

Bernie set my order in front of me and the delicious aroma of chicken and biscuits wafted up. Hell's Belles made the best food in town. At least my last meal would be a delicious one.

"It's nice to see a murderer with a hearty appetite," the grad student said.

I stopped mid-chew. "What did you say?"

"You're a murderer."

Before I could react, she was practically on top of me. She whipped out one of the chopsticks, which, I realized too late, made a handy weapon. She held it to my throat. "You killed my mother."

The stranger's glare now made sense. I'd only ever killed one woman, and that was my aunt Deci. I was looking at Deci's absent daughter, a pissed-off Fate-in-training.

I matched her stare. "She deserved it."

Our face-off was interrupted by my aunt. "Rebecca, I see you've met Nyx," Morta said. "Take a seat." Rebecca's chopstick pressed tighter against my throat. "You can try to kill him later," Morta snapped. "Right now we have bigger problems."

The pressure against my throat lessened, but my neck still throbbed. Rebecca wanted to kill me, but hadn't. Why?

The entire Wyrd clan had arrived while I was occupied with Rebecca—my two aunts, the remaining Fates, and Fates-in-training Claire and Naomi. There were always three of them—always exceptionally powerful, always female, and always from our bloodline. The Fates were not immortal. Every few hundred years, the old Fate would step down and her daughter would take her place.

They were down to two Fates, which was why they'd sent for the black sheep, Rebecca. One of the Fates-in-training would have to join the big leagues. I studied my three cousins. Which one would it be?

They took seats at a neutral table and Rebecca and I grabbed our stuff and moved to opposite ends. Morta gave Bernie a curt nod and Bernie turned the OPEN sign to CLOSED and dimmed the lights.

I tried to give Naomi a hug, but she stiff-armed me. Rebecca didn't even try to stifle her snicker.

"What happened to your arm?" Nona asked.

"Something bit it," I replied blandly.

"It's a wonder you have any blood left," Naomi said. It was the first time she'd spoken to me since she'd arrived.

I smiled at her, but she looked away.

While the rest of the family exchanged pleasantries, I was stuck on Rebecca's appearance.

"You don't look anything like Deci," I said casually. Before she'd died, Deci had mentioned the loss of a child. I'd thought she'd meant her child had died, but after meeting Rebecca, I realized it was a different kind of loss.

Everyone at the table fell silent.

"Don't be an ass, Nyx," Naomi said.

"I'm told I resemble my father," Rebecca said through gritted teeth.

Another long pause. What was the big deal?

"No one ever talks about you," I continued to charm her. Her gaze turned to acid.

"Rebecca is the oldest child in the Fates' line," Morta said. "She's been away."

"Except for me," I said cockily. "Technically, I'm the oldest."

Morta's slow headshake took a while to sink in.

I looked closer at Rebecca. "There's no way. You're older than me?"

"Apparently, smarter, too," she said snidely.

"What?"

"What everyone is tiptoeing around," she said, slowly, like she was speaking to a not–particularly bright child, "is that we're siblings."

"Siblings?" I had a sister? I was gaping like a trout. My family closet was full of secrets, and I never knew when another one would come spilling out.

"*Half* siblings," she emphasized.

"But we're cousins."

"That, too." She waited several beats for it to sink in. "Yes, our father was doin' sisters."

"Rebecca, language," Morta rebuked.

"Ever met him?" I asked.

Rebecca shook her head. "Never wanted to."

"Your mother didn't handle rejection well, which is why half of his face is melted off."

"He probably deserved it," she snarled.

Couldn't argue with that. "So where have you been?" I asked, but the other part of my brain was still grappling with the fact that I had a sister. One about as friendly as a feral cat, but still a sister.

For some reason, the question upset everyone at the table. "Why do you ask?" Rebecca replied.

"Why all the mystery?" I asked. "What did you do? Embezzle company funds? Murder someone?"

There was a long silence. I stared at Rebecca in awe. "You stole money from the Fates? You *are* your mother's daughter."

"You don't know what the fuck you're talking about," she snarled.

"Children, quit quarreling or I'll send you to bed without any supper," Nona said.

There was an unmistakable note of amusement in her voice. I'd been so busy exchanging barbs with Rebecca that I hadn't noticed my aunt watching us closely.

I snuck looks at my sister when I didn't think she was looking. Had my mother known about her?

"Give me a reason I shouldn't kill him," Rebecca said.

"He is your brother."

Her expression didn't change. "So?"

"He's the Custos," Naomi blurted out.

If anything, the news made Rebecca angrier. "I was supposed to be the Custos."

"You weren't around," I said. "So Deci gave the Book of Fates to me." I wasn't going to admit I didn't have the Book of Fates any longer.

She sneered. "You must have made her."

"Rebecca, you know it doesn't work like that," Nona rebuked her gently.

Morta cleared her throat. "Technically, Nyx is no longer the Custos."

I glared at her. "Is that why the Book of Fates is missing?"

"It's not missing," Claire said. "I have it." She flipped her blond hair triumphantly.

"You have it? But I thought there had to be some formal ceremony or something. Isn't that why Deci was willing to hand it over to me? Because she had no other choice?"

"We are Fates," Morta replied. "We always have other choices."

"My mother was doing you a favor," Rebecca said. "Being the Custos is an honor."

Being the Custos sucked, so why was I pissed that Claire had taken over? Maybe because it had made me feel like part of the family. The thought sickened me. Had I forgotten what this *family* had done to my mother?

"Your mother was evil," I said.

"Because she tried to kill you?"

"No, because she was working with a necromancer to free

Hecate," I said. "And dabbling in dark magic." And she killed her own sister, my mother, Lady Fortuna.

"She wouldn't do that," Rebecca said.

"She did."

My sister looked at her aunts for confirmation. After a long moment, Morta nodded. Rebecca's eyes welled with tears of sadness or maybe anger, but she shook them away. "You didn't have to kill her," she said in a whisper.

"I did." I wasn't winning any points in the good brother category, but I wasn't going to sit there and pretend Deci was a saint just because she was dead. Just because I'd killed her.

"So what now?" Rebecca asked, after she got her emotions back into check. "What am I supposed to do?"

"Rebecca, you will be trained as the Atropos," Morta said crisply.

"What's an Atropos?" I asked.

Rebecca gave me a scornful look and then made a scissoring motion with her hands.

"You get to be a mini-Morta," I said sarcastically. "Murdering friends and family alike."

"You really don't get the Fates at all," Claire said. "It's not murder. Someone has to do it. The Atropos is called and must obey."

"Enough quarreling," Nona said. She stared at me. "It is done. Nyx has fulfilled the prophecy." *He, born of Fortune, shall let loose the barking dogs as the Fates fall and Hecate shall rise.*

"And?"

"And now we have to fix it," she replied. "That's why we're here, isn't it?"

"Yes," I said. It still hurt to talk, and my sister's chopstick hadn't helped. I put a hand up to my throat.

"But what about the rules?" Rebecca said. "He shouldn't even be alive."

"Screw the rules," the normally elegant Morta said. "We are at war. We need him. We will settle all debts after it's over."

My sister's stare let me know she planned to collect her debts: probably by slicing off my fingers one by one.

"We'll all help you," Naomi said. "Even if it means killing Wren."

I couldn't let my cousin kill her sister. If it had to be done, I would be the one to do it. I leaned back against my chair and closed my eyes, suddenly weary. It was a near-impossible task.

"Don't get too comfortable, son of Fortuna," Morta said. "We have work to do."

"Hecate has won," Nona said. "We can't defeat her, not without three Fates."

"Then get Claire up to speed," I said. "You concentrate on that and I'll concentrate on getting Hecate back into the underworld."

"Not the underworld," Morta said. "This time we must discover a more permanent solution."

"You mean kill her?"

She snorted. "Killing a goddess is not an easy task, Nyx. I don't mean killing her. I mean immobilizing her for a few thousand years or so."

"Say I find a way to immobilize her," I said. "Where would we keep her?"

"Don't worry about that," she said. "You find a way to trap her and we will take care of the rest. Agreed?"

I didn't really care what they did with Hecate, as long as she was out of the way.

She looked from her sister to me and back again. "I have

been wrong about many things," she said. "But I was not wrong about you. You are my sister's son."

"Then help me," I said. "We'll defeat her together. Or at least tell me how you contained her last time. It was the three tasks, wasn't it?"

"There were three items necessary to hold Hecate in the underworld," Morta said. "But we scattered them into the wind. We each took one of the items. D-Deci…" She stopped for a moment to regain her composure. "Deci was in charge of Hecate's Eye."

"Which is why Wren knew exactly where to find it," I said. "I had it in my hand and let it slip away." I'd handed it over to save Willow.

They ignored my dig at Deci. My aunts didn't want to admit Deci had been in league with Hecate.

"Find them and you will be able to trap her again," Claire said.

"She already has the bead," I admitted. "I traded the harpies for Claire, but I think it's the harpy's silver feather she really wanted." My cousin had been trapped in the underworld with Hecate, and I had freed her.

"We already know that," Morta said. "But the harpies will not help Hecate as much as she thinks."

"Why did you give her the bead?" Rebecca asked.

"I gave it to her in exchange for Willow, but Hecate screwed me over." They didn't have to say it aloud. I knew what an arrogant idiot I'd been.

"How'd that work out for you?" Rebecca asked sarcastically.

"If she gets the third item, there will be no stopping her," Nona said.

"What exactly is the third item?"

"Medusa's mirror," Nona said. "There's no way she will get her hands on it."

"Where is it?"

"Please don't be offended, Nyx, but perhaps it is better you don't know," Morta said.

She had a point.

"We can't kill Hecate, anyway," I said. "At least not while she's still walking around in Willow's body."

"Why not?" Rebecca asked.

I glared at her. "If anyone at this table touches Willow, I will hunt you down and make you suffer."

"Jeez, touchy," Rebecca said.

"I like Willow, although Nyx usually has terrible taste in women," Naomi said.

Claire gave a snort of laughter. "So true." Her blond hair shone in the dim light.

"I wasn't the one getting all chummy with Hecate in the underworld," I snarled.

"I agree. Willow's off-limits," Naomi continued, as if we hadn't interrupted her.

I gave her a grateful look, but she ignored me.

"Hecate has Hecate's Eye, but I don't know how she intends to use it," I said.

"Get it back," Morta said.

"I'll try," I said, "but the Houses are getting nervous. They might decide to align with Hecate."

"I doubt they fear her more than they fear us," Morta said.

"Maybe," I said. "But you have to admit the Fates are at their weakest right now."

Morta glared at me, but I glared back.

"We are temporarily hampered," Nona admitted. "But

Rebecca's home and Claire has taken over as Custos. We'll be back to full strength soon."

"In the meantime, it might not hurt to make a few overtures," I said.

"Anything else?" Nona said. "You should rest."

"No time for that," I said. "I'll start talking to the Houses as soon as I can."

Our little family meeting broke up not long after. Rebecca looked like she wanted to kick me in the balls as a good-bye, but instead, she whispered something to Claire, who laughed.

Naomi didn't even bother to look at me before she left. Instead, she made a beeline for the door, ignoring everybody else.

I was weary, not just because I was now mortal, residing in a two-hundred-and-twenty-year-old body. Sometimes, the sheer enormity of what I had to do would overwhelm me. Then I'd want to give up, but I knew I couldn't. Knew I wouldn't. I had to succeed.

Chapter Nine

After my meeting with the Fates, I updated Talbot and his dad.

"Any word from Doc?" I asked.

"He'll turn up," Ambrose assured me.

"Hecate's tough, too," I said. "I hope nothing has happened to him."

"It's going to be a back-alley dog fight," Ambrose said. "She won't fight fair, but Doc can take care of himself."

"My aunts seem to think they have an ace in the hole," I told him. "Something Hecate needs to return to full power."

"Interesting," Talbot said. "I don't suppose they told you what it was."

I gave him an expressive look. "My aunts aren't in a sharing mood right now." I'd screwed up Talbot's relationship with Naomi already, but I wasn't going to do any further damage.

"Are they ever?" Talbot asked. "How was Naomi?"

"Icy," I replied. "But I can't really blame her."

He tried not to look as lovesick as he sounded. "Did she ask about me?"

I shook my head.

"What about the other Houses?" I asked.

Ambrose shook his head. "It's not looking good," he said. "They think we're doomed to failure."

I appreciated his use of "we." "You mean they think *I'm* doomed."

"It's possible we can turn the tide of opinion," he said. "We just need the right ally."

"Can you get me a meeting with someone from the House of Zeus? Maybe even the head of the House of Zeus?"

"Maybe," Ambrose said. "Luke Seren doesn't like to mingle with the other Houses."

That didn't sound promising.

A few days later, Ambrose handed me a folded slip of paper. "Meet here at four p.m."

"I'm meeting the head of the House of Zeus at the library?"

"He starts on time," he warned. "So don't be late. Nyx, do you know how to do the polka?"

"No, why?"

"You might want to learn."

When I got there, the library parking lot was nearly full.

I took Ambrose's comment as a hint and followed the sound of the music into the library branch community room.

Dancers twirled in cheerful red, black, and white Scandinavian costumes. There were a few rebels in blue.

The group was mostly senior citizens. They were learning traditional folk dances along with the polka.

At the front, an attractive man dressed all in black led the group through their paces. He shouted encouragement, beamed at his star pupils, and stopped occasionally to show the slow learners hiding in the back the correct way to do the step.

A row of fold-up chairs were lined up against one wall. I took a seat and watched the dancers. Which one was Luke?

An elderly man in shorts and a Hawaiian shirt sat in the chair next to me. His prosthetic leg clanged against the metal chair, but it barely made a sound over the blaring music.

The song ended and the man in black called for a five-minute break. The dancers crowded around him like he was the geriatric answer to Justin Bieber.

I waited, but no one approached me.

I turned to the guy next to me.

"Luke?"

He snorted. "You want Casanova over there." He pointed to the instructor, who had his arms wrapped around an attractive older woman with soft white hair and eyes the color of lupines.

My companion glared at them.

"That your wife?" I asked.

"My girlfriend," he said. He tapped on his prosthetic leg. "Least she was until this happened."

"There more important things than dancing," I said.

"Tell that to Ginger and Fred," he replied. I didn't tell him that I'd seen Ginger Rogers and Fred Astaire dance once when I was an extra on a movie set back in the thirties.

When I chuckled, he held out his hand. "Fitch."

"Nyx," I said in reply.

"The son of Fortuna? It's an honor."

I looked at him incredulously. "Not many people say that, at least not these days. I had you pegged as a mortal."

"I'm a minor god," he confessed. "And my specialty isn't one especially revered today."

"Which is?"

"I'm the god of moderation."

"No wonder I've never heard of you," I said.

"Not that kind of moderation," he corrected gently. "Although a little moderation would not hurt you a bit. I moderate when things get sticky among the gods."

"So you're like Switzerland?"

He nodded. "My job is to see if you and Hecate and come to an agreement. I'll act as an intermediate."

"Is that why I'm here?" I asked. "You can tell Hecate to go fuck herself."

"Not a very peaceful message," he said. "But it's a start."

"I thought I was supposed to talk to Luke."

"Luke is more of an interested party," Fitch said. "I'm neutral. I talk to both sides and try to get them to reach an understanding."

I stared at him. "You're going to try to talk to Hecate? She's on a rampage."

He nodded.

"She'll kill you."

His affable expression vanished, replaced by something cold and deadly. For the first time, I sensed the magic simmering below his benign surface. "She can try."

"I don't think there's any point in trying to mediate," I told him. "Either she dies or I do."

"You sure about that?"

"Yes."

"Did you know that Hecate has sent word to the Houses that there will be no more killing?" he asked.

"On one condition, right?"

"Right."

"Care to share what that condition is?"

57

Marlene Perez

"She won't kill any more members of the Houses if they turn you in," he said.

"And they're considering it?"

He nodded.

"What are my odds?"

"Right now, about fifty–fifty," he said. "They're as scared of your aunts as they are of Hecate."

That was something. I'd never thought my aunts' evil reputation would save my ass.

The music started again and we watched in silence.

The lesson stopped, and the dancers burst into applause.

"Any advice how to get Mr. Seren on my side?"

"Are you sure you want him there?"

"What do you mean?"

"Some god of light he is," Fitch replied. "Seren makes a good ally and a bad enemy. Trouble is you can't always tell which is which."

"Meaning?"

"Meaning watch your back. How do you think I ended up missing a leg?" Fitch struggled to his feet and made his way over to his girlfriend.

Luke Seren spent several minutes surrounded by his polka groupies before he wandered over to where I sat, like he had all the time in the world. Maybe he did.

I assumed I was being tested and waited patiently for the head of the House of Zeus to acknowledge me. I'd bet money he saw me the minute I came in, but Seren liked to play games.

He shook off his admirers and strode toward me.

"Nyx Fortuna," he said. "Did you enjoy the dancing?"

"Very much." Up close, Luke Seren looked older than I'd first thought, around sixty, swarthy, and theatrical. His cheeks were artificially rosy, his dark eyes enhanced by black eyeliner, and he'd last seen his natural hair color several decades ago. He had a moustache a walrus would envy.

When he held out his hand, I noticed he was missing the ring finger on his right hand. He caught me staring. "You met Fitch?"

I nodded.

"And he probably told you that I was responsible for the loss of his leg?"

I nodded again.

He wiggled fingers of his right hand. "He owes me a finger."

I felt like I'd been hauled in front of the principal for setting off a stink bomb in the john. I'd been enrolled in a public high school for exactly three weeks back in the fifties and had been sent to the principal's office several times. Rebelling had been my way of fitting in. It had ended when the Tracker had found me. I shut the memory away tight.

"At last I meet the one who well and truly set the cat among the pigeons," he said.

"Yes," I said. "And now I'm trying to fix it."

"And what does that have to do with me?"

"She already slaughtered dozens of your people," I said.

"I have no proof that Hecate was responsible."

"She's just warming up. The way I see it, she'll come after every House."

"Maybe," he said. "Maybe not. But tell me, if there is a war, why should I stand with you instead of Hecate?"

"You're scared," I said.

"Anyone in their right mind would be," he said. "She has it in for the House of Fates."

"You should join us because she's evil," I said.

I'd been saying the same thing over and over, but from his expression, I wasn't convincing him. "I'll think about it," he said. "And you should think about this. You let her out. How are you going to get her back?"

It was a good question. "I will stop Hecate or die trying," I said.

He nodded. "That much I believe."

Chapter Ten

It was after midnight and I sat in my bedroom, going over Sawyer's necromancy books. Sawyer had been a necromancer married to a Fate, but I'd liked him. And Nona was the least objectionable of my aunts.

Naomi's dad had been a nice guy, despite belonging to the House of Hades. He'd also fathered a daughter, Wren, with Hecate, the Fates' worst enemy.

I was sober, mostly. I needed my wits about me to understand what I was reading. Naomi had given them to me after he died. I'd made my way halfway through the stack and was on a chapter dealing with possession. The gruesome details weren't helping me fall asleep. I kept picturing Willow suffering as Hecate gradually took over her body until there was no room left for anyone else.

There was a brief mention of a necromancer using an elixir to reverse a possession, but the book didn't yield any other clues.

I turned the page and a photograph fell out. Sawyer, Nona, and a much younger Naomi beamed up at me. From the birthday candles on the cake in front of her, Naomi must have been about seven.

"I love that photo," Sawyer said. "What I wouldn't give to go back to that time."

I'd gotten used to him sneaking up on me. Almost. "I'm going to hang a bell on you," I said. "How long have you been here?"

"Not long," he said. "But there are lots of new souls milling about in Asphodel. What happened?" Asphodel was the part of the underworld where ghosts congregated. Asphodel flowers took their name from the place they grew. Even Hecate avoided that part of the realm.

"Your ex happened." Hecate was on a killing spree and I wasn't sure how to stop her.

"Hmm."

"That's it? Your wife and daughter are next on the list and all you can say is 'hmm'?"

"I'm not the one you're really mad at."

"I'm mad at everyone," I replied. It was true, but mostly, I was mad at myself.

"Anger isn't going to get you anywhere," he said. "Get your keys. I want to show you something."

I did as he asked, but was still half-asleep when I started the Caddy. Sawyer's voice provided directions and a running commentary as we headed a few miles outside of Minneapolis.

"We're heading back to the wildlife preserve?" I asked.

"Shut up and drive," he said. "It's not exactly easy to stay in the world. I need to concentrate."

I pulled up in front of the same conference room where Hecate killed the members from the House of Zeus.

Instead of heading to the conference center, Sawyer directed me elsewhere. "Take that hiking trail and follow it."

Stumbling around in the dark didn't seem like a plan. "Illuminate," I said. A sparkling silver light lit the path. After walking a long time, I heard the sound of running water and a waterfall came into view.

I inhaled. "Someone should have written a poem about this place."

Sawyer's voice was amused. "Someone did."

"Why are we here?" I said, looking around.

"You said you wanted to defeat Hecate," Sawyer said. "This is where Wren was born."

"She wasn't born in the underworld?"

"The Fates hadn't defeated Hecate when Wren was born. Hecate roamed free, tormenting the mortals as she saw fit."

"You think that's why she slaughtered the naiads and satyrs here?"

"No," he said grimly. "I think she slaughtered them because the House of Zeus refused to help her when she was in labor. Wren almost died before she was even born."

Hecate was an evil crone, but Wren had been an innocent baby. What was that old saying? Know your enemies? But guilt seemed to be Sawyer's motivation.

"You want me to feel sorry for her? Wren had a choice. She slit my throat because her mother told her to."

"Nyx, I want you to promise me you won't kill Wren," he said.

He wasn't trying to help me. He was trying to protect his daughter. I'd cared for Wren once and she was Naomi's sister.

"I won't, Sawyer," I said. "Not unless I have no other choice."

"Don't...have...time...for..." Sawyer's voice sounded like he'd entered a tunnel.

"Sawyer, are you there?"

"I'm back," Sawyer said.

"Any hints about how I'm supposed to dial up a specific dead person to talk to?" Thanks to my aunts, almost everyone I loved was dead.

My question hung in the air, unanswered. "Sawyer, are you listening?"

"I'm busy, Nyx," his voice finally replied.

"So am I," I said. "You know, trying to prevent the apocalypse in the form of one pissed-off goddess."

"And?"

"Tell me what you know," I said. "Anything that might help stop her."

"I don't know how your aunts trapped her last time," Sawyer admitted. "They didn't trust me enough to tell me, but I know Deci came up with the solution."

"Deci's dead."

"Then find another way," he said.

"I'm trying," I said. "Do you remember anything about the three items of power the Fates took from Hecate?"

"There is a legend that one of the harpies grew a feather."

"Not exactly earth-shattering." They were bird women. Feathers came with the territory.

"Let me finish," he said. "It was a magical silver feather that gave the owner unimaginable power. It was said that one of the minor goddesses took the feather and became even more powerful."

"Hecate," I said. It would explain her attachment to the harpies. She was probably hoping they'd grow a second feather. Or a whole pillow full of silver feathers.

"Nyx, you can't…" His voice faded before he told me what I couldn't do.

"Sawyer?"

But he didn't answer. He'd given me something to go on, though. Deci.

I had a couple of old books of my mother's, but I'd read them a thousand times looking for clues to find my thread of fate. There was nothing there to help me with my current situation.

That is, until I really looked at what I had thought were doodles along the margins.

There was a sketch of an asphodel and a list of ingredients. The flower had been heavily inked in.

When I was little, I had found a dried asphodel pressed between the pages of one of my mother's books. I showed it to her and asked her what it was. "A memory," she replied softly. "But it is also a rare black asphodel, which you can find in only one place."

"Where?" I was curious.

"Somewhere I can never go again," she said. Tears welled in her eyes and I stopped asking questions.

I'd lost my mother. I couldn't lose Willow, too. I closed the book and finally fell asleep.

In the morning, I had a shift at Eternity Road. Talbot wasn't there, but Ambrose was in his office. I told him I'd been chatting with my dead uncle, which elicited a raised eyebrow. "How long have you been able to speak to the dead?"

"Not long," I said. "Know anything about how that works?"

He shrugged. "I'll keep my eyes open."

"Why can't I hear anyone else?" I asked. "Only Sawyer. Not Jasper, or Deci, or..." My voice broke, though I tried to control it. "My mother." If I could talk to Sawyer, maybe he wasn't the only one from the realm of the dead. Maybe I could even speak to my mother. I had so many questions for her, but mostly, I wanted to hear her voice.

"Maybe you're not listening closely enough," he replied. "Try mediating."

I snorted, but he was serious. He marched me to an empty storage closet and shoved me in. "Try it, Nyx," he said. "Try talking to someone you loved and see if you get a response."

"What about my shift?"

"It can wait," he said. "Now try. Sometimes you need to let the dead speak."

I felt like an idiot, but I started by saying her name. "Lady Fortuna. Mother?"

There was no answer. I tried several times, but my mother didn't answer. I almost gave up. There weren't many people, living or dead, whom I'd loved. But then a name came to me.

"Amalie." The name of my dead girlfriend.

I said her name what seemed like a thousand times. Death was cold, but the room grew almost unbearably warm the last time I said her name. Sweat poured off me.

Her perfume permeated the room and her voice sounded in my ear. "My love."

"Amalie?"

"You called and I came," she said.

"I didn't expect you to," I said. "It's my fault you're dead."

"Still the same old Nyx," she said. "Blaming yourself for the actions of others."

It hurt to hear her gentle voice say my name, but it was a welcome pain. "I've missed you."

"And I you," she replied. "Your powers have grown."

"What makes you say that?" Talking to the dead was a skill I wasn't sure I wanted. Could I talk to my mother? Did I want to know her secrets?

"I have never been able to hear your voice before."

"I didn't know I could call to you," I said. "Are you at peace?"

"I am," she said. "But why did you call me?"

"To say I loved you. To say I'm sorry. To say good-bye."

I felt a cold kiss on my lips. "I already knew. Farewell, beloved."

"Good-bye, Amalie."

And then she was gone.

Talking to the ghost of my dead lover had shaken me more than I wanted to admit. I made it through the rest of the day in a daze. I could summon the dead.

Chapter Eleven

After work, Talbot and I went to the Red Dragon, my favorite seedy bar, to see if there were any rumors floating around in the magical community.

Two of his old frat buddies were at a booth, but they pretended not to see him when he waved.

"Cowards," I said.

Talbot shrugged. "Can't really blame them," he said. "Hecate has everyone scared."

I tried chatting up some of the locals, but they were silent and sullen.

"We're persona non grata, even at the Red Dragon," Talbot said. "We've sunk to new lows."

The bar's floors were usually sticky with old beer and other things I didn't want to think about, but the drinks were cheap and cold.

"I wish you'd waited to say that until after I'd had a drink," I said.

The place was nearly empty, but the bartender ignored

us until I reached around the bar and filled a pitcher of beer from the tap. "Hey, you can't do that," he said.

"This should cover it," I said. I tossed a twenty at him. "Now that I have your attention, we're looking for some information about Hecate."

His face went white. "Don't say her name here," he said. "I don't know anything. Just drink your beer and get out."

I raised my voice and addressed the bar. "Anybody here know anything about Hecate or her demons? We'll pay generously for information."

Most of the patrons stared at their drinks, but one guy muttered, "There's not enough cash in Minneapolis to get me to say anything."

I gave him a look and he added, "Not that I know anything. I want to keep it that way."

Everyone was too scared to say anything, but I wasn't about to let a perfectly good pitcher of beer go to waste. Talbot and I found a booth far from the other patrons.

The Red Dragon was where I'd first met Elizabeth in the men's bathroom, a random meeting that turned out to not be random at all.

The thought of my ex depressed me even more.

"Feeling sorry for ourselves, are we?"

"I'm screwed seven ways to Sunday," I said. "I might as well drink."

"Any excuse," Talbot muttered.

"I just had a conversation with my dead girlfriend," I said. "How's that for an excuse?"

"Someday you're going to have to face your demons," he replied.

"Faced them. Stabbed them."

"Very funny," he said. "You know that's not what I meant."

I knew what he meant. Everyone would leave me eventually. Or Hecate would kill them. Unless I killed her first.

"Let's get out of here," I said to Talbot. "Nobody is going to tell us anything."

I'd been staring at the pitcher of beer in front of me, but the noise in the bar stopped. I glanced up. Hecate stood in front of me and smiled at me with Willow's lips.

"I have a present for you, lover," she purred.

I raised a hand to strike, but Hecate's next words stopped me.

"Make one move and I'll kill everyone here," she said. "Including your little girlfriend."

I glanced around. Where were the demons? Hecate never left home without them. I spotted three total.

It wasn't likely Hecate would kill Willow's body, but her soul was another story. I hoped Willow could hold out until I could find Hecate's body and force her back into it.

"What do you want?"

"You dead, of course," she said. "But you just won't die. So I'll settle for finding your father."

"My father?" The longer I kept her talking, the less likely it was that she'd kill everyone at the Red Dragon. Out of the corner of my eye, I saw the bartender and a couple of the regulars inching their way to the back door. One of them stumbled and sent a glass tumbling to the ground. It shattered and Hecate's head turned toward the sound.

"I don't know where he is," I said. Desperate to keep her attention, I added, "But I can pass along a message to Sawyer if you'd like."

Her eyes turned back to me. "He's dead."

"Dead, but not gone," I said.

"You're bluffing," she said. "You can't call the dead."

I'd finally made her smug smile disappear. "But I can."

"Prove it and I won't kill these people."

"You're not exactly known for keeping your word," I said.

"True," she said. "That's a chance you'll have to take."

Talbot's white knuckles and the scared looks of the patrons convinced me to give it a try. "Sawyer, you there?"

"In a bit of hot water?" His voice sounded in my ear.

"A bit," I said. "Your ex would like to speak to you."

"Showing off, are we?" he said. "What does she want?"

"He wants to know what you want."

Hecate said, "I want to see him, hear him, touch him."

"That's impossible," I said.

Hecate gave a nod to one of her demons and he grabbed the nearest bar patron and squeezed his neck.

"Tell her to stop," Sawyer said. "I'll do it, but I'll need your help."

"He says to stop," I repeated. "Give me a minute and he'll materialize."

"One minute," Hecate agreed. The demon dropped his victim and the man fell to the floor, gasping.

"Nyx, you'll only have one shot at this," Sawyer said. "When I appear, she'll be distracted. You must attack her. She won't expect it. It's the only way anyone will get out of this bar alive. Nod if you understand."

I gave a short nod. "Now concentrate. Summon me," Sawyer continued.

Did my dead uncle really think I could summon ghosts?

"We haven't got all day," he said gently.

"Sawyer Polydoros, I summon you," I said. Nothing happened. I took out my athame and sliced it across my arm and repeated the phrase as the blood dripped down my arm.

Sawyer's form came into focus. He was little more than a chalk outline, but it was enough to throw Hecate off. "Sawyer, is it really you?" she asked.

I stared at her, stunned by the soft note in her voice. I gripped the glass pitcher of beer by the handle, reassured by its heft.

"Hecate, please let the naiad go," he said.

Her face went blank. I used the pitcher to club her over the head. She fell to the floor. Her demon companions growled and came at us at a run. One demon grabbed Talbot and pulled back his arms while the other punched him in the stomach. I wanted to grab Hecate while she was still unconscious, but Talbot needed me. I sliced the neck of the demon who was using my friend as a punching bag and Talbot took out the other one. The bar patrons took the opportunity presented and ran for the door.

The third demon, a female, picked up Hecate and ran. We followed the demon outside, but a strong wind blew us forcefully backward.

By the time the wind died down, Hecate and the demon had vanished. "We lost her," I said.

"Why do you think she's looking for Doc?" Talbot asked.

"I don't know," I said. "He must have something she wants. We need to find him before she does."

"What now?" Talbot asked. "What do you think the present is?"

"Nothing good."

It had been a hell of a night, even for me. I bought a couple of bottles of absinthe and took them to go. The bartender glared but didn't say anything.

A drunk stumbled into us on the way outside. "I know something," he whispered. "I seen some things."

Talbot curled his lip, either because of the horrible grammar or the horrible smell emanating from the man.

I ignored him, but he followed us down the street. "I do know something. It's your present."

I turned and faced him. "What do you know?"

"Give me one of those and I'll tell you," he said. He pointed to the bottles.

I took a swig from the absinthe and his eyes followed me greedily. "Information first."

"People are disappearing," he said.

"We already know that." I started walking again.

"I know where they're taking them," he said.

I handed him the bottle. "Show us."

"It's too far to walk," he said.

"We'll drive," I said. "And there's another bottle in it for you if it pans out."

I tossed the keys to Talbot. I'd had a few too many swigs of absinthe. "Don't scratch my car."

The drunk took regular swigs off the bottle as he directed us. I wasn't exactly surprised when we turned into the same riverfront community.

"It's that house up there."

The drunk seemed like he'd grown roots in the backseat, but I opened the door and yanked him out. "You're coming with us."

"You think it's a trap?" Talbot asked.

"Probably," I said. "Or maybe he really did see something."

The house sat back from the main street and we had to hike up a long drive to reach it. There were no lights on or cars in the driveway. "Are you sure this is the place?"

The drunk took a swig for courage. "I'm sure."

I peered in the window. No sign of life. I had a feeling Hecate had been there, but I didn't get any sense of demons or magic or anyone or any*thing* alive behind the doors.

I started to pick the lock on the back door, but Talbot pointed to a security sign in the window.

"If Hecate was here, the alarm's already off," I said. "And if she wasn't?"

"Run like hell," I told him. The lock clicked open and we entered a designer kitchen. Nothing but the best for a goddess. The smell told me that there was something dead in the house.

Talbot had a pen flashlight and he shone it around. "What is that smell?" he choked, but we both knew.

Hecate had been here. We were too late. She was long gone.

We found the bodies upstairs in one of the bedrooms. Tria Prima symbols were smeared in blood all over the white walls and white silk comforter.

"It looks like something ate them," Talbot said.

"Demons?"

"Bite marks are too small," he said.

"Let's get out of here," I said. "I'll call Trey. He can do the cleanup by himself this time."

Our companion threw up half of his absinthe in the hallway. I waited until we were in the Caddy to call Trey. He didn't sound surprised.

We dropped the drunk off at the Red Dragon. He practically fell out of the car.

Talbot helped him to a bus bench to sleep it off.

"Why do you think that drunk helped us?"

"I think Hecate was impatient," he said. "She wanted you to see what she'd done. She got the drunk to help it along."

Back at the apartment, I scrubbed the black demon blood off my face and hands in the kitchen sink. "I'm running out of clothes," I said.

"You'd have plenty of money for clothes if you stopped drinking so much," Talbot said.

"I drink because I'm a failure," I said.

"So what?" Talbot replied. "Everyone fails."

"I failed. Epically."

"The difference between success and failure is that the people who succeed get knocked on their asses and then get up again. The failures stay there and feel sorry for themselves."

I glared at him. "You have no idea what I've been through."

"No," he replied. "But you don't even seem to *care* what everyone else has been through."

My anger faded as quickly as it had come. "You're right. So why don't you tell me?"

"Haven't you ever wondered anything about me?" he asked.

"Of course," I said.

"I was in love once," he said. "Before Naomi. But she was a mortal."

"Like Elizabeth," I said. "What happened?"

"It worked out about as well as it did with you and Elizabeth," he said.

In other words, not well at all.

Chapter Twelve

I'd been slacking off at work, so I spent the morning dusting and stocking shelves. I even did a little side browsing. There were still a few of my mother's charms still missing, and although my thread of fate had been located, I still wanted the missing ones.

I touched the silver chain that always hung around my neck. I'd found a black cat carved from Indian ebony, a little coral fish, an emerald frog, a diamond-studded key, and a horseshoe made of moonstones. There were two missing: the miniature book and an ivory wheel of fortune.

I was halfway into my shift when Luke Seren sent a message to Ambrose that he wanted to meet with me. I wasn't sure why Luke hadn't sent it to me directly, but I was relieved to get a response.

"What does that mean?" I asked Ambrose.

"He's considering his options," he said.

"What do you know about Luke?" I asked. Ambrose knew everyone in town worth knowing and a few people everyone wished they didn't know.

"Political," Ambrose replied. "There's been a power play from occasional challengers to his position and he's managed to come out on top."

"Ruthless?"

"He meets the very definition," Ambrose said. "But we desperately need allies and many in the Houses are scared of defying Hecate."

"But he's not?"

"Afraid? No. But that doesn't mean he wouldn't switch sides in the blink of an eye if it suited him."

"So you don't trust him?"

Ambrose shook his head. "I don't. But we need him if we want the House of Zeus on our side."

"Agreed," I said. "But the slaughter at the wilderness center has Luke spooked. What can you tell me about the structure of the Houses?"

"I see you're prepping for this meeting with Luke," he replied.

"It certainly got me thinking," I told him.

"That's a nice change of pace," Talbot said.

"Very funny," I said.

Ambrose ignored us. "There's a leader in each House," he said. "The position is often hereditary, but not always."

"How is a new leader chosen when one dies?"

"There's a vote," he said. "There was a vote called already, but the House of Hades is giving their candidates a month to campaign. It's like a local election."

"I read about all that," I said. The books I had at the apartment told me a few things about the history of the Houses, but pretty much stopped in the fifties. The eighteen fifties. "What can you tell me about the contenders for the head of House of Hades?"

"There's Danvers," Ambrose said. "But his ill health is making the members nervous about backing him. There's a young guy named Johnny Asari, who says he's a direct descendant of Osiris."

"The Egyptian god of the dead?" I asked skeptically.

"A lot of people are buying it," Ambrose said.

"Johnny Asari is a dick," Talbot said helpfully. "He was at college the same time as me, but he pledged a different frat."

"Anybody else?"

Ambrose looked at me like he was deciding something. "There's a rumor floating around that the son of Hades is in town."

"The son of Hades has no interest in becoming a leader of a magical House," I said evenly. "But maybe his half sister is up for the task."

The conversation ended without us coming to any conclusions. I met Luke at the Bean Factory in St. Paul, which was the location he'd chosen. It was a little out of the way for me, which is probably why he'd chosen it.

Luke was already there when I arrived. I ordered a red-eye and then joined him.

"Thank you for meeting me," I said.

"I hear you captured a chimera," he said.

"You're well informed," I said.

He preened, taking my comment as a compliment, which wasn't necessarily the way I'd intended it. I didn't like people knowing my business.

"I am," he said. "I have to be if I want to stay on top."

I studied him as he sipped his tea. What would he do to stay on top? Luke Seren was drawn to power, but there were thousands of ambitious magicians in the Twin Cities.

He had a tiny scar near the open V of his shirt and another on the palm of his hand. On closer inspection, it looked like his missing finger had been removed with a knife.

He noticed my stare. "Hunting knife. Childhood game gone awry," he said. His tone was light, but the expression on his face forbade further inquiries.

"I was hoping that you would lend your support," I said. "Hecate has some running scared."

Luke gave me an appraising look. "You are impetuous," he said. "Many in the Houses believe your impetuous nature will get you killed."

"I've been dead before," I said.

"Impetuous and cocky," he said. "Why would I want to support you? It's common knowledge that you and your aunts don't get along, you've managed to wreak a considerable amount of havoc in the short time you've been in Minneapolis, and you set free a vengeful goddess."

Everything he said was true. "Yet you're still here," I said. Luke Seren was a hard man, despite his courtly air with the ladies.

He seemed to come to a decision. "You are also the son of Fortuna," he said. "And I feel the need to have some luck on my side right now. I will help you."

"What about the other Houses?"

"Trey Marin seems impressed with you," he replied. "Which means you have the House of Poseidon and the House of Zeus on your side." He kept his eyes on his teacup.

"I've never met the leader of the House of Hades," I said.

He glanced up swiftly. "The House of Hades is currently without a leader," he said.

"Why?"

"A sudden illness," he replied. "Alzezar was very old. Most

people had forgotten about him. There is a faction that wants to bring Danvers into power."

"That psycho? He's in no condition to lead anyone," I said.

Luke Seren smiled. "Thanks to you."

We shook hands. I was satisfied that Luke Seren would be our ally, but discomfited by the notion that my new friend had an ulterior motive.

Outside, I came face-to-face with my cousins and sister.

"Nyx, what are you doing here?" Naomi asked.

Had they been following me? I glanced at my sister, but she looked away. "I could ask you the same thing."

"We," Claire said gaily, "have been shopping." She held up multiple bags as proof.

"Were you in the Bean Factory?" I asked.

"I told you he was suspicious," Naomi said to Rebecca. The three of them giggled madly, like it was the funniest thing they'd ever heard.

It wasn't an answer.

"We were going to stop for coffee," Rebecca said, after she finally stopped laughing. "Want to join us?"

"Really?"

"Really," Naomi said. "You can fill us in on your meeting with Luke Seren."

"Shopping, my ass," I said.

They laughed again, but I held the door to the coffee shop open for them anyway.

They were Fates-in-training. They couldn't help snooping.

We ordered coffees and pastries and grabbed a table.

"Before I forget," I said to Naomi. I reached in my pocket and offered her the photo I'd found in Sawyer's things.

"I found this in one of your dad's books," I said. "I know

Sawyer would want you to have it." He wouldn't shut up about it, in fact.

I held it out, but she didn't take it. Her eyes narrowed. "How do you know?"

"I—I just assumed," I stammered. Now was not the time to tell her that I was having daily chats with her dead father.

She accepted the photo and stared down at it. "Thank you."

I thought the time might be right to put in a word for my best friend, who was pining for my cousin. "When are you going to forgive Talbot?" I asked Naomi.

"Eventually."

"He didn't do anything wrong," I said. "Except having poor taste in friends. You shouldn't punish him for my actions."

"That's not what I'm doing."

"Isn't it? You're punishing him for being loyal, but that's a good quality."

"You've made your case," Naomi said. "Now tell us what happened with Luke Seren."

She obviously didn't want to talk about Talbot, so I filled them on my meeting until the order arrived.

Claire and Rebecca went to get our food at the pickup window. I took the opportunity to grill Naomi.

"So what's the real reason for the sudden thaw?" I asked.

She avoided my gaze. "No reason."

"Naomi, tell me the truth."

She looked up. "It turns out"—she gulped—"that you were right about Aunt Deci. The aunts found out she'd been in league with Danvers for years."

Danvers and, by association, the Fates' mortal enemy, Hecate.

"How's Rebecca taking it?"

She shrugged. "Badly, but she promised to give you a chance."

Rebecca and Claire came back with two trays piled with food.

"Elixir of the gods," Claire said after she took a long sip of her iced coffee.

"Not exactly," I said wryly.

Naomi frowned. "The aunts aren't manufacturing that anymore."

She made it sound like they'd had a choice. The recipe for the elixir was gone, and if I had anything to say about it, it would stay that way. But thinking about elixir had reminded me of something I'd read recently.

"Nyx, are you okay?"

"Just thinking about something." I'd read about a necromancer who had used an elixir of some kind to reverse the possession. What if the Fates had done the same thing, only using the rare and powerful black asphodel?

I knew how the Fates did it. I knew how to save Willow. The hard part would be finding the elusive black asphodel. "You don't happen to know where I can get a dozen black asphodel flowers, do you?" I asked.

"What?" Claire said, confused.

"Doesn't exist anymore," Naomi replied.

There was a flicker of something in Rebecca's eyes, but when I stared at her, she looked away. Whatever she knew, my sister wasn't going to share with me.

"I can ask Mom, if you want," Naomi volunteered.

"That's okay," I said. Rebecca knew something and Sawyer had mentioned that Deci had come up with the solution. I needed to make a visit to Deci's, but I didn't want to advertise the fact.

Chapter Thirteen

My conversation with the junior Fates had shaken something loose from my brain. The next morning, I stopped at Hell's Belles for a couple of black coffees and eggs and bacon to go.

I woke Talbot up, but handed him one of the coffees. "I brought breakfast."

"Nyx, it's six a.m.," he groaned. He took a sip of coffee with his eyes still closed. "You better have remembered the biscuits."

I handed him a container. "Gravy's in the bag."

We munched silently.

"We're going to break into Deci's house," I said.

"Bad idea, Nyx," Talbot said.

"Do you have a better one?"

"No," Talbot admitted.

"It's my only lead to find the black asphodel," I said.

"The Fates will be pissed," Talbot said.

"You're right," I said. "But what they don't know won't hurt me." It was empty. Yesterday, Rebecca had mentioned she was staying with Claire.

We took the Caddy to Magician's Row, the street where Minneapolis's most prominent magical lived.

Deci had been Danvers's neighbor. Danvers's house was a fortress, but the place looked abandoned. I parked and approached the house. Someone had thrown a rock through the front window and shards of glass still lay on the grass. The door hung drunkenly on its hinges. I peered inside.

Even his henchman Lurch had deserted the premises, but the inside was worse than the outside. The place had been tossed.

Next door, Deci's lime and pink Victorian looked just as empty, but someone, probably Rebecca, had picked up the mail and watered the lawn. There were new wards on the front door.

"Let's try the back," Talbot suggested.

The back door was ajar.

The kitchen was empty, but I heard a faint sound from somewhere in the house. The sound was louder when we walked down the hallway.

"Someone's here," Talbot said.

I nodded and drew my athame, but wasn't prepared to see Rebecca on her hands and knees, sobbing as she scrubbed her mother's blood out of the floral carpet. I tried not to look at the rust-colored stain.

She jumped to her feet and had a weapon in her hand lightning fast. This time, it was a mop handle. "What are you doing here?"

"What are *you* doing here?" I repeated her question back at her.

"What's it look like?" she snapped. "Cleaning up a murder scene."

I flinched. "It was self-defense."

"Yeah, that's what you said." Her voice was emotionless, but there were still tears on her eyelashes.

I didn't want to leave her alone, but her glare told me she didn't welcome company.

"I hate to ask, but can you help me with something?"

"If you hate to ask, then why are you?" she asked.

I turned to leave, but she stopped me. "Just tell me what you want."

"Is it all right with you if we search the house?"

She gave me a weary look. "Why don't you try telling me the truth for a change?"

"It takes two," I snapped.

She shrugged. "What do you want to know?"

"I want to know where I can find black asphodel," I said. "It's the only way I can reverse the possession and save Willow before Hecate destroys her. I know Deci used an elixir of black asphodel last time the Fates trapped Hecate."

"Our father gave the flowers to her," Rebecca said. "Ask him."

"Doc's missing," I said. My research had led me right back to Doc. My father had been a badass in his time, although if legend was true, kind of creepy. Books on mythology were filled with stories of him, and not much of it was good. Nothing I read revealed the way into Asphodel. Other than death, that was.

"We're screwed," Talbot said.

"Not necessarily," I said.

Rebecca frowned. "That's all I know, I swear."

"I mean we can find the place they grow. My mother once said that black asphodel grows only one place, a place she could never go again."

"I've been here almost every day and I haven't found anything about the flowers, but you're welcome to look."

"You grew up in this house?"

"Yes, of course I did," she said.

"Have you been in the basement?" I asked Rebecca. I repressed a shudder. It had been filled with wraiths the last time I was there.

"No," she said. "Didn't have any reason to. There's just a bunch of old junk stored down there."

"Let's go," I said.

Rebecca stayed upstairs while Talbot and I headed for the basement. It was ill-lit, damp, and full of canned goods, but I had a feeling we'd find a clue about the location of the asphodel. Instead, we found Danvers slumped over in his wheelchair.

He didn't move when we entered the basement. "Is he dead?" Talbot asked.

I reached out for his wrist to check, but a bony claw clamped around my arm. "You did this to me," Danvers croaked.

He was barely recognizable. The curse had aged him. His good looks had disappeared along with his tan. He now resembled a white grub.

I'd been nearly dead when I'd cursed him, but it had taken hold. His skin was mottled red in some places, black in others. One of his hands had twisted into itself and lay useless at his side. He looked worse than when I'd seen him hovering at the gate of the underworld.

"Why are you here?" I asked.

"No reason," he said, but he avoided looking at a garish cookie jar, which was sitting just out of reach on the metal shelf.

"Did you have your hands in my aunt's cookie jar?" I asked.

He glared at me.

"How did he manage to get down here without anyone seeing him?" Talbot asked.

"And the stairs from the kitchen are steep. It would be hard to manage in a wheelchair, unless..."

"Unless what?" Danvers snarled. "You're the reason I'm in this chair."

"Unless you knew of another way," I said. "A secret tunnel, perhaps."

I opened the cookie jar. There was a house key on a metal infinity keychain.

"Wrong as usual," Danvers cackled.

"Oh, I don't think so," I said. He was transfixed by the key in my hand. He wanted it for some reason. And if Danvers wanted it, so did I.

I put it in my pocket. I was almost certain it was what Danvers had come to find. That still didn't explain how he'd gotten into my aunt's house undetected.

The basement was lit by one lonely bulb. I couldn't help but wonder if a wraith was going to jump out at us, but there were only cobwebs in the corners. Except for one corner, which seemed remarkably free of spiderwebs and dust.

I leaned one arm against a loose brick in the wall.

Danvers snickered when nothing happened. He was several inches shorter than I was and the curse had shrunk him even more.

I pressed again, this time lower, and was gratified by the sound of gears grinding.

"Wonder where this leads?" I asked Talbot casually.

He glanced back at Danvers. "What are we going to do with him?"

"We need to stash him somewhere for a while," I said. "I'm sure his blushing bride would like to spend some quality time with him."

The curse had turned Danvers's malevolent magic inward. From what I could tell, he didn't have any magic left. He was helpless. I didn't feel sorry for him. He'd beaten Willow, allowed Hecate to possess his wife, killed over a dozen naiads, and wore loud golf shirts.

"As much as I would like to kill him," I said, "I'm not going to." I had to hold on to the hope that Willow would make it out of Hecate's possession alive, which meant I'd leave Danvers still breathing long enough for her to decide what to do with him. After I got a few answers.

Danvers wheezed out something about my lack of balls.

"I am, however," I continued, like he hadn't insulted my manhood, "going to make him scream. Unless he provides some information."

Danvers snorted. "You can try."

I gripped my athame and embedded it in his thigh. "Now you're going to tell me where I can find black asphodel."

"Wh-why do you want it?"

"Is that why Hecate trashed your place?" I asked. "You're holding out on her?"

He tightened his lips and refused to speak. I twisted the knife in deeper.

"I'll tell you," he said. "The only place it grows is in Asphodel."

"How do I get there?"

"Not my problem," he said. I yanked out the athame and held it out. "Should I do the other leg, so you have a matching set?"

"I'll tell you," he growled. "You already know how to get to Hecate's realm. Keep going and you'll reach Asphodel."

"That's it?"

He nodded.

"You're lying," I said. "Hecate was looking for something. What was it?" I polished the handle of my athame with the end of my shirt. "You can tell me now or I can hand you over to Hecate."

"A charm," he said, defeated. "You can't get in without it."

I held out my hand. "Cough it up."

He took off his watch. "I need a screwdriver or something to pry it open."

I spotted a rusty toolbox in the corner and rummaged through it until I found a screwdriver.

He used it to pry off the face of the watch and took out a small plastic ghost, the kind you found in abundance around Halloween.

"You're kidding," Talbot said.

"Completely serious," Danvers said. "Go into Asphodel without it and the spirits will rip you to shreds." His oily smile surfaced like scum on a rain puddle. "Still could happen."

After he handed it over, he lapsed into a sullen silence.

"What should we do with him?" I asked Talbot. As much as I loathed Danvers, I couldn't abandon him.

"I have a friend who does in-home care," Talbot said. "He can handle Danvers. Carlos is with the House of Zeus and he owes me a favor," he added when he noticed my doubtful look.

"Babysitting a broken-down necromancer? That must be a big favor he owes you."

"It is," Talbot replied. He didn't elaborate.

He grabbed Danvers's wheelchair and pushed him through the hidden door.

"Danvers and Deci must have been plotting together for years," I commented as we walked.

"Quit talking about me like I'm not here," Danvers grumbled.

"Only a matter of time," I replied.

We went through a tunnel until we came to a dead end.

"Where's the lever?" I asked Danvers.

He scowled and refused to answer.

"I'll find it," I said. I finally located the brick that stood out a little more from the others. I pushed it in and a door slowly opened to reveal another basement.

I'd never been inside his house, but I was sure we'd made it to Danvers. There was an elevator in the basement, which led to his third-floor bedroom. The golf trophies confirmed we were in the right place, as well as the black satin sheets and décor reminiscent of early porn movies.

"Home sweet home," I said. Danvers had retreated into a stubborn silence.

We left him in his room. "Stay here."

Talbot made a quick phone call while I snooped. The house had been carefully wiped clean of all magic.

What had Danvers done to get on Hecate's bad side? Or maybe she just didn't have a good side.

We waited for Talbot's friend Carlos in the living room. Sitting on an uncomfortable black leather couch, I tried to picture Willow in this house and failed.

Talbot's friend Carlos turned out to be a model-gorgeous guy with full lips, dark eyes, and dark wavy hair that was carefully messy.

"One of your frat buddies?" I said in a low voice, but Carlos heard.

"Hardly." He smiled at me and I was nearly overwhelmed by the force of his charm.

"Knock it off, Carlos," Talbot said. That's when I realized that Carlos was a Mesmer, a magician who was able to compel with only his charismatic smile.

Carlos's smile decreased in wattage. "Sorry," he said. "It's just a habit when I meet new people."

I stuck out a hand. "Nyx Fortuna."

He shook it vigorously. "I've heard of you, of course. Your tarot poker games have become a local legend."

I changed the subject. "Are you sure you want to take this on?"

"Are you kidding me? I share an apartment with three other guys. Talbot, are you sure you want to waste a favor on this?"

"You haven't met the patient yet," Talbot warned. We took the stairs to make the introductions.

The sound of hoarse chanting came from his bedroom.

Danvers was in front of a small altar. A basin of blood was in his hand and judging by the cuts on his wrists, the blood was his.

"Girlfriend not taking your call?" I asked. I yanked the basin out of his hands and dumped it in the adjoining bathroom's sink.

"I'll bandage those cuts," Carlos said.

I was surprised when Danvers allowed it, but realized his magic was gone and he was as susceptible to Carlos's charms as any mortal.

"We should be getting back," I said.

"Go ahead," Carlos said. "I've got this handled."

"Call me or Nyx if you have any problems," Talbot said. Carlos and I exchanged phone numbers.

"Call me if you see anyone unusual," I said. "We have to seal the tunnel between the two houses."

After we went through the entrance to the basement, we sealed it closed and warded it, then did the same on the other side.

"Think it will hold?" Talbot asked.

"Danvers is in no shape to break those wards," I said. "The bigger question is why did he want the key?"

"The real question is what the key is for," Talbot said.

We went upstairs to find Rebecca. She was sitting at the kitchen counter, staring into a cup of tea.

"Do you know what this is for?" I asked. I held up the key I'd found in the basement.

"Probably just a spare," she said.

"I doubt Danvers would come sniffing around for a copy of the key to your front door."

She held out a hand. "Let me take a look." She examined it. "It's not our house key. I've never seen it before."

"I've read the Book of Fates over and over, but I didn't see anything about a key. It was about as exciting as my grocery list."

"Which reads 'beer, absinthe, beer, and chips,'" Talbot added.

"Can't help you," she said. "Maybe ask Nona or Morta."

I pocketed the key. "I guess we'll take off then."

She returned to staring at her tea and didn't lift her head when we left.

"You think Danvers knows more than she's telling us?" Talbot asked me once we were back in the Caddy.

"I'd count on it," I replied.

Chapter Fourteen

I'd thought it was hard to find my way into Hecate's realm until I looked for Asphodel. I took the plastic ghost and attached it to my mother's necklace with her charms and used the Hell's Belles basement entrance.

According to Danvers, I needed to walk until I came to the wall. I'd never ventured past Hecate's castle before. There'd been no reason to, but once I passed it, the air became lighter and sweeter. With the charm, I would be able to pass through the wall and move into the Field of Asphodel.

I wandered around the underworld for hours without finding Asphodel. Finally, I stopped and said, "Show me the way to Asphodel."

I saw a gleam of white in the distance and headed for it. After about an hour of hiking, I reached a gray stone wall, which was high enough that it blocked my view of what was on the other side. I got a toehold and pulled myself up and over. I dropped down with a heavy thud and lay there while I caught my breath.

Soft sunlight warmed my face. I sat up and looked around.

The ground was covered in white flowers as far as the eye could see. I'd reached Asphodel.

I headed for the field of the fragile white flowers. White asphodel grew in abundance, but there was no sign of any black plants. Some of the dead souls feasted upon the white asphodel while others flitted aimlessly about. The spirits ignored me.

I touched the plastic ghost hanging around my neck and was rewarded with a sharp prick on my finger. It was only a drop of blood, but it was enough. The spirits converged upon me, hungry for blood.

"Stop!" I commanded and the spirits subsided. I was shocked. Not only could I summon spirits, but I could command them.

"Very good," Doc said. I turned to face my father. "Your powers are growing, Nyx."

I didn't expect to find him hanging out in Asphodel, but that's where he was. He was Hades. The underworld was his to command.

"What are you doing here?" I asked him.

"I could ask you the same thing," he replied.

"I've been all over looking for you," I said.

"Here I am," he said. He acted like he didn't have a care in the world, but I could tell something had happened to him. His salt-and-pepper hair had gone white.

"Is this where you've been the whole time?" I asked. "I thought Hecate had you."

"She tried," Doc replied. "She was not successful."

"Obviously," I said, "or you wouldn't still be in once piece."

"I'm impressed. Not many venture into Asphodel. At least not the living," Doc said. He was remarkably calm. The twitching and shaking were noticeably absent. Maybe Asphodel was good for him.

"I need black asphodel to trap a soul."

Doc went still. "Whose soul?"

"Hecate's."

He rubbed his right arm. "You want the black flowers for her?"

"You helped my aunts trap her the first time," I said.

He hesitated before answering. "I supplied a few ingredients."

"Can you do it again? And where are you going to get black asphodel?" I asked. I gestured to the field we stood in. "All I see is white flowers."

"Don't worry about it," Doc replied. "The asphodel elixir must be mixed with your blood. Hecate will be expecting a trap, but she won't be expecting this one."

"Why not?" I was skeptical. Hecate had been two steps ahead of me from the beginning.

"The black asphodel only grows one place," he said. "And I'm the only one who knows the location."

"I need at least a dozen of those flowers," I said. "Can you be a little more specific?"

"Let's take a walk," Doc suggested. "I'll show you."

"Where are we going?"

"Here," he said. He touched my shoulder and we were standing in a field of black asphodel. The sky was the color of ash and a single white poplar tree stood like a lonely ghost in the distance.

"Where are we?"

"A part of the underworld that even Hecate doesn't know about," Doc replied. "Your mother is the only other person I've shown this place to."

My father was trying to connect to me, but whenever he mentioned my mother, it only reminded me how he'd abandoned her to the Fates.

"Is this where you got the asphodel for the elixir?"

He nodded. "Let me show you my home," he said.

One of my father's many nicknames was The Rich One. Hades was known for his wealth, so I had expected something ostentatious, but instead, he led me to a simple one-story structure at the edge of the asphodel field.

It was desolate but beautiful. I bent and sniffed one of the blooms. It had a sweet, spicy scent.

"Is this where you go when you disappear?"

He nodded. "Yes, it was built for me a long time ago."

I hadn't thought, not really, about how long a god must live. And I'd been whining about putting in a couple hundred years.

Once inside, I surveyed my father's home. He was showing me his secret place and I wanted to learn what I could. It was tiny, for a god, and sparsely furnished. The walls were plain white, but several paintings hung on them.

I felt comfortable there and I realized it was because I was surrounded by my mother's things. There was a vase of her favorite flowers, a garnet ring she'd worn when I was small.

"This still has your bite marks in it," Doc said. He held up a small wooden rattle.

I recognized a carved wooden flute. When I was a child and scared of the things that came for you in the dark, my mother would play it and sing me to sleep at night.

I snatched up a miniature book charm, which I'd been searching for since my mother's death. "Do you know how long I've looked for this?"

He nodded. "I knew why, too."

"Did you know she'd hidden my thread of fate in the athame?"

He shook his head. "I had no idea. That was my first athame, and I gave it to her when I found out you were coming. We were so happy."

"Then what happened?"

He touched his scarred cheek contemplatively. "Your mother found out about Deci. And Rebecca. And that was that." The sorrow in his voice almost made me reach out to comfort him. Almost.

But then I remembered my mother and I had spent our lives on the run because of his cowardice and lust.

"Let's get the asphodel and go," I said.

"Is there anything here you'd like to have?" he asked. My eyes went to the miniature book and an ivory wheel of fortune. The charms still missing from my mother's necklace.

I grabbed the missing charms and placed them on the necklace. "I can't believe I have them all." The miniature book and the ivory wheel of fortune joined the black cat carved from Indian ebony, the little coral fish, the emerald frog, the diamond-studded key, and the horseshoe made of moonstones. "Finally." I touched each charm gently.

"Please, take anything you'd like," he said. "Take it all."

I cleared my clogged throat. My mother's presence permeated the room. "I thought the aunts were the ones who had the charms."

"I didn't trust them," Doc said. "I wanted to keep them safe."

"Too bad you didn't feel the same way about your wife and child."

"I am trying to make amends," he replied. "In my poor way."

"Hecate's daughter Wren said you left Hecate to die," I said.

After a long moment, he nodded. "She was ambitious," he said. "She wanted to rule the underworld. I was not willing to let that happen."

"That's why she is doing all this?"

He nodded gravely. "I'm afraid the sins of the father have indeed been laid upon the children."

"But you still won't help me stop her?"

He shook his head. We picked the flowers in silence.

There was nothing else to say, except "Take me home."

Chapter Fifteen

My father insisted that we brew the elixir at midnight on a full moon. We were in my kitchen. It was around 10 p.m. and we still had two hours to kill before we could start cooking up the stuff that would, I hoped, free Willow and trap Hecate.

"A little theatrical, don't you think?"

"It will maximize the strength of the potion," Doc replied. He sighed. "There is so much I need to teach you."

"Kind of late for that, don't you think?" I slammed down the pot I'd been holding.

I'd invited Rebecca to join us, but she'd declined the invitation with a smirk. "No daddy/daughter bonding time for me, thanks," she'd muttered.

"Do you think you'll be able to find Hecate's physical form?" Doc asked. He seemed oblivious to my simmering resentment.

"Shouldn't be too hard," I replied. "Hecate, at least her body, can't leave the underworld." The goddess had found a way around her imprisonment by possessing Willow, but her form was stuck.

"The underworld is a very big place," Doc said. "And you said you'd already searched Hecate's castle."

"I'll find the body," I said. "I have to."

I was well into my fourth or fifth beer when there was a thump in the hallway outside my apartment.

I drew my athame and looked out. At first, I didn't see anything. I heard a sound again and stepped out into the hallway. There was a body lying near the stairwell. Something about the dark hair and thin frame looked familiar.

I rolled her over. It was Rebecca.

Her nose was bloody and swollen and her arm hung at an odd angle at her side, probably broken, but she was alive.

"Met your ex tonight," Rebecca said, right before she collapsed.

Doc carried her to the couch and set her down gently. The bone of her right arm poked through her skin. There was dried blood on her face, her jeans, even in her hair.

"We should set her arm before she wakes up," Doc said calmly. "Find me some newspaper or a small board, and an old T-shirt if you have one."

"We?" The thought horrified me. When he stared at me, I collected myself. "Last week's newspaper is still on the kitchen counter." I rounded up a ratty tee and handed it to him. Doc brought out some adhesive tape from the depths of his ratty trench coat and scooped up the newspaper.

"You'll need to hold her steady," he said. "It won't take long."

"Okay." I watched as Doc fashioned a makeshift splint.

It was turning out to be a hell of a family reunion. Other than a whimper when Doc first started setting her arm, Rebecca didn't stir.

A few minutes later, he said, "You can let her go now."

"How is she?"

"Got any alcohol?" Doc asked.

I snorted. "That's how well you know me," I replied. "I always have booze."

"Unless you've drunk it all," he said.

I guess he did know me, after all. I handed him a bottle of vodka, thinking he was going to sterilize the bandages or something, but instead, he took a swig.

Rebecca stirred. "Steady, now," Doc said. "You've been injured."

"Where am I?"

"Nyx's apartment," Doc replied.

She tried to sit up and winced. "I remember now."

"What happened to you?" I asked.

"A couple of demons jumped me," she said.

"Was Hecate there?"

"No, why do you ask?"

"You said something about my ex, and since she's currently possessing Willow, I thought..."

Rebecca shook her head. "You thought wrong. I was talking about the redhead. Naomi's sister."

"*Wren* jumped you?"

Rebecca grinned weakly. "That's what I thought," she said. "She looks like an angel, doesn't she?" She touched her nose gently. "But I gave as good as I got."

"Your arm is broken," Doc told her. "You should rest."

"We need to warn the others," I said. I grabbed my cell and dialed Naomi's number. When she picked up, I explained what happened.

"I'm coming over," she said.

"Don't go anywhere," I replied. "It's not safe."

"I'm right next door, at Talbot's," she said. "I'll call Claire and the aunties and then I'll be right over."

I started to say something, but she hung up on me.

Talbot and Naomi entered the apartment hand in hand, which was one bright note in an otherwise dismal evening.

Doc was glancing at the clock. I checked it, too. It was just after eleven—still plenty of time to make the elixir.

I filled Talbot in while Naomi checked on her cousin. She wet a kitchen towel and used it to clean the dried blood from Rebecca's face.

"Everyone has to be very careful," I said. "Wren is dangerous."

Naomi overheard me.

"Wren won't hurt me," Naomi said. "Despite everything, she's my sister."

"It's the rest of us I'm worried about," I said. I slammed my beer down. "You still think Wren is going to come back and say sorry? That's not going to happen."

"So what's the story?" Rebecca said. "Exactly how many of your exes want to kill you?"

"All of them," Talbot quipped.

"Only Wren," I clarified. "And she actually did kill me."

"I need to go home," Rebecca said. "Gotta feed my cat."

"You don't have a cat," Naomi said. "What did you give her?" she asked Doc.

"A mild sedative," he replied. "She shouldn't be moved."

"She's out of it anyway," Naomi said. "And it's safer for her here."

A soft snoring came from the couch.

My sister looked smaller, gentler when she slept. "Probably all the drugs Doc gave her," I muttered. I grabbed a spare blanket from the closet and covered her up.

I'd wring Wren's neck the next time I saw her.

"It's time, Nyx," Doc said reluctantly.

"Time for what?" Naomi asked curiously.

"Cooking lesson," I said. "While Doc and I do that, why don't you two go through the books on that shelf and see if you can find anything to kill a shitload of demons in one fell swoop."

Doc was already in the kitchen.

I got out a beat-up old stockpot I'd found at Eternity Road. "Will this work?"

"I'd prefer to do this without witnesses," he said in a low voice.

I shrugged. "Rebecca's sound asleep and Talbot and Naomi are trying to find a spell."

He frowned, but started to get out the ingredients.

"Hecate knows you're alive," I said. "Won't she come after you?"

"Don't worry about me," he said.

"I don't want anyone to get hurt," I said. "Are you sure this is the right thing to do?" We had to do something. I would deal with Wren, too, when the time came.

"You don't have a choice," Doc said. "Hecate needs to be contained either way."

"What if the elixir doesn't work?"

He looked grave. "You know Willow better than I do. Would she want to suffer, knowing Hecate is controlling her body? Knowing others are suffering?"

"No," I said. "She'd want me to end it."

"Then that is what you must do," he replied. "One way or the other."

I turned my attention back to the elixir. "How does it work?"

"The spell forms a giant magical spiderweb," he explained. "Or a net. It'll trap Hecate, but free Willow."

"You're sure it will do the job?" I asked.

"Yes. It takes a lot of magic to possess a mortal," he explained. "Once Hecate enters the trap, it will drain her powers and Willow will be able to break free."

"Why are you so sure?"

"Because it worked on me," he said.

"Someone drained you of your powers?"

"It won't happen again," he said. I believed him. "We're going to trap her."

"How do you know she'll show up?"

"Because her body will be the bait."

"Hecate knows we might try to take her body," I said. "She doesn't seem to care. She won't let go of Willow."

"You just haven't given her the right incentive."

My father's plan was to find Hecate's physical body and steal it. She'd be so pissed that she'd either give up her hold on Willow's body to get her own back or she'd come looking for us.

"And how do you expect me to find Hecate's body?" I asked. "I'm sure she didn't leave it lying around unprotected."

"But you found a chimera guarding the underworld," he pointed out. "My guess is the body is there."

"Seems reasonable that she'd leave her body where she felt safe," I acknowledged. "Or because she hasn't figured out how to use the bead yet. But that's the first place I looked."

"If she could leave the underworld on her own, she would," Doc said. "It's there somewhere."

"Anywhere else you can think of?" I asked. "The cave where Wren was born was empty, too."

He shook his head. "She probably has some nasty booby trap waiting for anyone dumb enough to touch her body," he warned.

"Or maybe she *wants* us to take the body out of the underworld," I said. "Maybe it's a trick."

"It could be," he admitted. "But it seems to be your only chance. Otherwise, she'll just keep sending demons until one of them manages to take you out."

"According to the Fates, Hecate already has everything she needs to end her banishment in the underworld."

"The Fates have been wrong before," he said.

"So now that you've met Rebecca, what do you think?"

"I always knew about Rebecca," he said.

"That's a comfort," I said. In a strange way it was. He'd abandoned her, too. No wonder Deci had hated my father. I hated him, too, sometimes. When I wasn't feeling sorry for him.

"Nyx, this must be difficult for you, finding out you had a sister," he said. "I wanted to tell you, but…"

Difficult?

"Try disappointing, infuriating, amazing," I said. "And you kept it from me."

"I'm sorry," he replied.

"Let's just make the elixir and get this over with," I snapped.

He gave me a long look. "Where's the vodka?" he asked.

I grabbed the bottle off the antique tea cart that served as a makeshift bar.

Doc took it from me and then poured a healthy amount into two glasses. He handed me one and then tilted his in my direction. "Cheers."

He poured the rest of the vodka into the stockpot he'd brought with him and then sprinkled the black asphodel in.

"That's it?"

"Not exactly," he said. "May I borrow your athame?"

I handed it to him and he made a tiny cut along the thumb of his left hand. He held it over the pot and blood dripped onto the flowers. He turned on the burner. "It has to cook on low for exactly one hour."

The air turned noxious, but my father continued to stir the elixir, seemingly impervious to the smell.

"The second Hecate tries to take possession of her own form, the elixir will start to work," he said. "Now all we need is the bait."

"What's the one thing that will bring Hecate to our doorstep?" Talbot asked.

That was my cue. Time to go snatch a body.

Chapter Sixteen

Talbot and I took the Hell's Belles entrance to the underworld. Hidden in the basement storage room were an altar and an express entrance to the underworld. It was quicker, but was also more likely to be heavily guarded by demons.

"Did you and Naomi find a way to kill the demons en masse?" I asked as we cut through the kitchen to the basement altar that was the shortcut to the underworld.

"I may have found something," he said. "But I'm not sure it'll work."

There was no sign of Hecate's hounds. I didn't even hear a bark. I assumed they were guarding their goddess's body.

We crossed over, not far from Hecate's castle. A purple haze masked a moon the color of blood. Twisted black trees lined the path. The wolfsbane, mandrake, belladonna, and dittany had flourished since my last visit and threatened to overrun the path.

It was easy to get lost on the path, but Naomi had left a few magical bread crumbs the last time we were here.

"There was a mention of demons unable to stand silver and

salt," Talbot said, "so Naomi made me something special for them. Silver, salt, and a nasty little spell. It should melt the skin off their bones."

"I hope she's right," I said.

Hecate's palace seemed to be empty, but I caught a glimpse of a skittering thing, black and thin as a shadow.

Another of the insectlike creatures joined its friend, and then another. The marble floor echoed with the sound of hundreds of the insects.

"Got any bug spray?" I whispered.

"What do you think they eat?" he whispered back.

"Let's not find out." I sent a fire bolt into the middle of the creatures. The flame spread until the smell of roasting insect filled the room. They let out high-pitched squeaks as they burned.

The sound brought a horde of demons running. Talbot lobbed the ball of silver and salt into the middle of the throng. It exploded. The demons shrieked as their skin bubbled.

We raced through the castle, checking each room for Hecate's physical form. I found the locked door where I'd first encountered the chimera.

I tried every unlocking spell I knew, but the door wouldn't budge. I sliced open my palm and held it over the knob. "Open," I commanded.

The door creaked open and we stepped into the room.

Hecate's body was in a white aspen bed carved with Tria Prima symbols. She was dressed in a simple white gown, but the bottom was festooned with more of the Tria Prima symbols. Her long dark hair fanned out on her pillow and her skin was as pale as her dress.

"She looks dead," Talbot said.

"I wish."

We stood there staring at the body of the goddess. "Let's get this over with."

"Maybe she's booby-trapped," Talbot said. He pointed upward. There was another of the skittering black insects hanging above the bed. The thing looked at us with its tiny red eyes.

I sent a bolt of flame toward it. It dodged the fire. Instead of running, it jumped, landing on my face. It felt like I was being stabbed by hundreds of tiny knives. Talbot managed to pull it off me. He threw it on the floor and stamped on it, but the insect still twitched. I threw my athame and skewered it.

"What are those things?" Talbot asked.

I shrugged. "An underworld bedbug?"

I checked, but didn't spot any more of the insects.

I grabbed one of Hecate's arms and her eyes opened. They were opaque and unseeing. I dropped her arm and took a step back.

"Think she knows we're here?"

Talbot shrugged. "I think we should hurry. One or two demons might have escaped and rushed to tattle."

I repressed a shudder and picked up Hecate at the knees. I slung her over my shoulder and we started the long hike back home.

We didn't spot any demons, unless you counted Bernie, who was in the kitchen when we came topside, dragging Hecate's body with us.

"Son of Fortuna," Bernie said. "Please use the back door when you leave." Which I took to mean there were demons waiting for us at the front entrance.

We took the rear exit when we hauled Hecate's body out

of the restaurant and into the back of the Eternity Road van. Doc was in the driver's seat, and he started the vehicle when he saw us.

"I've literally become a body snatcher." I grunted as we set our burden down. "Not my highest point, career-wise."

Talbot laughed, but then sobered quickly. "She's going to come after you with everything she has." He closed the back doors and Doc floored it.

"Let her," I said. "This is the only way Willow is going to be free. She wouldn't be in this mess if it weren't for me."

"You don't know that," he replied. "Hecate was looking for a way out of the underworld. You had nothing to do with putting her there."

"She has a grudge against my entire family," I said.

"You know you're giving her what she wants," Talbot said. "By taking her body out of the underworld, all Hecate has to do is climb back in and she's truly free. She won't need Willow anymore."

"I have something planned," I said.

"What are we going to do with the body?" Talbot asked. "We need it close so Hecate has another container."

"We're taking the body to Parsi. They have the perfect spot to stash someone."

"Dungeon?" Talbot guessed.

"Zoo," I told him.

My aunt Morta was there waiting for us. She'd even brought a body-size dolly with her. Talbot and I heaved Hecate's prone form onto it and followed Morta. Doc trailed behind us and kept his distance from Morta. She didn't even acknowledge him. Maybe she didn't realize he was there. Doc had the ability to fade into the background when he wanted to.

"You are surprisingly resourceful, son of Fortuna," Morta said.

"So you think it will work?" I asked.

She shrugged. "Stranger things have happened."

It didn't take long for us to relocate Hecate's body to her new prison. It was decidedly less luxurious than her palace in the underworld. The rest of Morta's "guests" went silent when we entered the corridor with the body of the goddess.

The plan was to free Willow and to trap Hecate, this time so she couldn't possess anyone ever again. Hecate's body was the bait.

"What now?" Talbot asked.

"We wait for Hecate to realize her body is missing." It shouldn't take long. We'd killed a dozen of her strongest demons.

Aunt Morta's lackeys provided a couple of folding chairs. We sat in front of the warded room and waited.

Chapter Seventeen

I spent an uncomfortable night, dozing on a folding chair in the basement of Parsi Enterprises. I waited for Hecate to show, but she never made an appearance.

At around 9 a.m., Nona wandered down. "Why don't you take a break?" she suggested.

I hesitated and she gave me an exasperated look. "You don't think I can handle anyone who shows up?"

I'd unintentionally hurt her pride. Nona was still raw from Sawyer's death. "Of course you can take care of things," I said. "Maybe I'll check in on Rebecca."

"She's here," Nona replied. "Why don't you take her across the street for some tea? She looks terrible."

I found Rebecca in Morta's office, sitting in Morta's chair.

"She hates it when you sit in her chair," I said.

Rebecca grinned. "I know."

Nona was right. Rebecca did look terrible.

"Shouldn't you be resting?" The bruises had faded, but there were dark rings under her eyes. "It looks like someone used a Sharpie on your eyes."

Rebecca put her feet up on Mona's desk. "Nona send you up here to babysit me?"

"Probably," I said. "I've been sleeping on a folding chair all night. Want to grab a cup of coffee?"

"Don't tell me you want to bond?"

"I want to ask you something," I said.

"Okay," she said. She moved slowly, but I was amazed at how fast she'd already healed.

Across the street, I ordered two red-eyes for me and a hot tea for Rebecca.

Rebecca took a sip of her tea and then added a dollop of honey. "What did you want to ask me?"

"We're going to trap Hecate," I said. "But if it doesn't work, if I can't get her out of Willow's body, I want you to do something for me."

"What?"

"Kill Willow."

She gaped at me. "Fuck, Nyx," she said. "You've threatened the life of anyone who looked at the naiad wrong. Why'd you change your mind?"

"I was in Asphodel," I said. "A bunch of spirits milling around. It's quiet. Serene. Better than sharing a body with Hecate."

She met my eyes. "Why me? Why not one of the other Fates?"

"Naomi is too softhearted," I said. "And I don't know if Claire has what it takes to kill someone."

"But I do?"

"Yes."

She nodded. "I'll do it. But only if there are no other options."

On our way back to Parsi, I spotted one of Hecate's demons watching us from the shadow of a building.

"Snooping for your boss?" I asked the demon.

He sneered at me. "You pissed her off."

"I thought she was already pissed off."

"She was only playing before," he said. "She wanted me to let you know she's getting rid of the naiad."

Rebecca hissed. "You cockroach."

"She might want to rethink that." I kept my voice even, but it took an effort.

"Why's that?" I'd managed to surprise him.

"Because I have her body," I said. "And Willow's continuing existence is the only thing keeping me from building a great big fire and tossing Hecate's body into it."

"You're lying," he said.

"Want to take that chance?" I said. "If I were you, I'd scurry back and tell the boss lady."

We watched him leave. "I guess we'll have company tonight," Rebecca commented.

"If that doesn't get Hecate here, nothing will," I said.

In our absence, one of the Fates' flunkies had brought a couple of folding cots and set them up near the cage where we'd stashed Hecate's body. I persuaded Rebecca to get some rest, but she wouldn't leave the building. "I promised you," she said. "I'm staying."

My sister was stubborn. Instead of arguing with her, I stretched out on one of the cots. "You take first watch."

I'd dozed off, but a small sound woke me up. In the cage across from us, the Phoenix cawed softly and then ruffled its feathers.

Willow/Hecate walked in. Her hands were bloody. I had a feeling I knew what had happened to the security guard. Rebecca was still in the cot next to mine, but she was awake.

"You have something of mine," Hecate said, "and I want it back." Willow's complexion was normally a translucent blue, but ropy green veins ran under the skin.

"How about I trade you for it? Willow's body for yours."

I grabbed her arm and smeared the elixir on her forehead, lips, and cheeks. "*Expello*," I commanded. "Get the hell out of Willow's body." I added. Her eyes rolled back in her head and she slumped forward.

"Where am I?" Willow said. "Nyx, what happened?"

It had worked. Willow was free, but something still held me back from celebrating.

She flung herself into my arms. She felt like Willow.

"Nyx, you saved me. I'm so grateful." She sounded like Willow, but I still wasn't sure.

She kissed me, a wet passionate kiss full of nymph magic. My suspicions were correct.

"Kiss me again," I commanded, struggling to keep my voice sound like that of an eager lover.

She did. My grip on her tightened. She mistook it for passion and put her head on my shoulder. "Let's go home."

"I don't think so, Hecate." Willow, the real Willow, had made a *Pignus Sanguinus*, a blood oath to her loathsome groom. She was bound by honor, and by magic, to remain faithful. She wouldn't have risked her life or her honor to kiss me, no matter how much I wanted her to. And not once had ever she used nymph magic to seduce me. She hadn't needed to. She wasn't Willow.

Willow's face changed and for a second, something dark and deadly swam in her eyes. Hecate's voice came out of Willow's mouth. "You thought it would be that easy to reverse a possession? I've seen that little trick before."

"I know," I said. "But you haven't seen this." I tightened my grip even more before I used my athame to cut my hand.

She'd taken my blood when Wren slit my throat. "You wanted my blood so badly," I said. "You're about to get a bellyful." I smeared my blood onto her lips and began to chant. She tried to spit it out, but I held her jaw tight as my blood ran into her mouth.

A trickle of a chartreuse substance came out of her mouth. Her body slumped and I caught her in my arms before she fell.

A piercing scream cut the silence. Then another and another. I couldn't tell if it was Willow or Hecate screaming in pain, but the possibility that it was Willow made me shudder. The noise continued, but weaker, like she was walking through a long tunnel.

"Jesus, Doc, did you know?"

"I did," he admitted. "But I didn't want to tell you."

"Why not?"

"I didn't think you'd go through with it if you knew Willow would be in pain."

I glared at him. "You're right."

Forced out of Willow's body, Hecate's spirit headed for home. Hecate was forced back in her own body, which we'd covered with more of the black asphodel elixir. I smeared more of my blood onto her skin and watched as the elixir crystallized into long strands and bound Hecate tight.

Hecate was trapped inside a crystal web. The more she struggled, the tighter the strands wound around her body. Her eyes were black with fury and she screamed over and over, muttering command after command, spell after spell. As fast as she uttered spells, I repelled them.

I threw a counterspell at her. A strand covered her mouth and she tried biting through it, but it held fast. The strands wrapped around her until she looked like a mummy. She fought until she didn't have any breath left. Eventually, she stopped struggling.

"Is she dead?"

"No," I said. "But she won't get out of that, not in a thousand years."

Willow's prone body lay on the floor.

"Willow?"

Hecate was gone, but Willow was cold and unmoving. I laid my head on her chest and listened. There was a faint thump, but it was so weak. The knowledge that I'd failed to save her was a lump in my throat.

I wrapped her in my jacket and fumbled for the healing amulet. Panic blanked my mind, but I finally remembered the words to the spell.

I completed the ritual and then waited, but there was no change. I wasn't going to let my aunts snip Willow's thread of fate.

"Damn it, Willow, just breathe."

She leaned over and retched. More of the foamy yellow substance came out of her mouth.

"Nyx, where am I?"

"Don't talk," I said. "I'll get you to the water."

A naiad healed best surrounded by water. I ran to the Caddy with Willow in my arms and then broke several traffic laws to get her to the lake.

I threw the Caddy into park and carried her to the water's edge. I stripped off our clothes and dove into the water. She sank into its healing depths with a grateful sigh.

She floated, encircled in my arms, for a long time. Her color gradually returned.

"Better?"

"Yes, thank you."

"Do you remember anything?"

Her eyes narrowed. "Danvers."

"You're safe now," I said.

"But my dear husband is not."

"It's not the right time to go after him," I said. "We have bigger problems."

I explained everything that had happened since Hecate had possessed her.

"You did that for me?"

I don't know what I expected, but it wasn't the slap that landed hard on my jaw.

"What was that for?"

"You're an idiot," she said fiercely. "We have to fix it. We have to make it right. I'm not worth it."

"You are to me." A lock of dark hair fell into her eyes and I tucked it behind her ear.

She touched my jaw again, softly this time.

"Willow, I—"

She put her hand on my mouth to stop the words. "There is no time for sentiment."

"There's always time," I said. I bent my head and tried to kiss her, but she blocked it.

"I made a vow, remember? The *Pignus Sanguinus*. I am not free."

I nodded and instead, rested my forehead on hers, until we were eye to eye, nose to nose. Her lips were a breath away. It took a minute, but she pushed me away.

"No, Nyx," she said. "There will be no more of that. You have things you must do. And so do I."

"You need to rest," I said. "Regain your strength."

"Where is my husband?"

"Why do you want to know?" I asked.

"I will find him, with or without your help," she said. "Please."

Not even a god could resist Willow when she wanted something. And she wanted Danvers's head. Preferably on a platter with an apple in his mouth, like the pig he was.

"I'll take you to him."

She slipped on the robe Hecate had put on her, but not without a shudder, and I pulled my tee and jeans back on. We headed to Magician's Row.

Danvers and Carlos weren't home. Willow headed straight for the master bedroom. She rummaged through the closet until she found what she was looking for. It was a simple green dress, long and flowing.

She stripped, not bothering to check to see if I was watching. I was. She put her dress on and then kicked Hecate's robe aside. "Burn it," she said. "I never want to see it again."

I scooped it up and took it to my car. It might be useful to have a Tria Prima robe. Carlos and Danvers showed up as I locked the Caddy's trunk.

The curse had done more damage than I imagined. Danvers was covered in pustules and his once-strong frame had shrunk. He no longer had the strength to push his own chair. Carlos was at his side.

Carlos drew me aside. "It's only a matter of time," he said. "He has a week, maybe two. What happened to him?"

"Nothing he didn't deserve," I replied. Carlos's attention wandered and I looked over. Willow had a firm grip on her husband's wheelchair. Danvers had the good sense to look terrified.

"You may go now. He's my husband," Willow said sweetly to Carlos. "I'll take care of him."

Carlos looked at me, but I shrugged. "I went to the wedding."
And hated every minute of it.

"I shouldn't leave him alone," he replied uncertainly.

"He won't be alone," Willow said. "I'll take care of him."

He took one look at her dark hair tumbling down her back
and her luscious lips and nodded. "I'm sure it will be okay.
After all, you are his wife."

I snorted, but quickly repressed it when Willow elbowed
me in the ribs.

Carlos gave Willow one of his Mesmerizing smiles, but she
didn't even blink. "Thank you for your service."

"Rich guys have all the luck," Carlos muttered enviously.

Luck? Danvers would be lucky to make it through the
night alive.

Willow sweetened the deal by reaching into Danvers's wallet and handing Carlos more cash than he made in a year.

I had an idea what Willow had planned for her husband,
but I wouldn't interfere.

"Willow, maybe he's already suffered enough?"

She glared at me. "I'll decide when he's had enough."

"I know he killed your sisters," I said. "But…"

"But nothing," she said. "I am still under the *Pignus
Sanguinus* as long as my husband lives." The blood curse
Danvers had insisted on in order to insure Willow would
remain loyal.

The blood curse was driving me insane. I wanted Willow.
Maybe she was right and I wanted only the things I couldn't have.

"Please leave, Nyx."

She wasn't going to change her mind. I did as she asked
and left.

Chapter Eighteen

Hecate had been trapped and we'd won, but the sense of unease I felt never lifted, despite my becoming the magical version of a *Tiger Beat* poster hunk. The Houses treated me like a rock star for trapping Hecate, even though many of them had sided with her.

Things gradually returned to normal, or at least what passed for normal. Members of the Houses stopped spitting when they saw me and, instead, nodded and smiled with a "Buon Fortuna, Nyx Fortuna."

The entire Wyrd family had been invited to a party hosted jointly by the House of Poseidon and the House of Zeus, held at Trey Marin's house. It was across the lake from Elizabeth's house.

I went because I thought there was a chance I might see Willow there. And for the free liquor. Trey's home was almost hidden by trees, shrubs, and a wild profusion of flowers.

The house itself was big, but not too flashy. It looked like it had been there as long as Minneapolis had been a city. A uniformed naiad answered the door and ushered me in with a seductive smile.

Trey's house was decorated simply, but expensively. Hand-carved furniture, simple lines, and nautical artwork.

I was early. Only a few guests had arrived and because of the warmth of the evening or their personal preference for the outside, they were out on the terrace.

It looked like Trey was expecting a crowd. Rows of tables had been set up on the back lawn. I watched them from the floor-to-ceiling windows in the great room.

There was no sign of any of my family members or Willow.

A server handed me a glass of champagne. I turned to join the party outside and almost ran into Trey.

"She's not coming," Trey said.

"Who isn't coming?"

"My niece," he said. "That's who you were looking for, right?"

There was no point in denying it. "Yes, but why won't she be here?"

"She is a recent widow," he replied. I wasn't going to have to kill Danvers after all. Someone had beaten me to it.

"We talked about it and decided it would not be seemly."

"Seemly? Nobody mourns Danvers," I said. "Not even his wife."

"She is my niece, Nyx," he said. "I know you don't understand how the Houses work, but believe me, the House of Hades would not appreciate openly showing glee at one of their members' death."

I shrugged. "I don't really give a fuck what the House of Hades thinks."

"Rumor has it that you are more involved in that House than you'd like to admit."

I stared him down. "You know what they say about rumors." Hades was my father, but I didn't want any part of that inheritance.

"Shrug it off all you'd like, but you must realize that some members of the House of Hades do not like the idea of Hades's heir coming in and taking over."

"There's not a chance in hell of that happening," I said. I wasn't sure about Rebecca's interest in lording over the House of Hades, but I was even less sure if the magical world knew who her papa was. It had evidently gotten out who mine was.

Despite my earlier interlude with Willow, there was a hollow aching inside me. I wanted to be dancing with her in front of everyone. I wanted to hold her hand and smile at her the way Talbot smiled at Naomi.

The sun had gone down while we were talking. Fireflies lit up the darkness, more than I'd ever seen.

I spotted Willow in the woods edging the lake, dancing with the fireflies.

"Gorgeous," I said. "Excuse me."

I tried not to attract attention, but was stopped every few minutes by people wanting to shake my hand. I was as patient as possible, especially since some of them had cursed my name and the House of Fates only a few days ago.

I made the excuse that I had to go to the bathroom and then snuck back out through the front door and then cut through the neighbor's yard to avoid the party entirely.

She was still there.

"Willow, you look beautiful." She was dressed for the party in an emerald silk dress and summer sandals.

She took my hand and led me deeper into the trees, where

it was quiet and dark. She kicked off the tortuous heels and then slipped out of the silk dress.

Her bare skin gleamed in a sliver of moonlight. She shook out her dark hair and a tiny smile crossed her face. "Thank you, son of Fortuna," she said.

She held out her hand, but I grasped it and pulled her closer into a tight hug and then kissed her with all the passion I'd been denying.

She unbuttoned my shirt. Our gazes stayed locked while she stripped me. She laid my clothes carefully on a nearby bush and then stepped into my arms. I slid my hands down to her hips and kissed her.

She moaned into my open mouth. I picked her up and she wrapped her legs around my waist.

Somehow, we ended up in the lake. A drop of water trailed down her neck and settled into the hollow of her throat. I licked it away and she moaned again.

Making love in the water was slippery work, but we managed. Much later, we lay on the shore and let the warm night air dry our skin.

Willow's mood shifted when the sounds of revelry drifted over the water.

"It's time you went back to the party," she said. She handed me my shirt and pants.

"Come with me," I coaxed.

"I am happier here," she said. "You go ahead."

I kissed her good-bye and then watched as she dove back into the lake.

The party was in full swing when I returned.

As the evening progressed, the party became louder and more crowded. The backyard was full of the magical community, including those who had turned their backs on the Wyrd family only days before. Luke Seren manned the grill, while Trey circulated.

My aunts held court in the center of the room. My aunts were both attractive and didn't lack for admirers. Nona looked like a hot soccer mom barely old enough to have a daughter Naomi's age and Morta had the ice-queen thing down pat. She could freeze someone's balls off with one look, but some guys liked that.

With her eyes, Morta gave the order to join them, which I ignored. Rebecca and Claire sat in a couple of chairs a few feet from her and Naomi had been cornered by a sweaty mage in purple shorts and a bad haircut.

Talbot and I stood watching the crowd. My attention was caught by a guy wearing board shorts and a loose white cotton shirt. A trio of naiads surrounded him. I couldn't hear the conversation, but he said something and the naiads burst into gales of laughter.

"That's Johnny Asari," Talbot said. The sour note in his voice made me give him a long glance, but he didn't elaborate.

A few minutes later, the stranger approached us. "Talbot, I thought that was you. You've lost a few pounds."

Talbot blushed. "Johnny." His voice was cold.

"Man, you're not still pissed about that girl?" Johnny asked. "That was ages ago. College. Bygones."

From Talbot's expression, he was still pissed about that girl, whoever she was. I'd grill him about it later.

"And you must be the man of the evening, Nyx Fortuna," Johnny said. He held out his hand. I didn't take it. He had wavy dark hair that fell into his eyes when he spoke, which was a mannerism I suspected he practiced in the mirror at home. He had dark brown eyes with full lashes and his skin was the color of a walnut.

"Nyx, I hear you play a mean game of tarot poker," Johnny continued. "We should play sometime, both of us having the eye on the prize and all."

He was talking about the leadership of the House of Hades, but I feigned ignorance. "What prize?"

He smiled and his teeth gleamed white against his tan skin. "All of them."

We were getting sideways glances from several people at the party. I didn't feel like giving them anything else to talk about, so I just said, "Excuse me, Johnny, we need to speak to my cousins about something."

Talbot extricated Naomi from the sweaty wizard while I went to say hello to my family.

I kissed Nona's cheek. "How are you?"

"Sad," she answered honestly. "And I'd like another drink."

Nona hadn't recovered from Sawyer's death very well. Her words were slurred.

"How about a glass of lemonade?" I offered.

"As long as there's vodka in it," she replied.

"I know a little bit about trying to drink away the sadness," I told her softly. "It doesn't work."

"I know," she said. "But I want vodka anyway."

I shrugged. I wasn't going to try to babysit a Fate. I got her the vodka and lemonade, but asked the bartender to water it down. Nona would be humiliated if she got publicly shit-faced, and she was well on her way. Since I was already at the bar, I got myself another drink as well.

When I returned, Talbot and Naomi had disappeared.

Probably making out in Trey's broom closet or something. Or maybe he just wanted to avoid Johnny.

I handed her drink to Nona. Morta glared at me. I glared back. Nona was seconds away from crying. "You'll feel better if you eat something," I told her. "I'll be right back."

I went up to Luke. "Can I get a couple of hamburgers?"

"Anything for our conquering hero," he replied.

I was beginning to hate the sound of that word. "I'm not a hero. I had a lot of help. Talbot, Ambrose, my father." The last part slipped out, and I regretted it when Luke's eyes blazed with curiosity.

"I've been meaning to ask you about that," Luke said.

"Ask away," I said, but my tone said the opposite of my words.

Luke studied my face for a moment and decided to, at least on the surface, change the subject. "Are you an ambitious man, Nyx?"

I took a long sip of my cocktail. "Do I seem ambitious to you?"

"You seem driven. Haunted, even."

"Not the same thing," I replied.

My answer seemed to please him, because he hummed a little tune as he flipped my burger. "No desire to follow your father? Take over where he left off?"

"I have no desire to rule the underworld," I said. "Or the House of Hades."

"There are others who don't feel the same way," he said. "You need to be careful who you trust." His gaze went to Johnny Asari, who was trying to charm my sister.

"Johnny's welcome to it. I have enough on my plate."

"Speaking of which," Luke said, "here are your burgers." He slid expertly cooked patties onto plates and beamed. "It's been a pleasure speaking to you. One last question, though. Is Hades really your father?"

Fitch and his date arrived as I was trying to think of a way to diplomatically tell Luke that my paternity was none of his business. "Excuse me," I said. "I see someone I want to say hello to."

I delivered the burgers to Nona and then made my way over to Fitch. I felt Luke watching me.

"Fitch, you made it," I said. We shook hands and then he introduced me to his date, the same woman I'd seen Seren dancing with.

"Wouldn't miss your celebration for anything," he said. "Would we, Ruth?"

"Nyx Fortuna," I said.

"Where are my manners?" Fitch said. "Nyx, this is my dear friend, Ruth Delaney."

"Once Fitch told me he knew you, I wouldn't stop pestering him until he made the introduction."

As we talked, Fitch's attention was on Luke Seren at the grill.

"Think I'll grab Ruth and me some grub," he said. "You two stay here and get acquainted."

He ambled over to Luke and slapped him on the back. The other man flinched, but gave Fitch a smile.

They had an animated conversation. To the casual viewer, they appeared to be having an amiable conversation, but Fitch's jaw was tense, even when he smiled.

"They look like two old friends," I commented to Ruth.

She looked startled. "They are. They should be. They're brothers."

"They don't look anything alike," I said.

"Different fathers," she explained.

"I thought they hated each other," I said, despite the evidence in front of my eyes. Fitch and Seren were still laughing. Something about the way Fitch smiled at Luke bothered me, but I couldn't explain why.

The smile in Ruth's eyes faded. "The two aren't mutually exclusive. You should know that." Her gaze went to the table where my aunts sat. Morta's eyes gleamed with pleasure as she accepted the credit for toppling Hecate, but Nona looked like she wanted to be anywhere besides the party.

I couldn't argue with that. I realized I hadn't asked Ruth anything about herself. "Which House are you with, Ruth?"

"House of Fates," she said. "Although I'm not one of the more popular members."

Which meant she wasn't one of the group currently sucking up to the aunties. "Why not?"

"I'm a fortune-teller," she said. "There aren't many of us left. Not real ones anyway."

Anything that reminded my aunts of my mother had been stamped out. Her status as the fourth Fate had been erased by my aunts and time.

There was more to Ruth than I'd previously thought. Fortune-tellers had been loyal to Fortuna. She'd had to be a fighter to survive.

"Give me your hand," Ruth said. I held out my left hand, palm up. She took it in both hands and stared down at the lines there. She touched the fleshy part near my thumb.

"A very overdeveloped Mound of Venus," she said.

Even I knew that meant I loved sex, food, and drink. "That's not exactly a secret," I said. I winked at her.

Her smile was adorable. "No, not a secret, but true nonetheless."

I watched her as she studied my hand. I could see why Fitch was so infatuated with her.

"You seem to have gained a life line recently," she said.

I nodded. "Very recently."

She bit her lower lip as she concentrated on the reading. She traced the fate line with her forefinger.

"The past leaves its mark," she said. "But the future is still about possibilities."

Her hands trembled in mine and her face paled. "You ran straight toward your fate," she said. "Your blood still boils with the need for revenge."

"'I will seize Fate by the throat,'" I quoted softly. She wasn't telling me anything that a hack couldn't figure out after listening to rumors and a few minutes in the same room with my aunts and me.

"The Fates will fall as foretold," she continued. "But you shall fall with them. She will bring you to your knees."

"She?"

Something black flew into my face. It was a tiny bat, not much bigger than a moth. I swatted it away, but several more followed. A stream of bats rushed me and then flew into the night sky.

"Where did they come from?"

Ruth dropped my hand.

The party went silent. Nona made an urgent gesture to join her. I excused myself from Ruth and went to see my aunt.

"What's wrong?" I asked in a low voice.

"It's a bad omen," Nona said. "All those bats."

As superstitions went, it was one I'd never heard of, but an icy finger touched the back of my neck. I shuddered.

"Don't tell me you're superstitious," Talbot said.

"You of all people should know how whimsical the hand of Fate is," she said. "Some things even the Fates cannot prevent."

"What does it mean?" I asked.

"Death. Destruction," Claire said in a low voice. "And Rebecca saw it in the tea leaves, too."

That explained my sister's habit of staring at teacups.

The party was in danger of fizzling, but Luke had other ideas. He dropped his barbecue tongs to take center stage.

"I'm sure we've all dealt with superstitions before," Luke said loudly. "So we know there are many ways of interpreting this."

Did he just dis my aunts? From Morta's expression, she thought that Luke had offered her a grave insult.

"Trey, I think it's time for another round of champagne," Luke continued blithely.

I found a quiet spot to think. There was a bench in an arbor not far from the main terrace. As I watched the magical Who's Who laugh and drink, a sense of dread lingered. For me, Nona's vision had cast a pall over the party.

Despite Hecate's imprisonment, unanswered questions weighed on my mind. What was the key for? I'd tried the locks on several doors at Parsi, but I hadn't been to my aunts' menagerie. What better place to hide a weapon against Hecate?

"I've been looking everywhere for you," Talbot said.

I lifted a glass of champagne. "Here I am."

"You're not letting that omen thing get to you, are you?"

"It's not that," I said.

"Then what is it?"

"I can't stop thinking that it's not over."

He clinked his glass with mine. "You know what they say. It's not over until it's over."

I drained my glass. "Will it ever be over?"

He didn't have an answer.

Chapter Nineteen

Two in the morning and the party was still going strong. Despite the omen, my friends and family were having a good time. My enemies, too. Too bad I couldn't always tell the difference.

Talbot and Naomi talked to his dad, the aunts were occupied terrorizing the heads of Houses, and Claire argued with Carlos about something. He gave her a smile and I could practically hear her tell him not to try that Mesmer shit with her. My sister and Johnny were the two who held my attention. The music slowed and Johnny grabbed Rebecca's hand and coaxed her to dance. After a few minutes, she put her head on his shoulder and he whispered something in her ear.

Despite my earlier interlude with Willow, there was a hollow aching inside me. I wanted to be dancing with her in front of everyone. I wanted to hold her hand and smile at her the way Talbot smiled at Naomi.

I snuck out of the party and drove around aimlessly. The Caddy and I traveled the streets together, the purr of its engine a comforting sound.

I ended up at Parsi Enterprises. On impulse, I broke into

the building. I could have asked my aunts to show me the creatures they held in the lower levels, but I wasn't sure they'd agree. I brought the key I'd found at Deci's house with me. I had a feeling it opened the cage to something or someone the aunts preferred to keep hidden.

I wasn't worried about the security guard, but I wasn't sure I could get past the wards without being detected. I went through the loading-dock entrance and slipped in without a problem. There was a keypad in the elevator, but I'd watched Morta punch in the code. It took two tries, but I got the numbers right and the elevator carried me into the depths of the building.

The only light came from dim bulbs along the hallway, but the cages were dark. The aunts had decided to keep Hecate at Parsi, instead of returning her to the underworld, where she could gather power.

I checked on Hecate. Her room was colder than the others and for a brief moment, I thought I saw a movement out of the corner of my eye.

I gripped my athame and waited, but nothing happened. It was just a shadow, I told myself, or the air-conditioning kicking in. I waited, but she was unmoving, wrapped tightly in the black crystal strands we'd used to imprison her.

I left her there, certain that she was immobilized. My breathing sounded loud as I walked along. There was a presence awake somewhere in the bowels of Parsi Enterprises.

The sound of whispering turned to a plaintive song I followed the sound to a part of the menagerie I hadn't visited previously. There was someone standing motionless behind a locked door. I managed to take the wards off.

I slid the mysterious key into the lock. It fit. The handle turned and I stepped in. The room was a simple one, no window with the only light coming from a bulb dangling from a chain, a cot in the corner of the room. It looked like a nun's cell. Or a prison cell.

A woman stood in the center of the room and stared raptly into whatever was on the wall opposite the door.

She was tall, elegantly thin, and pale. Snakes coiled in her blond hair, but at my entrance, they slithered out. She had thickly lashed eyes and lips round as an apple that made me want to take a bite out of them.

Medusa. The snakes in her hair hissed, but she didn't turn her head.

"Son of Fortuna," she said. "What brings you here?"

"Curiosity," I said.

"Which killed the cat," she replied. Her attention didn't stray from the wall. I wanted to see what had held her so transfixed. On the wall opposite her bed, there was a small obsidian mirror mounted to the wall. The silver frame was engraved, but I didn't want to chance looking at it. Legend had it that whoever looked into Medusa's mirror would see their true selves, which often led to madness. The alternate story was that Medusa's gaze would turn you to stone. I didn't chance it, so I kept my eyes away from hers.

"What does the mirror do?" I asked her.

"Many things," Medusa replied.

"You are powerful enough to tear down this entire building," I said. "Yet you allow my aunts to hold you captive."

"I have all I need here," she replied.

"You're here willingly?" A goddess, kept in a basement like a pet? It didn't make sense.

"Nyx Fortuna, tread lightly," she said. "You ask too many questions. The mirror's spell holds me here."

"You are a powerful goddess," I pointed out. "Why don't you break the mirror's spell?"

"If I could break its spell, I would," she said. "Instead I am trapped here, staring in a mirror."

"At least the view is good," I said. Legend went that Medusa was hideous, but in reality, she was breathtakingly gorgeous. Hecate had probably spread that rumor.

"You assume that I like what I see."

"What do you see?"

"The truth," she said. "It is not always palatable."

I couldn't imagine seeing my screw-ups every day in the mirror, replaying over and over.

"If I ever am free of the mirror," she said, "I will come looking for those who imprisoned me with the mirror."

"My aunts?" I guessed.

She shook her head and the snakes hissed. "They have given me shelter," she said. "And because of that kindness, I will not kill you tonight."

Medusa's mirror was one of Hecate's items of power, but I'd have to kill Medusa to get to the mirror, which would be even more of a daunting task than taking on Hecate had been. Besides, the mirror was safe where it was. Medusa and her snakes would guard it and I wouldn't have to worry.

"Good night, Medusa," I finally said. I'd found the one person in Minneapolis who was lonelier than me.

"Good night, son of Fortuna," she said. "And please remember, I may not be so merciful the next time you visit."

I shut the door softly on my way out. I was barely out of the room before the plaintive singing started again. I let out a wry laugh. I'd never have guessed that my aunts' kindness to a deadly goddess would eventually save my life.

Chapter Twenty

I hadn't seen much of Willow since the night of the party. She had gone into hiding. Or she was avoiding me. Or both.

I searched every lake, river, and stream in Minnesota, starting with her lake. I finally found her on my second trip back to her home. She was sunning herself on some rocks by the river, just outside the cave where she sometimes slept. And sometimes did other things. My treacherous memory supplied me with images of what those things had been. Seeing her wasn't helping my head. Anyone, any male at least, got a little light-headed around a naiad.

She skinned a fish, a walleye, I think. Her expression didn't change when she saw me, but she gripped the knife a little tighter. There was no guarantee that Willow wouldn't kill me when she heard what I had to say.

"Leave me in peace, Nyx Fortuna," she said. "I have things to do."

"I just want to help you." Who was I kidding? I wanted her.

"Help?" she repeated. "It does not help me to see you right now."

"I don't understand," I said. "I thought we were friends."

"I would be your friend," she said. "I only need some time."

"I will wait for you," I said. I didn't want to be her friend, but I'd take what I could get. I wasn't sure I could stand not touching her.

"Don't." The single word popped the tiny bubble of hope in my chest. Lucky in cards, unlucky in love. "I've been thinking of moving on, anyway."

"You mean leave Minneapolis?" Willow had made it clear we didn't have a future together, but there was a hint of sadness in her voice.

"Hecate has been taken care of." Strangely, after my years of roaming the world, I was starting to think of Minneapolis as home. I wasn't sure I liked the sensation.

I stared at Willow. There was something different about her. I'd been so consumed by lust the night of the party that I hadn't been paying close attention.

Naiads had the ability to drive men mad with lust, but they'd seduce them and then kill them without thinking twice. A necklace of men's teeth signified social status in a naiad colony.

But Willow had always worn a simple necklace made of river stone. She might weave in a few spring wildflowers or some greenery. At least that's what she used to do.

Now she wore a set of men's teeth, still bloody at the roots. She noticed my gaze and lifted it up so I could get a better look. My stomach roiled.

"My dearly departed husband's," she said with a satisfied smile.

Willow was the one who'd killed Danvers.

She'd ended the blood oath. Willow was free. But she

wasn't the girl I'd come to love. I'd turned her into this. A killer of men. A queen. She'd killed Danvers. It's not that he didn't deserve it, but murder changed a person. I should know.

Her eyes were full of ambition and pride. She was beyond me now. There was no turning back. My dream of a life with her was impossible. Once she'd experienced the bloodlust, she'd never be satisfied with a little place near the Driftless.

I'd been a fool to think I could ever be happy.

I didn't regret helping Willow to save herself, even though my actions had freed Hecate, just as the prophecy foretold.

"Can I kiss you good-bye?"

She nodded. I kissed her softly on the nose, the forehead, and finally the lips. She kissed me back until I said the wrong thing.

"I love you," I whispered into her ear.

She stiffened and pushed me away. "Don't say that to me ever again," she said, "or I'll add your teeth to my collection."

I dropped my arms and she turned and headed toward the lake. With each step, she moved faster and faster until she was running, arms wide as if greeting a lover. Then she dove into the water and disappeared.

I sat on my favorite bench and stared at the water until the sun came up, but she never returned.

Chapter Twenty-One

A week after we'd captured Hecate, Rebecca stopped by the apartment on her way to Parsi. Her arm was still in plaster and someone had drawn a complicated protective hex on it.

"Nice art," I said. "Who did it?"

She looked down. "Johnny. I ran into him last night at the diner."

Ran into him, my ass. Johnny Asari was making a play for my sister.

"I hope you have better luck than I do at love," I said.

"You saved her," Rebecca replied. "You saved the whole city."

It didn't make me feel any better. Willow's rejection still stung.

She changed the subject. "How's it feel to be a rock star?"

I popped the top on a beer. "Grand."

One of the things I liked about my sister was that she never ragged on me about my drinking. She probably hoped I'd fuck up my liver and keel over, which, since I was mortal now, could actually happen.

I offered her a bottle, but she waved it away. "It's a little early for me. I'm on my way to work," she said. "Which brings me to why I'm here. The aunts want you to come back to Parsi Enterprises."

I wasn't surprised by much these days, but she'd done it. "To work?"

"Of course to work," she said.

"Why?"

"They've decided we need to stick together," she said. "Wyrd family united and all that."

I studied her face. "I'll think about it."

"It's a solid offer," she said. "You can't work at Eternity Road forever."

"Why not?" I asked. "The aunts want me back in the bosom of the family, but they don't trust me with their secrets." The two items of power were the harpy's silver feather and Hecate's Bead. Nona had told me Medusa's mirror was the third item of power, but the aunts knew more than they were telling me.

"They don't trust anybody," she replied. "Including me.'

"What's the real story about why you left?"

"You mean why did I steal the money?"

I nodded. "I'm assuming you had a reason."

"You're the first," Rebecca said. "What makes you think that?"

"You don't strike me as someone dumb enough to double-cross the Fates for the hell of it."

"I'm not," she said. "I had my reasons. Maybe someday I'll tell you about them."

A silence fell, but she didn't make a move to leave.

"Something else on your mind?"

"I had an interesting offer and I wanted to talk to you about it," she replied.

"Then talking about it means you know, talking about it," I hinted.

She made a face. "Smart-ass. Johnny Asari asked me out and I wanted to know what you think."

Was my sister really asking me for dating advice? "About Johnny? Talbot thinks he's a dick, but there was a girl involved in that decision-making process."

"There usually is," Rebecca said dryly. "So you're cool with it?"

I didn't tell her I already knew about her and Johnny. I was touched she'd considered my feelings at all. "You're worried that I'd be offended because Johnny wants to take over House of Hades? Don't be. I don't want it."

"That's not what he thinks," Rebecca replied.

I shrugged. "I can't help that."

"The aunts are furious about it," she confided. "And we haven't even gone on our first date."

"They're usually pissed about something," I said. "Do what you want. What your heart wants."

Rebecca gave me a peck on my cheek. "Maybe you should take your own advice."

Maybe I should. It hadn't worked out for me so far, but I was the son of Fortuna. Luck was in my nature.

"I thought you hated me," I said.

She met my eyes. "What can I say? You're growing on me."

After she left, I finished the beer and hit the streets. Eternity Road was located in a less-than-desirable location in Minneapolis, but I liked it. It had become home to me, the only home I'd known in two hundred years.

I hadn't given up on finding Baxter. Part of me felt responsible for him. Hecate probably would never have noticed him if it weren't for me.

We'd already gone through the house Hecate had

commandeered. It had been a scene of vile depravity, blood-soaked rooms, and the stench of despair, but no Baxter.

I drove by the morgue. Baxter's car was long gone, of course, probably collecting dust at the police tow yard. He could be anywhere, if he was even still alive.

I'd driven halfway around Minneapolis without any luck. I decided to search Morta's for the silver harpy feather. Hecate had been contained, but I'd learned the hard way to hedge my bets.

Morta lived downtown so I pointed the car in that direction. I used a quick *obscura* spell and slipped in without anyone, including the security guard, noticing. I listened, but didn't detect anyone else in the apartment.

I let the spell slip away. I needed to concentrate on my snooping.

The portrait of my mother still hung above the fireplace. In it, she wore a red dress and the silver chain with the charms that I now wore around my neck.

I headed for the bedrooms and collided with Claire in the hallway. The collision left both of us disconcerted, but Claire recovered first.

"What are you doing here?" she asked.

"I could ask you the same thing," I replied.

"This is my mother's apartment," she reminded me unnecessarily. "*I* have a key."

There was something twitchy about her, though. Like she'd been caught doing something wrong.

She didn't ask me why I was there, either, which I found interesting.

"Aren't you supposed to be at work?" I asked. "Tangling webs and all?"

"I'm the boss's daughter," she said. "And I was on my way. Morta asked me to pick up something for her."

She was lying. She wore blue jeans and a Minnesota Twins tee. I'd wear that to Parsi, but Claire never would. She favored power suits and expensive jewelry when she was at the office.

She tried to step around me, but I blocked her way. "Want to tell me what you're really doing here?"

She deflated. "Same thing as you. Looking for the harpy feather."

"So you did find something out from the Book of Fates?"

"Not much," she said, "but enough to know my mother has it."

"Why were you looking for it?" Suspicion was clear in my voice.

"I just wanted to know where it was," she said. "Don't worry. I wasn't going to take it."

I'd been suspicious of Claire, but now I was curious. "Why do you want to find it so badly?"

She shrugged. "They never tell us anything," she replied. "They tell us that we are the new generation of Fates, but then they keep things from us, like we're children."

I studied her face. "I'll make a deal with you," I said. "If I find it, I'll let you know."

She flashed a grin. "And if I find it, I'll do the same."

I was getting woozy from all the warm fuzzy family time I'd had. We walked out of the building together and I escorted her to her car. I watched her drive off, wondering if I'd been wrong about Claire all along.

A sudden gust of wind nearly knocked me off my feet. I thought I heard a snicker, but when I looked around, there was no one there.

Chapter Twenty-Two

A few days later, Claire, Naomi, and Rebecca walked into Eternity Road. Rebecca and Naomi carried a bottle of wine in each hand. Worse yet, Claire held a stack of board games.

Talbot and I exchanged a glance. "Uh-oh," he said.

"Family bonding night," Claire announced.

"We used to do it all the time when we were growing up," Naomi said. "Minus the wine."

"Speak for yourself," Rebecca said. There was a hint of a smile at the edge of her mouth. "Nyx, it's time you joined us."

What had brought on the sudden urge for my company? My sister had thawed toward me, but I was still wary.

"Have fun," Talbot said wistfully.

I stared at Naomi. "He's coming with us. He's my brother, at least as close as I'll ever get to one, so he's in or I'm out."

Talbot gave me a grin. "I guess I could close the store early."

She sniffed. "I'll encourage your little bromance. We're playing at your place, then. And you're buying the pizza."

"Fair enough."

They followed me up the stairs to the apartment, but I noticed that Talbot and Naomi were lagging behind.

"Naomi, hurry up," Claire called out, but Rebecca nudged her. "Don't be an idiot."

I gave my sister a look. "Playing matchmaker?"

"She was miserable," Rebecca replied. "It'll work. Trust me."

Strangely enough, I did.

I unlocked the door, frantically trying to remember if I'd left underwear on the floor. Normally, I didn't give a shit, but Rebecca was bound to notice. The idea that I worried about impressing my sister made me a little queasy.

I was relieved that the apartment was relatively clean, if you ignored the empty bottles piling up on the kitchen counter.

"Did you have a party last night?" Claire asked, staring at the bottles and cans littering the room.

Rebecca snorted with laughter, but didn't say anything. Surprisingly, my sister was polite enough to ignore my empties. Or maybe she just didn't care.

"Make yourself comfortable," I said. It was after 7 p.m., but it was still hot, so I went through the apartment and opened all the windows.

Talbot and Naomi finally showed up, holding hands.

"Let's get the game started," Rebecca said. "I call Scottie dog."

"Whenever we play Monopoly and Becks gets the dog, she always wins," Naomi explained.

"Not this time, *Becks*," I said. "We're rolling for it."

The pizza arrived and we settled in. When I chose a soda instead of absinthe, Talbot grinned at me, but didn't comment. I wasn't trying to stop drinking, I was trying to win. Rebecca was a ruthless player and I needed my wits about me.

I won the roll of the dice and got to go first.

"Luck is on your side, Nyx Fortuna," Rebecca said. "But I have skill on mine."

"So how do you stay so young-looking?" I asked my sister. "If you're older than me, I mean?"

"How do you know it's not the same way you look so young?" she replied.

"I doubt your mother defied the Fates and a prophecy and hid your thread of Fate," I told her. "So how do you really do it? A little of Gaston's go-go juice?" The orange nectar of the gods had kept the Fates' Tracker alive long enough to torment me.

She raised an eyebrow. "Didn't you read all of the Book of Fates?"

"Not enough time," I said. "I died, remember? Claire inherited it."

Claire gave me a look. "I'm not giving it back."

"I was supposed to have it," Rebecca said.

"You can have it," I said. "There are just some things it would have been nice to know."

"Sorry, it's a trade secret," Rebecca said. She rolled the dice and got snake eyes.

"Now who is lucky?" I bit into a slice of gooey cheese pizza.

"Is that what they call it?" My cousin elbowed me hard in the stomach.

Talbot and Naomi were so busy kissing that he wasn't paying attention to the game. "Talbot, it's your turn."

"While you were drowning your sorrows, I was doing some research," he said smugly. "I know where Wren is."

Part of me still had a soft spot for Wren. My inclination was to let her go. She had been under her mother's thumb.

Maybe she could have a life of her own, now that Hecate was trapped.

The soft summer wind picked up and blew the Monopoly money all over the room. Rain poured down like liquid silver, coming faster and faster. I shut the windows while everyone else gathered up the money.

"Should we start over?" Rebecca asked.

Naomi shivered and Talbot wrapped an arm around here.

"Weather's changing," she commented. The air turned cold. There was a sudden cessation of sound.

Something hard hit the roof. I looked out to see hail, larger than I'd ever seen, slamming to the ground.

Rebecca shivered. "Something's wrong," she said.

The air had gone electric. "Storm's coming," Naomi said.

"Not just any storm," Talbot said.

"Storm god," I said. The sky was purple and getting darker.

"A storm god?" Talbot asked. "No, it's just a little crazy summer weather. Happens all the time in Minneapolis."

"Not like this," I said. "I'm telling you this is the work of a storm god." The wind screamed in my ear. *Where is she?*

"Which storm god?" Claire asked.

"The pissed-off one," I said. "Now move. Talbot, where's your dad?"

"At home," he said. "At least he was ten minutes ago."

"Find him," I said. "Gather up all the magical items at the store and then take them and everyone you can find into the basement."

"What are you going to do?" Rebecca asked.

"I'm going to try to stop him."

"I'm staying with you."

"Me, too," Claire said.

I didn't have time to argue with them.

"Talbot, find your dad, please," I repeated. He hesitated, but finally tugged on Naomi's hand and they headed for Ambrose's apartment.

Rebecca and I took the narrow stairs that led to the roof. The door wouldn't budge, but Rebecca shoved me aside and sent a spell whizzing through the door. It popped open and the wind tore it off the hinges. The door flew into a growing funnel cloud. We were pelted with rain as we went.

There was every possibility we'd end up in that funnel cloud, but somehow we stayed on the roof. For every step we took, the wind beat us back two. The tornado sirens wailed a warning as we struggled to stay upright.

The sky was filled with clouds like dark smoke, but the sun still shone through in spots. Tornado weather.

The storm god appeared, riding a black storm cloud in the shape of a horse. "Bring her to me," he said. His voice boomed like thunder. Boreas, the god of the cold north winds, had a voice like thunder. His long black hair, streaked with frost, streamed in the wind. A bolt of lightning struck not far from where we stood.

"What does he want?" Rebecca said.

"Not what, who. He wants Hecate."

"She's not here," Rebecca said.

"Obviously," I replied. "But he doesn't know that. Unless…" I trailed off, struck by an even more horrifying possibility.

"Unless what?"

"Bring me the goddess." Boreas said. He accentuated his request with another bolt of lightning.

"What goddess?" I shouted, but my words were swallowed by the wind.

"He's trying to kill us," Rebecca said. "Why?"

I tested her theory by moving closer to Boreas. At that range, he shouldn't have missed, but the next bolt he sent landed several feet away.

Why was Boreas attacking us?

"He's not trying to kill us, he's trying to stall us," I told Rebecca.

"Why?"

"He's just the diversion," I shouted.

"Diversion for what?" Rebecca yelled.

"Someone is trying to break Hecate out," I said. "His job is to stall us."

"The aunts," Rebecca said. "They're at Parsi. Let's go."

My sister caught on quickly. When we tried to leave, Boreas sent a gale-force wind to stop us.

"Since when is the god of the north wind on the side of a murdering psychopath?" I yelled.

The building shook with the force of Boreas's fury. The hail came down faster and faster, morphing into huge jagged icicles. The air went frigid enough that I could see Rebecca's breath.

"He'll tear the city apart," I said. "We have to stop him first."

Stopping a god, even a minor one like Boreas, wasn't going to be easy.

I tried to send a compulsion spell his way, but it didn't even slow him down.

A gust of angry wind knocked me off my feet and I struggled to get up again. I was dragged along the ground, but grabbed ahold of the building's ledge and clung. The wind howled in my ears as I tried to think, hitting on and discarding spells. I tried fire, but he summoned a downpour and put it out.

I sent a fireball his way while Rebecca lobbed a trash can at his head. I was desperate enough to try to remove the air around him. No air, no wind god. I wasn't sure if the spell would remove the air near us, too. I filled my lungs.

The spell was complicated. As I started to utter the words, Boreas caught on to what I was doing and sent a gale-force wind my way. Rebecca did her best to block the worst of it, but I was pelted with a two-by-four, a street sign, and a city trash can.

It felt as though my face was going to be ripped off, but I clung to the edge of the roof as I spit out the last words of the spell. Boreas fell out of the sky and the wind died.

My lungs burned. I gasped for air until fresh oxygen hit my system. I crawled to the center of the roof. The storm had ended, but we were wet and shivering. The water was ankle high and seeped into my Doc Martens.

"Are you okay?" I panted. "Your arm?"

"I'm okay," she said. She winced as she put her arm back into the sling. "Holy shit, that was some storm." Her lip was bleeding and two enormous bruises dotted her cheeks. "Good work stopping it," she added.

"Thanks for running interference," I said. "Let's go!"

Our shoes made a squelching sound as we ran. Outside, the building next to Eternity Road had been flattened, reduced to toothpicks by the twister. Broken glass littered the sidewalk.

There was a painful scrape on my leg from where I'd been dragged. I limped as I led the way to my car. The wards had held, but a large tree branch blocked the road. I pushed it out of the way, using a combination of magic and body strength.

The Caddy was covered in debris, but most of it was small enough that Rebecca and I cleared it away.

As I drove across town, I saw downed power lines, flooded roads, and wrecked cars.

"Can't you drive any faster?" Rebecca snapped.

"If I wreck the Caddy, we won't get there any quicker," I said. I clicked on the radio and searched for the news. It wasn't good.

The Stone Arch Bridge had been blown apart. At least three people had died, and more were missing.

"Hurry," Rebecca urged. "The aunts always work late. They might still be in the building."

As powerful as they were, the Fates were not invincible.

"Someone from the House of Zeus had to be involved," I said. I clutched the steering wheel tightly.

"What makes you say that?"

"Boreas had help," I said. "Luke warned me that Johnny couldn't be trusted."

"That doesn't mean anything," she said.

"Unless it does," I replied. "Although all the wind gods are from the House of Zeus."

"You can't think Johnny had anything to do with this?" I stared at my sister. There had been a strange note her in voice.

"You can't be in love with him already," I said.

"Of course not," she said. "But Johnny and I are old friends."

The information surprised me. "You two knew each other before?"

She nodded. "In college." The news that my sister went to college surprised me almost as much as her relationship with Johnny.

"Old friend, huh? Tell me the truth, Rebecca," I said. "It's important."

"I may have some feelings for him," she said.

I wanted to shout at her not to be stupid, that of course he couldn't be trusted, but not that long ago, I'd told her to go for it. I'd gotten soft since I'd stopped running. And romance wasn't my forte, anyway.

"And if he did betray us?"

"Then he's dead."

I didn't know what to say. I changed the subject. "We're here."

"Park near the loading dock," she ordered.

I threw a quick ward over the Caddy after we exited. Rebecca ran for the building while I followed at a slower pace.

Buildings all over Nicollet had been obliterated. The wooden structures were in pieces, turned into toothpicks for the gods. Cars were scattered, upside down and sideways, like an enormous petulant child had a tantrum and thrown his toys.

Naomi's bad omen had come true. Death and destruction were everywhere. And I had brought it to Minneapolis.

Chapter Twenty-Three

Despite magical wards that should stop a hurricane, even Parsi Enterprises had taken a hit. Half of the building had been blown away.

The windows in the lobby were shattered. Rebecca and I paused long enough to take in the damage. There was the trunk of a bur oak tree blocking the stairwell. It must have been at least forty foot tall when upright.

"Can we move it?" she asked.

"Not without help," I said.

"Good thing we're here, then," Talbot said.

I turned around. Claire, Naomi, and Talbot stood there. "I thought I told you guys to head to safety."

"I got my dad out," Talbot said. "He's already organizing supplies."

"We need to check on Hecate in the basement," I said. "And then see if we can find anyone in the building."

Naomi blanched. "Mom was working late."

"We'll find her," Talbot soothed. "Maybe she's already home. Call her cell."

Naomi's expression was blank as she surveyed the devastation of her family business.

Hecate had won. The fates had fallen and it was my fault.

"It isn't your fault," Talbot said.

"Quit doing that," I said.

"What?"

"Trying to read my mind. That's not what I was thinking," I lied.

Naomi dialed her mother's number. "Voice mail."

"Keep trying," Talbot said. "It's late. Maybe she already went to bed."

With the extra help and magical assistance, we were able to move the tree.

"We need to split up," I said. "Look for survivors. I'll take the basement." I was certain Hecate had escaped, but I wanted to be sure.

Naomi let out a little sob at the word, but Claire didn't show any emotion.

"Naomi can go with Nyx," Talbot said.

Naomi shot him a hurt look, but he ignored it. If the aunts were upstairs, they might not be alive, and Talbot didn't want Naomi to be the one to find the bodies.

"Naomi can come with me," I said.

"Claire can go with Talbot," Rebecca said. "I'm fine on my own."

"No," I said sharply. "Nobody goes alone."

My sister gave me a look, which I matched. Finally, she looked away. I'd won the staring contest. "I guess it won't hurt to tag along with Claire and Talbot."

"Where did they put Hecate?" Naomi asked.

"We're headed there now," I said.

"Where are Mom and Aunt Morta?" Naomi fretted.

"Maybe they went to the basement when the tornado siren sounded," I said.

From deep in the bowels of what was left of the building, I heard a bone-chilling scream.

"We have another problem," I said. "The menagerie is loose."

I didn't have to remind her that there were some very dangerous magical creatures roaming through Parsi Enterprises. The lights were off in the basement. The only sound was the drip, drip, drip of water, probably coming from a busted pipe.

"Illuminate," I said. A ball of light appeared and gave enough light to see in front of us.

Naomi moved closer to me. "There's something waiting in the shadows."

"There always is," I replied. "Naomi, stay here. I'm going to check out the cages."

"You're not going anywhere without me," she said. "Nobody goes anywhere alone, remember?"

I picked through the rubble. The building had been destroyed by someone who knew how to remove magical wards. There was a trail of blood and gore leading away from the lamia's cage, but it was Hecate that concerned me.

The room was empty. Someone had released her from her prison while Boreas whipped up the tornado.

Next, we checked the room that housed Medusa. She was gone. The mirror had fallen off the wall during the tornado and lay on the floor.

I grabbed it without looking into it and slipped it inside my jacket.

The menagerie was on the loose and they were almost as dangerous as Hecate.

"Hecate's gone," Naomi said. "We need to look for Mom. She might be in her office, trapped."

We headed for the main office. Trevor, the receptionist, was facedown in the lobby. The back of his head had been bashed in and brain matter leaked out of his shattered skull.

Naomi choked back a sob.

We headed for the executive offices. Nona wasn't in her office. I saw the growing panic on Naomi's face. "Maybe the others already found her," I said.

We checked on Morta next. The desk was upside down, but no Morta.

A pair of golden scissors lay on the floor, abandoned. Morta was lying motionless next to them.

Hecate stood over her. Her head whipped around when we entered.

"What did you do to her?"

She gave me a vicious smile. "Now you know what I needed your blood for, son of Fortuna."

"You used my blood to hurt my aunt?"

"The spell called for the blood of Hades, but it turns out his son's works just as well. You were twice warned, son of Fortuna," she said. "You ignored the warnings. The Fates have fallen."

I ran toward her and fumbled for my athame. I stabbed my palm and coated the blade in my blood. "Maybe it'll do the trick for you, too." I aimed for the heart, but only succeeded in a glancing blow, enough that black blood dripped from her shoulder.

She screamed. "Boreas!" The wind god blew into the room

and swept her up into his arms. Her long dark hair settled over her like a shroud before they both disappeared.

Naomi and I stared at each other, stunned.

She ran to Morta and looked for a pulse. "She's still breathing, but she's pretty badly injured. Can you try a healing spell?"

"I'll try," I said. Blood was everywhere. Even as I said the words of the spell, I could feel Morta's life slipping away.

"We need to find your mother," I said. Nona would know what to do.

Naomi picked up Morta's scissors. "I'll keep these safe for her."

There was a low groan from the hallway. Nona leaned against the wall, breathing heavily.

"Mom, I've been calling you and calling you," Naomi said. "Are you okay?" She was trying and failing to keep the panic from her voice.

"I'm not injured," Nona said. She sounded dazed, though, and there was a purple bruise already forming on her forehead. "Where is Morta?"

Naomi and I exchanged glances.

Nona's gaze sharpened. "She's dead. That's why Naomi has the scissors."

"You don't know that. Morta was still breathing a second ago." Why was Nona so calm?

"I do," Nona said. "Her scissors would never have left her hands otherwise."

"She loaned them to me once," I pointed out.

"Yes, loaned," Nona emphasized. "Never abandoned. And she only loaned them to you to trick Gaston."

"We should still try," I said. "Call nine-one-one."

Nona shook her head and a tear splashed. "It's too late. My sister is dead."

The scissors vibrated in Naomi's hands and then disappeared. "What just happened?"

"You have taken Morta's place. You are the new Atropos," her mother said. "From now on, you will cut the thread of Fate."

Naomi shook her head. "No," she said. "No."

"Naomi, your aunt would be proud that you are following in her footsteps."

"But I'm supposed to follow in *your* footsteps," she replied. "Like you wanted."

I gave her a questioning look, and she corrected herself. "Like *we* wanted."

"I need to see if I can get some of the beasts back into the cages," I said.

"You can't go alone," Naomi protested.

"You have to stay here with your mom," I said.

"Nyx, danger," Sawyer's voice sounded in my ear. I broke into a run.

Rebecca and Claire were walking toward us. They were near the receptionist area when I noticed a dark figure behind Claire. The lamia advanced, fangs already extended.

"Claire, look out," I cried. But the lamia was already on her. She'd escaped from the basement prison and wanted revenge.

I strained to keep her sharp teeth away from Claire's neck. Naomi sent a spell over, but it didn't even slow the lamia down. Rebecca tried to pull the lamia away, but the vampire threw her across the room.

I had seconds to decide: heart or head. I drove my athame into the lamia's neck, but she didn't stop. Her long fangs pushed closer to Claire's skin. The smell of her breath was intense, dry with despair, hot with longing.

I grunted and struck again. This time I separated her neck from her shoulders. I leaned against the wall and tried to breathe.

"Are you okay?" Naomi asked.

"Not even a scratch, thanks to Nyx," Claire replied.

"Nyx?"

I nodded, still short of breath.

"What else is on the loose?" Naomi asked her mother.

"Everything," Nona replied. "We need to be extremely careful."

"Can we get them back into their cages?"

She shook her head. "Doubtful. It took all three of us for most of them. And as you can see, I'm the last Fate standing. The girls aren't ready."

"I'm ready," Rebecca said.

"Me, too," Claire said.

"Ready or not, here I come," Naomi told her mom.

We helped Nona to her feet. "I must check on one of our guests," she said.

I shook my head. "Hecate is gone."

"Not Hecate," she said. "I must go alone."

We argued with her, but she wouldn't budge.

"Naomi and I will go with you," I said. "We'll wait outside. You have five minutes. If you're not out by then, we're coming in."

She headed for the cage the Fates had warned me away from on my first visit to the menagerie.

The wards were gone and the round wooden door had been blown off and lay on the floor several feet away. The salt was scattered to the winds.

The door had a thick iron dead bolt on it and salt encircled the door. The garlands had been shredded and the ancient runes written on the wall were broken.

"It's long gone," I said. "Whatever it is."

"A basilisk," Nona replied. "And it hasn't left."

Naomi repressed a gasp. "They can kill with a glance."

"I'm aware," Nona said dryly. "I have the most experience with this creature." She gave Naomi a brief kiss on the cheek. "See you in five minutes."

We waited, but Nona never came out.

"Stay here," I said.

"I'm coming with you."

"Stay here," I said again. "Something's wrong."

Inside the cage, it was dark, but I could see Nona's prone form. She'd been stunned by its glance or maybe by poisonous venom.

The basilisk hissed once. I threw my athame without looking, using the sound as my guide.

It struck the basilisk, who hissed again, this time with pain, but it wasn't down.

I tried again with a spell.

There was a thud as it dropped, but the floor was sticky with its venom. If any of it had absorbed into Nona's skin, it would be too late to save her.

I stuck my head out. "Naomi, I need towels, blankets, cloth, anything you can find."

She nodded once and then took off at a run.

I returned to Nona's side.

"Nona, are you okay?"

She tried to move and let out a moan. "What happened?"

"I'm not sure," I replied carefully. "Is the floor dry around you?"

It wasn't easy to fool my aunt. She caught on right away. "The venom," she said. "It's all over my skin."

I didn't know what to say.

"Naomi is getting towels," I said. "We'll get the venom off your skin. There's still time."

We both knew I was lying.

"My sister was wrong, you know," Nona said.

"Wrong about what?"

"Your kind heart isn't your greatest weakness. It's your greatest strength."

"That's not how I see it."

"You will," she said softly.

"If you say so," I said.

"I did it for her," Nona said.

I thought she was talking about Naomi. "She knows you love her."

She shook her head. "I wronged my sister, but I have tried to right the wrong. Forgive me, son of Fortuna, for her sake."

"Nona, I…" I trailed off. I didn't know what to say to her. Pictures of my mother flooded my mind: the joy on her face as she danced with the naiads under the summer moon; her grave expression when she gave me my father's athame; and finally, the pain in her eyes as she lay dying, stabbed by her own dagger.

Still, the reborn, sober Nyx was trying on something new: forgiveness.

"I forgive you," I said. "I hate to leave you, but I'll be right back."

She bit back a sob. "I'll be here."

I rubbed a garland of white flowers all over my skin. They were supposed to protect from basilisk poison. Naomi came back with two blankets.

"I broke into the emergency supplies," she said. "Where's my mom?"

I handed her a garland that had managed to stay intact. "Rub this all over your skin," I said. "I'll carry her out."

I picked Nona up. She was already burning up from the poison.

I took her into the hallway and placed her gently on the blankets.

It was a slow death. Naomi held her mother's right hand. I held the left. There was no sound except Nona's breathing as it slowed.

Naomi dropped her mother's hand and picked up the golden shears. Her hand trembled as she held the scissors. I wanted to ease them away from her, to tell her she didn't have to, but she did. At least if the Fates had a chance of survival.

Nona was gone. The last Fate had died. Another time, another person, I'd gotten my wish. I had wanted my aunts dead. That person was gone. Now all I wanted was for Nona to sit up and smile at me.

The thing that I thought I wanted more than anything had happened and I found I didn't want it at all. Someone else had felt that need for vengeance, the need to see as much of their blood spilled as my mother's had. Be careful what you wish for.

"It's done," Naomi said, before collapsing into a ball. "There's nothing left for me. They're both dead." I dropped to the floor and wrapped my arms around her. As I held my inconsolable cousin, I realized then what a great burden being a Fate truly was.

Chapter Twenty-Four

A roar reminded me that there were still several mythic animals loose inside Parsi.

"We need to go," I said.

"Go where?" The despair in Naomi's voice nearly ended it right there. I wanted to curl up into a ball next to her. Instead, I hauled her to her feet. "It's not safe here, Naomi. Let's move. We need to find the others and get to safety."

I led her through the basement to the top floor, where the corporate office was located. Shards of glass from the broken windows littered the carpet and all around was the smell of death.

Rebecca, Claire, and Talbot were in the Human Resources offices, searching under the overturned furniture for survivors.

"Anyone live?" I asked.

Talbot shook his head. "No one survived. The only good thing is that the tornado hit after five. Most people had already left."

"But not the aunts," Rebecca said, after a glance at Naomi.

I shook my head. "Time to leave," I said. "There are things out there. Things we don't want to run into."

Talbot's gaze went to Naomi immediately. "What's wrong?"

She threw herself into his arms. He murmured comforting words into her ear as she sobbed.

"My mother?" Claire said. "Or Aunt Nona?"

"Gone."

She gasped. "Both of them?"

"We've got to move now." I'd killed the basilisk, but who knew what else was still lurking at Parsi.

Rebecca put an arm around Claire, but she seemed strangely unmoved by Morta's death. Maybe there was a reason Claire had been with Hecate all those months.

I thought my cousin was as cold as her mother, but as we walked down the stairs, she sank to her knees. She saw me watching and righted herself before I could offer her a hand.

We made it out of the building without incident, but Talbot had to carry Naomi, who was prostrate with grief.

Talbot followed me in the van with Naomi and Claire. Rebecca, to my surprise, decided to ride back with me. The torrential rain had turned into a warm summer drizzle.

We made a brief stop at Eternity Road to pick up Ambrose and as many supplies as we could fit into the two vehicles.

There were two dead demons in the store.

"Dad?" Talbot broke into a run.

"In here, son," Ambrose replied.

We followed the sound of his voice into the office. Ambrose had a gouge near one eye and smears of black demon blood on his shirt, but other than that, was okay.

We updated Ambrose as quickly as possible.

"We can't stay here," I said. "It's the first place Hecate will look."

"There's a box of emergency supplies in the storage room,"

he said. "Talbot, grab every blanket, pillow, and scrap of cloth you can find. Nyx, you need to get as many healing amulets from the display as you can carry."

We stared at him in astonishment as he barked out orders.

"Get moving, kids," he said. "This is war."

The word galvanized us. We packed up and headed to the abandoned fort. It had been a part of history once, but now stood empty and neglected. The windows of most of the buildings had been boarded up in a futile attempt to keep out the rats and other creatures. We had our choice of buildings, but some were in better shape than others. We left the one with the caved-in roof to the rats and raccoons.

A street kid had brought me to the Dead House when I first came to Minneapolis. It was where he'd tried to feed me to a troll, but I still had a fondness for the place. It had the added benefit that I'd never taken Wren there, had never even mentioned it to her.

Damp and rotting or not, the buildings were better than sleeping outside. We were exhausted, wet, and cranky. An overturned car blocked the road, so I parked about a block down and we walked.

"What a dump," Rebecca said when she caught sight of the base.

"Beggars can't be choosers," I said. A barbed wire fence surrounded the place, but I showed them where to slip through a hole in the fence.

"At least it has a roof and four walls," Talbot said grimly. Naomi had stopped crying, but had sunk into a quiet funk.

I tapped the stone troll's nose when I walked by. He stood outside the Dead House, the building where they used to store the bodies. Jasper, the street kid I'd met when I first came to

Minneapolis, had lured me there to feed me to the troll, but I'd managed to defeat him.

"I'll be right back," I said. I pried open the boarded-up window and slid through. I went around and opened the front door.

"Welcome home," I said.

Rebecca snorted.

"Be it ever so humble," Talbot said.

Jasper's camp stove was still there. Maybe the stone troll had scared off any scavengers. I fired it up and the room warmed quickly. Naomi was in shock.

"I'm going to clean up a little," Rebecca said to Claire and Naomi. "And then I'll get you settled." She managed to clear out most of the trash within minutes. My sister was efficient.

"Have you checked out the other buildings?" Ambrose asked. He arranged a load of blankets on the ground.

"No," I said. "I think we should get some sleep and check them out at first light. We're going to need the space."

"For what?" Claire asked.

"There will be others wanting to hide from Hecate's wrath," I explained.

"We're not hiding," Talbot quipped. "We're just regrouping."

It was only a few hours before dawn. "I'll take the first watch." As tired as I was, I wouldn't be able to sleep.

The others settled in to try to get a few hours of rest, but I kept a watchful eye. Too many of the Wyrd family had died already.

The sun came up without incident, except that I learned that Naomi snored like a grizzly in midhibernation.

Ambrose and I went through every building. We decided that the old hospital would make the best place to take any injured.

"You can count on casualties," he said grimly.

"Already have."

"I'm sorry about your aunts, Nyx," he replied.

Not as sorry as I was. Aloud, I said, "We have to find some way of stopping Hecate. Any word from Doc?"

He shook his head. "He'll turn up. He's impossible to kill."

"I hope so."

"Nyx, he's Hades," Ambrose said. "I know it's hard to tell, but Doc can take care of himself."

The word got out that refugees from Hecate could find shelter at the old fort. At first, it was just one or two, but within a week, there were almost thirty magical creatures staying with us.

We'd warded the perimeters and set up a system that would alert us of a demon presence, but the precautions were not going to stop Hecate if she really wanted us.

We'd all found separate spaces to sleep. Rebecca and Claire shared a room, Talbot and Naomi shared another, and Ambrose took what used to be the mortician's office. I slept on the floor in the room where the troll had tried to kill me.

Naomi had spent most of the day inside. I decided to change that. No matter how much we scrubbed, we couldn't get the smell of death out of the rooms. Despite that, we all wanted to stay close together, at least in the same building.

"Come take a walk with me," I coaxed. "I need to salt the perimeter anyway, and I can't carry the bag by myself."

She gave me a look. "Quit trying to make me feel sorry for you," she said with a gleam of her old humor. "I'm busy feeling sorry for myself."

"Please?"

"Okay, I'll go," she said.

Outside, the sun beat down on us as we walked along in silence. I stopped to reapply the salt near the fence and noticed it had been brushed aside. I bent down to look. Part of a footprint marred the border. It was possible one of us had done it, but I reinforced it with a spell, just in case.

"I'm sick to death of cutting threads of Fate," Naomi said. "Sick of death."

Naomi's new job as the Atropos was making my funny charming cousin quiet and sad.

I dropped the bag of salt and gave her a one-armed hug. "We can change it," I said. "You don't have to be the Atropos forever."

"How?"

"After this is over, I'll find a way," I promised rashly. "We don't know everything about being Fates."

"I know I hate it," she replied. "I don't know how Aunt Morta stood it."

I hugged her again. She was frailer than before, worn thin by what she had to do. "We'll find a way to get you out of this gig."

She sniffed and then hugged me back. "Thank Hades the mortals don't believe in us anymore, or I wouldn't get any rest."

"You're lucky, you know," she added. "Fortuna had the fun part. Everyone loved her."

"Until they forgot about her."

"Better forgotten than feared."

"Hecate hasn't attacked yet," I said. "But it's only a matter of time. I injured her, but it's hard to keep a goddess down."

"Maybe she hasn't figured out where we are," Naomi said. "Or maybe Wren convinced her to leave us alone."

The hopeful note in her voice made my heart hurt.

"Hecate has the wind on her side," I said. I looked up at the sky. There were winged creatures circling above our heads. "Or maybe she already knows where we are."

The sight of the harpies hunting for me was a familiar one, but not one I welcomed.

"What do you mean?" Naomi said.

"Don't you see the harpies?"

"I don't see anything," she said. "The sun's in my eyes."

When I shaded my hand over my eyes to look again, they were gone.

Chapter Twenty-Five

We'd been holed up at the fort as the city regrouped. Word that the Fates had fallen had led to chaos in the Twin Cities, though. The magical community was choosing sides and doors were closing. Hecate had promised to make the world burn, and she was a goddess who kept her word.

Mortals as well as the magical were fearful. Rumors of dark rituals, human sacrifices, even a serial killer were whispered in the mortal world, while the magical world concerned itself with the news of Hecate's escape.

Hell's Belles was still standing, but had been deserted. Nobody knew where Bernie was, or if she was even still alive. A mortal stood on the corner with a sign proclaiming, THE APOCALYPSE IS NIGH.

I'd warded the boundaries of the abandoned fort and we started making preparations for an attack that never came.

"Where is she?" I asked.

"You wounded her," Ambrose reminded me. "She might be too weak to fight."

"But wounds heal," I replied.

He hoisted a five-pound bag of salt. "Where do you want this?" he asked me.

"The old mess hall for now," I told him. "Naomi and Talbot are working on a demon cocktail."

"Does it matter?" Talbot asked glumly. "Hecate will just bring more demons."

"If there was only a sign of where the harpy's feather is, we'd have a chance."

"Claire's been scouring the Book of Fates," he pointed out. "All we know is that Morta had it. She hid the harpy feather, obviously."

"But where?" I slapped a mosquito that was trying to suck on my neck.

"Nobody has a clue," he said. "I think the secret died with the Fates."

"And whose fault is that?" Naomi snapped. It was the first thing she'd said all morning. She was huddled on the cot.

"What do you want me to say?" I asked. "I didn't mean for any of this to happen."

"Yes, you did," she accused. "You came to Minneapolis to get your revenge."

"At first I wanted to kill the aunts," I said. "But that changed."

"Yet my mother and aunts are still dead," she said. "And my father." She turned her face to the wall.

"My mother is dead, too," I replied. "Instead of arguing, we need to fight. Or have you given up?"

Her shoulders tensed, but she didn't reply. I knew my question had hit home, though, when she got out of bed. "I'm going to see if I can help Claire."

Talbot murmured something in her ear and then kissed her gently before she left.

"What did you say to her?"

He choked back a laugh. "I suggested, diplomatically, that she might want to bathe."

A series of honks told us that Ambrose had arrived back with supplies. We went outside to help him unload.

"Any luck?"

He handed me a ten-pound bag of beans. "The shelves are almost wiped clean. The tornado scared the mortals and now they're stocking up for emergencies." He had to be careful which stores he went to. Some of them had already been taken over by Hecate's demons.

"I like beans," Talbot said cheerfully, but his father's next words wiped the smile from his face.

"Trey Marin is missing."

"You think something happened to him?"

"I think someone happened to him," he replied. "No one has seen him since he met with the other House leaders."

"What did Luke Seren say?"

Ambrose shrugged. "I didn't ask him."

"You think Luke is behind Trey's disappearance? But Luke said he was on our side."

"That's what he said," Ambrose said. "The question is do you believe him?"

"Why would Luke want to kill Trey?"

"Trey has been coming to your defense with the other Houses," Ambrose said. "He's done everything but take out an ad. Hecate would want that threat removed."

"What about Johnny Asari?" Talbot said. "I wouldn't put it past him to screw us over."

"Anyone else you can talk to about Trey's whereabouts?" I asked.

"His niece," Ambrose said. "But maybe you'd like to speak with her personally." He gave me a sly smile.

Despite the seriousness of the situation, I laughed. "I'm persona non grata with Willow right now, but if anyone knows where Trey is, it'd be her."

My mind was still worrying on the question of the harpy feather.

"I need to go into the city," I said. "There's someone I need to see."

He didn't bother telling me I'd probably get killed. He didn't have to. We'd been taking turns patrolling the city, searching out the demons preying on mortals and magicians alike. Any demon worth his salt would be itching to kill me. Hecate probably promised bonuses to whoever managed to kill me.

I needed to see Ruth Delaney. She was a fortune-teller. Maybe that was enough that she'd be loyal to Lady Fortuna. Loyal to me.

Ruth had a small shop not far from where Zora's used to be. The palm-reader symbol hung discreetly in the window, but other than that, it looked like a high-priced tea shop.

I peered through the window. She was alone. The store was decorated in white lace and blue floral prints. It looked like a doily convention.

Ruth sat on a blue silk divan and sipped a cup of tea. She set it down abruptly when I entered.

"What are you doing here?" she asked. "Are you crazy? There are demons everywhere, searching for the son of Fortuna."

"I know that, but I need your help. I want a reading, Ruth," I said.

"Not here," she said. "Meet me at the Greyhound station tomorrow. Fitch will come with me."

"It has to be early," I told her. Demons didn't particularly like the sun, although they could walk in it, if needed.

Customers entered and we both froze, but it was a group of mortal women. They gave me curious looks as they browsed. I must have looked out of place in the frilly shop.

"I'll take some of the Earl Grey," I said. It was the only excuse I could think of.

Ruth wrote something down on a receipt pad and then rang me up. "Your receipt, sir." I stuffed it in my pocket.

I was a block from her store when I nearly collided with Luke Seren. "Nyx," he hissed. "What are you doing here?"

I narrowed my eyes. "Looking for supplies," I lied.

He modified his tone. "Forgive me for my anger," he said. "I was concerned about your safety."

"I can take care of myself," I said.

"Did you happen to see Ruth today?" he asked.

"I went to her shop," I said.

"Why?" His questions were setting me on edge.

I studied him for a moment. "My cousin has just lost her mother," I said. "I thought maybe a cup of tea would brighten her day."

"Ah, yes, of course," he replied. "Tea is a wonderful restorative."

"Yes," I said. "We're all recovering from the betrayal."

He flinched, but recovered quickly. "Betrayal?"

He knew something. "Only a very few people knew where Hecate was imprisoned."

"Maybe you should look to Johnny Asari for that," Luke suggested.

"How would Johnny know?"

He made a steeple of his hands. "How do I put this delicately? Pillow talk."

I slammed him against the storefront wall. "Are you accusing my sister of something?"

"No, no, of course not," he said. "It's just…"

I set him down. "Spit it out."

"Don't you find that you tell your secrets to those you love?"

I stalked away without answering. I waited to get back to the Dead House to read Ruth's note. She'd written down an address and time. Six a.m. at the bus station on Hawthorne.

The next morning, I got a ride with Ambrose. We'd scraped the Eternity Road logo off the side of the van and repainted it. Now the van looked like a million other white delivery vans, instead of a bull's-eye for demons.

Ambrose dropped me off six blocks from the meeting point. He was headed out to replenish our zombie chow and maybe find some extra food and supplies for the rest of us.

The Greyhound bus station was only a few blocks from Hell's Belles. I'd reluctantly left my leather jacket with Talbot and felt naked without it, but it would have made me stand out like a sore thumb. I borrowed one of his hoodies. I hoped it would obscure my identity long enough to find out what Ruth could tell me.

As I walked along Hawthorne, I noticed Tria Prima symbols on most of the buildings. Despite my best efforts, Minneapolis was in thrall to a demon goddess.

The magical world hadn't waited long before choosing sides. Hecate hadn't given them much choice. Besides, I wouldn't bet on me, either.

I took a seat on a metal bench that faced the entrance and settled in. I waited for three hours, but Ruth and Fitch never showed up.

Chapter Twenty-Six

Two days later, I still hadn't heard from Ruth or Fitch. We were still holed up at the Dead House. The rest of our ragtag fighters were scattered around the fort, but the Dead House had become command central.

The wounded were housed in the old military hospital and the able-bodied were sleeping in the barracks. Word had got out that Hecate didn't play nice, mostly from the people who came to us with burns, bites, or missing limbs.

Doc and Willow had both turned up. The Korrigan I'd met at Hell's Belles arrived with six of his friends. Willow had sent a few satyrs and naiads to the abandoned base, but she didn't want to stay with me. She'd changed since Hecate's possession.

Willow was harder, colder, and it made my stomach churn to think of the things Hecate had done with and to Willow's body.

There was a secluded lake on the fort grounds. It was farther away from the Dead House and me, but Willow insisted she would be fine there. I couldn't really argue with her. She'd get sick if she was away from the water too long.

"Have you seen your uncle?" I asked. "Or know where he went?"

"The satyrs tell me Trey is wandering in the woods," she said.

"Is that something he usually does?"

"No, it is not," she replied.

"I'll go look for him," I said.

"If there is something wrong," she replied, "it is better if I am the one to find him."

I nodded. "Let me know if you hear anything."

"I will," she said.

There was nothing else to say, so I returned to the fort. I was inspecting the protective salt lines when I heard a shout.

"Nyx," Willow shouted my name from somewhere far away. "Nyx, help me."

I ran to the lake as fast as I could. Willow was waist deep in the water and she held her uncle Trey by the shoulders. He was unconscious.

I helped her drag him out of the water.

"He's been stabbed," she said. "But there's something else wrong."

"Let's get him to the hospital," I said. "Doc can patch him up good as new." I didn't know if it was true, but it helped to erase the lines of tension in her face.

We made a makeshift stretcher out of some branches and carried Trey at a run back to the hospital building.

"Doc!" I shouted. "We need you now!"

He met us in the center square. "Get him inside."

We followed him into the hospital wing with Trey. "Where'd you find him?" Doc asked as he checked Trey's vitals.

"He was in the lake on the south side of the fort," I said.

"The stab wound is superficial," Doc said. "But he's burning with fever."

Trey moaned and Willow grabbed her uncle's hand.

"Infection?" I asked.

"Maybe." Doc examined him closely. He finally found a bite mark at the nape of his neck.

"Is it bad?"

"I'm afraid so," Doc said. He glanced at Willow.

"Please tell us the truth, Lord of Bones," she said.

"Trey might not last the night," Doc said grimly.

"He has to," I said. "Since you won't fight, he's the strongest person we have."

"I'm better off tending to the dead and dying," Doc said. "But your magic is stronger than Trey's."

"Stronger than the great-grandson of Poseidon?"

"Yes," he said. He laughed at my doubtful look.

"Why is he so sick?" I asked. "What happened to him?"

"Something bit him," Doc replied. "I have a theory, but I can't even believe I'm thinking it."

"You think a flesh eater got to him," I said flatly.

"How did you know?"

"Because the only flesh eater I've ever met is missing," I replied. "And I'm pretty sure Hecate took him."

He studied my face gravely. "That's a problem."

"We'd have a fighting chance if you fought with us," I said.

"I won't fight, but I can show you a few things."

Doc treated the wound, which was already festering.

"Now what?"

"Now we wait."

"I'll sit with him," Willow said.

I didn't want to leave her alone with Trey, but Doc said, "If he has been bitten by a flesh eater, it'll be another day before we know."

I kissed her forehead. "We won't be far," I said. "Call out if anything changes."

Doc and I found an unoccupied room next door.

"So what did you want to show me?"

"Things the son of Hades should know," he replied.

Some of the spells I already knew, but I didn't want to tell him. He was smiling a real smile and the constant twitch had receded into an occasional jerk.

"Good," he finally said. "Now, are you ready for some real magic?"

"I thought that's what I've been doing for the last two hundred years." I was trying not to let my exasperation show, but a hint must have registered with him.

"I have a few tricks up my sleeve," Doc said.

"Show me."

It wasn't easy, but my father eventually taught me how to form a fireball. The first one looked more like a fire*fly* than a fireball, but I persisted.

"Your mother..." he started to say, then cleared his throat. "Lady Fortuna was like no one else, but she did not approve of dark magic, even for the greater good."

I nodded. "I know."

He met my eyes. "She would not have approved of what I'm about to show you."

He taught me a compulsion spell that would command even the most powerful necromancer. "This spell takes away another's will," he said. "It must be used only if you are desperate. Do you understand?"

"I understand," I told him.

"And, Nyx, if you go to war with Hecate, you must realize that I can't bring you back if you die again."

I nodded. "I understand." I didn't remind him that dying had been my goal all along.

Twenty-four hours later, Trey was still battling for his life and Doc was no closer to figuring out how to save him. I slipped out, looking for booze.

It was stupid, but I convinced myself that a quick run to the liquor store couldn't hurt anything. Taking the Caddy was out of the question, so I hoofed it.

I was out of absinthe, but would have settled for a cold beer. Who am I kidding? I would have settled for someone else's warm beer at that point, as long as there weren't cigarette butts floating in it. My quick trip turned into a duck into a seedy bar.

No one looked up when I walked in, not even the bartender. It was the kind of place where there were no clocks and only a few grimy windows, so when I finally staggered out, it had grown dark. I stopped at the liquor store and grabbed as many bottles as I could carry.

I took the roundabout way back to the Dead House. A narrow winding path cut through a forest and came out in the empty lot on the other side of the abandoned fort.

The path was shrouded by trees, but here and there, the moonlight broke through. I passed by a couple of pixies who were sweeping up the debris and broken glass along the path leading to the forest.

I stumbled over something in the darkness and leaned down to examine it. I told myself it was a raccoon bone, but it looked like a human finger, licked clean.

The dark magic Doc showed me saved my life. A snarling skeleton leaped upon me in the darkness. It was a man, or had been one once. He had me on the ground in seconds. A thick gob of drool hung from his mouth, and I twisted and bucked, but he held me fast. If he pinned down my arms, I was screwed.

A piece of broken bottle dug into my back. For a brief second I mourned my lost alcohol, but I had bigger problems. He clawed at my chest, frantic. He let out a hungry feral growl.

"Baxter?" I recognized him. The flesh eater who had disappeared. I had no doubt he was hungry enough to eat me. He wore only filthy dress pants, his skin smeared with blood and bits of gore. His brown hair was shaggy, his eyes were wild, and he bore little resemblance to the suave man I'd met at the morgue.

A moment of lucidity passed over his face. "Nyx, run!"

The bone I'd found made sense now. I probably looked like a three-course meal to a starving flesh eater. The brief moment of clarity disappeared. He was so strong. He tried to take a bite out of me, but got a mouthful of leather jacket instead.

I stretched out one hand and searched for something to use as a weapon. I found one unbroken bottle and grasped the neck. I swung it around and bashed him on the head.

"*Constrixi, Compellere, Pareo.*" I uttered the spell my father had taught me. For all my blustering, I'd used the spell the first chance I had. I understood what my father meant about the pull of dark magic. It had worked immediately and now Baxter was under my control. Heady stuff.

"Yes, my lord?"

"Nyx, Baxter, my name is Nyx."

"Nyx," he said. "What is your command?"

"Tell me what happened to you."

"Hecate captured me," he said. "I'm so hungry. I tried to resist, but she made me."

"Made you do what?"

"Eat," he said. "But only a bite. Had to leave them alive."

"Leave who alive?"

"All of them," he said.

"Follow me," I said. "And Baxter?"

"Yes, Nyx?"

"Don't you dare bite anyone," I said. "Especially not me."

He nodded.

Despite the spell, I made him walk in front of me.

"Jesus, Nyx, you should have let someone know where you were going." Talbot's lecture sputtered to a stop when he saw Baxter. "What happened to him?"

"I found him starving in the woods," I said.

"What did you do to him?"

"Nothing." The lie sprang to my lips all too easily, but Doc saw right through me.

"Undo it," my father snapped.

"Why did you show me if you didn't want me to use it?" I muttered.

Doc gave me a stern look.

"If I undo the spell, Baxter will tear your throat out and eat your brains," I said.

Doc snorted. "Like I can't handle a starving flesh eater."

Talbot leaned in and said to me, "I've never seen this side of him. Now I know where you get your cockiness from."

"We need to get him something to eat," I said.

Talbot and Doc looked at me in horror.

"Not *live* food," I said. "He survived on corpses."

"I'll take care of it," Ambrose said. He left with a shovel. Minutes passed while we waited, but he eventually came back with a couple of bags of something I didn't want to examine too closely.

"Now get rid of the spell," Doc ordered.

I waved my hand and muttered, "Release."

Baxter lunged for the closest warm body, but Ambrose was prepared. He threw the bag at Baxter, who ripped the plastic apart and shoved handfuls of bloody meat into his mouth. He chewed frantically.

I looked away, but couldn't shut out the slurping sounds he was making. When I glanced toward him again, he had tipped the plastic bag over his mouth and was sucking the bloody juice out of the bag.

"More," Baxter said.

Ambrose tossed him the second bag. The chewing was slower this time. I tried not to think of what, or who, Baxter was eating.

"Why would Hecate want Baxter's victims to live?" I asked.

"To create an army of flesh eaters," Ambrose said.

"She gets in your head," Baxter said. "Whispering that you can't cut it anymore. That you're nothing. That you should just take a bite." His dark eyes were full of agony.

"And?" Talbot said.

"And pretty soon I start to believe her. Nobody's looking for me. Nobody cares. Nobody will know."

"How many did you kill, Baxter?" I asked.

His answer surprised me.

"One."

"You're a flesh eater," I said. "How did you survive for so long without... food?"

"None *at first*," he emphasized. He looked at his hands. "She fed me sometimes," he said. "The same scraps she fed the harpies. But then..."

"Just tell us."

"I was so hungry that I would have eaten my own grandmother," he said. "And she brought this mortal in and told me to take one bite. I'm in chains. Starving. I couldn't stop. Hecate wasn't happy."

"Why did she want you to take one bite? Doesn't seem like that's enough to do real harm." I already knew the answer, but wanted him to say it Hecate wanted to spread the flesh eater disease and Baxter was lucky patient zero. The other flesh eaters had been hunted and killed long ago.

"To make more of me, of course," he said, confirming my suspicions.

"And did she?" Ambrose asked.

"After a while, I learned that if I could manage only a bite or two, I'd be rewarded. If not, I'd be punished. I learned quickly," he said.

"Where did they keep you?" I said. "I looked for you."

Maybe I hadn't looked enough.

"At first, they kept me at Danvers's house," he said. "I'd been there once before for his bachelor party."

"Then what happened?" Ambrose prompted.

"Danvers screwed up. He was supposed to be watching me, but instead, he was tormenting my potential victims, telling them beforehand what was going to happen to them. I escaped. I didn't get more than a hundred yards from the house before one of Hecate's demons spotted me. That was the last time I tried to escape." He shivered in remembrance.

"That explains why Hecate kicked Danvers to the curb," I said. "But you don't have to worry about Danvers anymore." There was a long list of people who wanted to kill Danvers, but it was too late. Willow had already done the job.

Baxter's story was enough to silence everyone in the room. A zombie outbreak would be enough to make the black plague look like a case of the sniffles.

Chapter Twenty-Seven

Later, after Baxter had time to clean up and change into some clothes Ambrose had taken from Eternity Road, we held a meeting at the Dead House.

"What are we going to do?" Talbot asked.

"Baxter, is there a cure?" I asked.

His stare made me realize how stupid the question was.

"I was a toddler when my mother was killed by a mob," he said. "But if there's a cure, I haven't been able to find one."

"So the only solution is to kill them?" I asked.

"It's the only one I know of," he replied. "Not one I'm particularly fond of, though."

"Me, neither."

We both knew that was the only solution, unless we could find something in the Book of Fates.

The confab broke up without finding a solution. I took a flashlight and a book on zombies to bed and poured over it, but didn't find anything that would help us stop Hecate from creating an army of flesh eaters.

The next morning I reached into the pocket of my leather

jacket and found a piece of paper I didn't recognize. I unfolded it and saw Alex's handwriting. He'd given it to me before he and Elizabeth had left Minneapolis. At the time, I'd thought it was a thank-you note and then I'd forgotten about it.

I stared down at a formula. The formula for making ambrosia. Without volition, a thought popped into my mind. I had in my hands the formula that could make me immortal again.

A phone number was written at the bottom, along with a message to call him if I ever needed anything.

I tucked it back into my pocket. My aunts would kill to get their hands on the formula. Gaston had killed Sawyer to get it. Or at least I thought that's why he'd killed him. Gaston had been a psychopath, so it was hard to understand his motivation.

The formula did give me an idea, though. Alex was a scientific genius. As much as I wanted Alex and Elizabeth to be as far away from Minneapolis as possible, I needed him.

I made the call. "Alex, I need a favor." He wasn't a medical researcher, but he was the closest thing I knew to one. And Doc could help.

Alex was ready to hop on a plane, but I tried to talk him out of it. "Can't you work on the formula to reverse the flesh-eating disease long-distance?"

"I have to come to Minneapolis," he replied. "I need to get blood and other samples from patient zero."

"Baxter," I said. "But it's smarter to do this long-distance." Safer, too.

"Nyx, I would do anything to help you," he said. My ex's brother sounded strong, but I knew that strength was a fragile thing. "I'll be there within twenty-four hours. Can you start by getting the lake house ready for me?"

I wanted to tell him to forget it, to stay wherever he was, safe and happy, but I couldn't. Instead I told him I'd meet him there.

The lake house was shuttered and dark, but I slipped in through an unlocked window. The wards I'd placed after Elizabeth and Alex had fled Minneapolis had held. Besides an ungodly smell coming from the kitchen and a layer of dust everywhere, the house was untouched. Only a family of mice had dared to take up residence.

Doc helped me set up a makeshift lab in the living room where Elizabeth and I had shared our first kiss.

"If there's no solution in magic," I asked, "what makes you so sure science will work?"

My father was the king of the underworld. If he didn't know how to stop a zombie invasion, I didn't have much hope that Alex would crack it.

"Magic and science go together," Doc replied. "Many of the old gods had trouble accepting that."

While we waited for Alex to show, I occupied my time by cleaning out the refrigerator. Alex and Elizabeth had left Minneapolis unexpectedly in the middle of the night, and there was a science experiment growing in the kitchen. I threw everything into a garbage bag and took it out to the curb, then scrubbed everything I could reach.

Afterward, I took a shower in the guest room where I'd stayed when I first met Elizabeth, and padded down the stairs barefoot and bare-chested.

A woman sat at the kitchen counter. She had dark frizzy hair and glasses, and wore a load of makeup, but I recognized her immediately. Elizabeth. My stomach lurched as I recognized my former girlfriend.

Marlene Perez

"What is she doing here?" I asked Alex, who was at the stove cooking. Doc had disappeared, which didn't surprise me.

"It's nice to see you, too," Elizabeth replied. "I thought you'd be glad to see me. I'm better now, you know."

"I want you to stay that way," I told her. Underneath the disguise, she did look better. Some of the scarring from the fire had faded and her eyes were clear and bright.

"Why did you come?" I asked her softly. "It's not safe."

"We want to help," she said. "You saved Alex and now we want to help you save everyone else."

She gave me a hug, then touched the charms I always wore on a silver chain. "I see you found your mother's charms."

A shiver ran through me at her touch. Our eyes met and she looked away.

Alex cleared his throat. "Want some eggs, Nyx? We've been traveling all night and I'm starving."

"Sure, Alex," I said. I took a seat as far away from Elizabeth as I could. "Where'd the food come from?"

"Doc brought it," Alex said happily. He slid a plate of eggs and toast over to his sister and then served me. "He even remembered orange juice."

"Speaking of Doc," I said. "Where is he?"

"In the basement," Alex replied. I glanced at Elizabeth, who was pushing around her food without eating it.

"Why the basement?"

He shrugged. "Dunno, but I think I'll check on him."

After Alex left, Elizabeth and I avoided looking at each other.

I shifted in my seat. "You're looking well."

She bit back a laugh. "Hardly."

"No, I mean it. You look…happy."

"I *am* happy," she said. "I wish you were."

"You do? You don't blame me for the fire? For what happened to you?"

"The Fates were entangled in my life long before I met you," she said.

"Dating me didn't help."

She put her hand on my arm. "It didn't hurt, either, Nyx. I don't regret it."

I covered her hand with my own. I didn't know what to say, but she didn't seem to expect me to say anything.

"Doc's rigging up space for the test patients," Alex said from the doorway. "Come check it out."

I'd never been in the basement at the lake house. We followed Alex down the stairs. Their basement was nicer than my apartment.

In a few hours, Doc had fashioned a makeshift prison.

We smuggled Baxter into the house a few hours later. Doc and Alex took turns drawing blood while Elizabeth and I watched from a safe distance.

"You're not hungry, are you?" I asked Baxter. I didn't want him taking a bite out of someone while we worked on the cure.

"I could eat," he said.

I held up the bags Ambrose had provided. "Lunch is served."

While Baxter ate, I cornered Doc. "Do you think we really have a shot at this?"

"I do," he said.

"But usually cures take years, decades even," I said.

"Don't worry, Nyx," he said. "We have magic on our side."

"I'll leave it to you, then," I said. I gave Elizabeth a hug. "Be careful, Elizabeth," I added. "Hecate is still out there."

"I'll be careful," she replied. "But don't worry so much. She doesn't know anything about me."

Doc looked up from the paper he was writing on. "Not strictly true," he commented. "I'm sure Wren told her all she knows of Elizabeth."

"Wren? What happened to Willow?" Elizabeth asked.

Baxter snickered. I shot him a dirty look.

"Long story," I said.

She waved a hand dismissively. "Never mind. Forget I asked."

"No, you should know," I said. "You'll be more prepared. Alex, too."

I settled in and related everything that had happened after they left Minneapolis, leaving out the more intimate details.

Elizabeth got the gist, though. "Nyx, I don't know what gets you into more trouble," she said. "Your penis or your kind heart."

"His penis," Alex and Doc replied at the same time. Baxter bellowed with laughter.

I grinned sheepishly. "I am a guy." I sobered quickly, though. "Elizabeth, I'm not kidding. You and Alex need to be extremely careful while you're here."

I was torn. I didn't want to leave them, but I needed to get back to the Dead House and check in.

"Go ahead, Nyx," Doc said. "I'll make sure no harm comes to your friends."

If a god couldn't keep them safe, I didn't have a shot in hell. I nodded and headed back to camp.

Chapter Twenty-Eight

When I got back, Luke Seren was parked outside the gates of the fort, behind the wheel of a shiny black Lincoln. I didn't open the gate.

Instead, I went over to his car. "What are you doing here?"

"I brought you some supplies," he said. "Frankly, I expected a warmer welcome."

"Let me see," I said.

He popped the trunk, which was full of food and blankets. "I can be your food tester if you're worried it's poisoned."

"Sorry," I said. "I appreciate it. We're a little on edge right now. In fact, you should probably go."

"I understand," Luke replied. "But at least let me help you carry these."

I studied him. "Why are you helping us?"

"It's despite my better judgment, I assure you."

His blunt response eased my fears. "I'll show you where you can put the groceries, but then I'll have to ask you to leave."

"I understand," he replied. "I'll make it brief."

In fact, Luke's visit was almost ridiculously short. He said hello to Ambrose, put down the bags of groceries, and then made his departure.

"I'll show you out," Ambrose said.

"No need," Luke replied. "I know when I'm not wanted. I'll be out of your hair shortly."

It wasn't more than five minutes later when I heard his car start up and drive away.

"Think he's gone?" I asked Ambrose.

"I don't think he wanted to stick around," Ambrose replied.

"Then why did he show up at all?" I asked.

"He's hedging his bets," Ambrose said. "If we come out on top, we'll remember he did us a favor."

"And if we don't?"

He shrugged. "Luke's a survivor."

We had more important things to worry about. I helped Ambrose store the supplies and then headed back to the Dead House.

Emmett Greenfellow was waiting for me there. When he saw me, he stopped and gave me a low bow.

"How did you get past the guards?" I asked.

He gave me a stiff bow. "It is of no import," he said. "You saved my life, Nyx Fortuna."

"I told you to forget about that." Gratitude made my skin itch.

"I cannot," he replied. "And that is why I came to warn you. You have been betrayed by someone. Hecate's followers are on their way here."

"How do you know that?"

"No one pays attention to me," he said simply. "I hear things. But you must warn the others."

"Thank you," I said. He didn't leave, so I asked, "Is there anything else?"

"I will stay to fight," he said simply.

"Thank you," I said again.

Emmett Greenfellow had given us a fighting chance by removing the element of surprise. When the magical world heard the Fates had been defeated, it didn't take long for them to realize helping us wasn't in their best interest of breathing.

"Hecate will be here soon. And I'm guessing she'll bring the flesh eaters," I told Doc and the others.

"We won't be able to hold them off," Naomi said. "Any luck on the cure yet?"

Doc frowned. "We're close, but we need more time."

"We don't have time," Talbot said. "We've contained an outbreak, but won't be able to for much longer. And who knows how many flesh eaters Hecate still has."

"I have an idea," I said. "It won't stop them, but it might slow them down."

"The flesh eaters?" Ambrose asked. "You think we should feed them."

"Exactly," I said. "If they're well fed, they might not want to fight."

"I saw a dead raccoon near the lake," Talbot offered.

"That should work," I said.

Rebecca and Claire went to the lake to look for fish, preferably dead ones, while Talbot and Ambrose made several trips to the garbage heap at the edge of the fort. It smelled putrid, but the flesh eaters would love it.

I occupied my time by pouring lines of salt throughout the camp. It was a myth that salt kept the demons away completely, but they didn't like it. It was fortuitous that my secret hideout was an abandoned military fort.

"How many flesh eaters to you think Hecate has?" Talbot asked as we lugged the bags and buckets of scrap meat to the pit I'd dug. I'd had help, of course.

"One flesh eater is too many," I said.

"She's been planning this for a long time," Talbot commented. "She recruited Danvers, set him up next door to Deci, lured Claire into the underworld. All of that takes planning."

"Do you trust her?"

"Hecate? Of course not."

"I meant my cousin." He'd known exactly who I was talking about, but wanted to avoid an answer.

"You don't, do you?" I persisted.

"Do you blame me? You don't trust her, either," he said.

"Of course not," I said. "It was either Stockholm syndrome or she's part of Hecate's plan and Claire will betray us."

"You're an ass," Claire said from the doorway. "You didn't even consider another possibility." She pursed her lips like she was trying to hold something in.

"Which is?" I asked.

What she said next left Talbot and me openmouthed, looking like fish out of water.

"The aunts knew exactly where I was," she said. "They should have. They were the ones who sent me there."

"You were spying on Hecate the whole time?"

"Yes, genius, I was the aunts' spy." With that, she flounced away.

"Your family is weird," Talbot said.

"Punny," I said. My brain was busy with Claire's bombshell. The aunts had sent me to find Claire, but in reality, they'd known where she was the entire time. In the underworld, with their worst enemy.

Claire came back seconds later. "Someone took down the wards," she said. Someone we trusted had betrayed us. Beware of those bearing gifts and all that.

Chapter Twenty-Nine

I rushed outside. Claire and Talbot followed close behind.

There were no stars out and only a sliver of a moon shone in the night sky. "Do we have time to get the wards back up?" Talbot whispered.

I shook my head and pointed to the tall weeds growing in between the buildings. Something was moving through them.

Hecate's group came quietly, but the rippling weeds alerted me. I sent up a bit of magical light, which signaled to the rest of the group that we had company. I watched the tall weeds in the center of the square sway as our enemies approached.

Talbot was the first one to join me.

"They're here," I said.

She sent the flesh eaters in first. They emerged from the tall grass, their mouths foaming, and screeched. As I had suspected, they were hungry, maybe starving. There weren't as many as I'd feared. With hunger and surprise on her side, she didn't need many. Our motley crew was braced for whatever was coming, thanks to Emmett.

The leader sniffed the air and caught the scent of the rotting flesh we'd put in the pit. He broke into a run, stopping occasionally to sniff the air. Another one, a female, let out a sound like she had a bellyful of gravel and trotted after him. Two dozen of their friends followed them into the pit.

"They'll try to climb out eventually," Talbot said.

"Already thought of that," I said. "Watch." The trap sprung. A warded silver net covered the top of the pit. The flesh eaters were trapped, but they didn't seem to notice. The sound of frenzied eating arose from the pit.

We waited, but no one else appeared. A blob moved across the sky. As it drew closer, I made out the harpies. They swooped in low, heading straight for Naomi.

"Watch out!" I cried. I threw a ball of red flame at Fleet Foot. She screamed and then the smell of burning harpy filled the air. It smelled a little like rotisserie chicken, if the chicken had been left out in the sun. Still burning, she dropped out of the sky and landed with a thud. One down, two to go.

Swift Wing headed straight for me, her talons spread wide, her mouth open in a horrible screech.

Talbot still held a bucket of entrails. "She's hungry," I said. "Maybe the rotting meat will distract her long enough."

"Long enough for what?" Rebecca asked.

"This." The harpy was within arm's reach. I took my athame and aimed for the heart. She fell with a thump. Her sisters screamed in anger, but I sent a bolt of magic their way. They exploded. Guts rained down, but we managed to avoid them.

The harpies were dead.

"What now?" Talbot asked.

Naomi asked, "Did it work?"

Before I could answer either question, the ground shook with the force of a giant's steps. Shock held me motionless as an enormous one-eyed man advanced. Hecate had a Cyclops on her side.

There were only hollow sockets where his eyes would normally be. His chest was bare, but he wore what looked like pajama bottoms. His one eye was located where his belly button would normally be.

"It's Femus," Ambrose said. "The last Cyclops. I thought he left this world long ago." His face was lit by wonder.

I gave him a tap on the shoulder. "Quit fan-boying and tell us how to defeat him."

"He can't see us," Talbot said. It was a false hope. Talbot was looking in the wrong place. The Cyclops's enormous eye had already latched onto us.

"His one eye is in his belly," I replied.

The giant was slow-moving, but each footstep created pockets of devastation. A second wave of flesh eaters ran with the giant, managing to avoid getting squashed. About a hundred demons joined the fray.

Dark shapes moved all around us, making it hard for us to see who was friend and who was foe.

"Illuminate," I said. The air around us glowed, lighting up the night sky enough so we could see. The demons shielded their eyes.

I took the opportunity to stab one of them with my athame.

It was impossible to watch out for my loved ones in the heat of the battle, but I tried. I wasn't the only one.

As I fought, I grappled with the idea of the traitor in our midst. It couldn't have been a coincidence that we'd had two visitors only hours before we were attacked.

Talbot was in the middle of the fray. His eyes went silverlight and he sent spell after spell at the demons, but he kept a close eye on Naomi.

Rebecca and Claire lobbed balls of the silver-and-salt mixture. I scanned the area, but there was no sign of Hecate. Naomi helped when she could, but her duties as Fate kept her busy.

Hecate had been confident enough that the B team would be able to defeat us. I expected to see some of the minor gods fighting on the other side, but none appeared. Either they were still withdrawn from the mortal world or they weren't taking sides. I hoped it was the latter. Even Boreas, who'd helped break Hecate out of Parsi Enterprises, was sitting this battle out.

Wren and Naomi rolled on the ground. Wren finally gained the upper hand and hit her sister in the face with a rock. Wren wrapped her hands around Naomi's neck and squeezed. I raced toward them, but Rebecca got there first. She grabbed Wren by her dark red hair and pulled. Clumps of hair fell, but Wren refused to let go. Rebecca bent Wren's neck back as far as it would go and she finally released Naomi to face Rebecca.

Rebecca smashed her forehead into Wren's. There was a crack as their heads collided. Wren dropped, probably unconscious. Rebecca kicked her body aside to get to Naomi.

The ground shook. I couldn't stop to see if Naomi was okay. I pivoted. The Cyclops was lumbering toward Talbot, whose attention was on Naomi. He had his back to the giant and didn't seem to realize the danger.

"Hey, ugly," I shouted, but the Cyclops continued to advance. I tried again. I gave him a hotfoot he wouldn't forget. He turned and ran toward me.

He knocked me to the ground. My head was ringing. I put up a hand, but before I could get the first word of the spell out, he was on me. He twisted my arm until I heard a crack.

It dangled there, useless, but I managed to send a white-hot fireball at the Cyclops. It hit his belly and his eye began to burn. The sound of a screaming Cyclops filled the air.

Hecate entered the battle, riding on the back of her three-headed dog, Cerberus.

Hecate was on my other side. She let out a war cry and brandished an axe as big as she was. She missed the first time she swung, but the second time, she hit flesh.

There was a scream that echoed in my mind until I realized it was me screaming. There was the crunch of bone and I shut my eyes against the pain. When I opened them again, there was nothing but a wall of red.

When my vision cleared, I looked over, numb with shock, to see a flesh eater munching on my severed left arm like it was turkey drumstick at the state fair. Hecate had hacked it off, just above the elbow.

The flesh eater gave me a bloody grin and waved at me with my own arm. Rage overrode the intense pain. I drew a raggedy breath and then another. My right hand started to tingle and a small fireball formed in my palm.

He stopped grinning when I sent it his way. He couldn't dodge it. The fireball glowed white as it enveloped his body and turned him to ash within seconds.

"That's for taking my arm," I said. His comrades were still there. We were outnumbered by the sheer number of flesh eaters, trolls, and demons in Hecate's army.

There was a strange numbness all over my body. I couldn't look away. There was an emptiness where my left arm used to be. The stump was at an odd angle and blood spurted from the torn arteries. I'd die of shock and blood loss if I didn't do something soon. As I felt my life draining away, I threw another fireball, this one bigger and glowing white, right into the center of Hecate's army.

The last thing I heard was the sound of Hecate's laugh rising above the chaos.

Then I died. Again.

Chapter Thirty

I woke up in the makeshift hospital at the abandoned military base. I recognized the graffiti on the walls. I'd been upgraded to a fold-up cot. I wondered who'd risked their life to find it for me, but I wasn't going to complain. It was better than sleeping on the floor, especially as much as I hurt.

There was the unmistakable odor of singed flesh, the ache of a missing limb. My left arm was gone.

My body screamed for alcohol. The DTs started, and I was a sweaty ball of pain that not even magic could cure.

I tried to sleep it off, but my dreams were filled with the sounds of screams and visions of bloody corpses. When I was awake, alcohol withdrawal hurt worse than the amputation. My eyesight was blurred by pain or by medication and visitors were fuzzy shapes.

A few days of sweating out the alcohol left me dehydrated and cranky. I would have wrestled a bear to get to some absinthe, but the blood loss and DTs left me too weak to leave my bed.

When I awoke again, my father was staring down at me.

"This is getting to be a habit," Doc said.

"Did you bring me back again?" It was an accusation.

"You're not done yet, Nyx."

"You told me that a piece of everything that makes me human dies each time," I said. "I'd rather be dead than an empty shell."

"You seem to be full of righteous indignation," he said. "So apparently, your humanity is still alive and well."

My father could be a smart-ass.

I remembered what had happened on the battlefield and looked down at my left arm. Or, more accurately, what was left of it. "I guess even Hades can't bring my arm back," I said.

"The flesh eater ate it," Doc said bluntly. "Naomi applied a tourniquet, which probably saved your life. They brought you here and I cauterized the wound."

That explained the smell. I owed Naomi big-time. I would have bled out before Doc got to me.

"I need to check the bandage," he said. "Make sure there's no infection."

I turned my face away as he unrolled the gaze. I winced and his hands stilled. "Are you in pain? I gave you a sedative. It should take effect soon."

"I'm fine," I said. "And no more sedatives."

"It's up to you," he replied.

"Where are the others?" I asked. "Rebecca, Talbot, Ambrose, Claire, Naomi? Are they safe?"

"Yes, they are safe," he replied.

"How many dead?" I asked.

He shrugged. "I'll let Ambrose fill you in on that." My father didn't think I was strong enough to take bad news.

He started to slip out of the room, but I stopped him. "Doc?"

"Yes?"

"Thank you."

"Get some rest," he said. He gave me a short nod before slipping out.

I was loopy from the pain meds and fell asleep almost before the door closed.

When I awoke, Ambrose and Talbot were in the room.

"How many people did we lose?" I asked.

Ambrose avoided the question. "We managed to do some damage."

"Not enough," I said.

"Probably not," he said. "But you killed her Cyclops."

I stared down at the spot where my arm used to be. The stump was bandaged, but a trace of blood had leaked through. "Yay me. What happened to Hecate?"

"Doc wounded her," Ambrose said shortly. "She ran."

"How?"

He shrugged like it was no big deal, but I was amazed. Doc had been adamant about staying out of the fight.

"He did it to protect you," Ambrose added. "He's pretty shaken up about it."

I deserved what had happened to me. I'd been so sure of myself, so cocky. My arm, or what was left of it, throbbed angrily. It was gone and there was nothing I could do about it.

"I wish you'd let me die," I told him.

"It wasn't your destiny, Nyx," he said gently.

"Who says?"

"Can I come in?" Naomi stood in the doorway, twirling her braid nervously.

"Of course," I said.

She gave me a gentle hug. "I couldn't bear it if anything happened to you," she said. "Not after Aunt Morta and Mom."

"I'm hard to kill," I replied.

She leaned away from me and looked into my eyes. "But not impossible," she said. "Remember that and try not to take any unnecessary chances."

"I will," I said. "I can't afford to lose any more body parts."

The sound she made was half laugh, half sob. "See that you don't."

I fell asleep soon after. I'd put a brave face on things for my cousin, but inside, I wanted to scream.

I slept for hours, but not even sleep took away the pain of losing a part of me. Something I still felt as my missing fingers tingled. Phantom feelings.

I woke up dry-mouthed and reached for the cup of water on the upturned crate that served as my night table.

"How's our hero feeling?" Talbot asked.

"Who says I'm a hero?"

"You're the closest thing we have to one," he said.

"Don't let it get around, but I've been working on something," I told him. "I just need a few days to figure out where it's stashed."

"And then what?"

"And then I use it on Hecate," I said. "Help me up."

"Nyx, you've lost a lot of blood," Naomi said. "You need time to heal."

"I haven't got any time. I need to fix things."

She stared at the stub where my left arm used to be. "No amount of magic is going to fix that."

I closed my eyes and slowly, the stub began to tingle, then warm and burn. I opened my eyes and saw a hand of flame. It glowed red, then green, and then finally turned ice blue before disappearing.

There was a long silence.

"How did you learn to do that?" Naomi asked.

"Doc taught me," I said.

She gave me an odd look.

"What?" I tried to cross my arms and then remembered it was in the singular now and stopped mid-cross.

"Most magicians, even the oldest and best, can't do that," she said.

I racked my brain. Had I ever told Naomi who my father really was? I hadn't. Was it forgetfulness or something more? I shrugged. "Doc can. And so can I."

Doc slept in a chair in my room. The missing arm throbbed a reminder of all I'd lost. I wanted something to drink, but I fought it. My hand shook with the effort it took not to reach for a bottle. I had the sweats. I threw up.

When I finished heaving, Doc handed me a cup full of smelly liquid. "This should help," he said.

"This smells like cat piss," I complained.

"Yes, it does," he said. "Now drink every drop."

I choked it down. "The cure is worse than the sickness."

"Give it a minute," he said.

It took ten, but the pounding in my head stopped. "Time for a strategy session," I said.

"Are you sure you're up for it?" Doc asked.

"I have to be," I said. "The longer we wait, the longer Hecate has to torture people."

Doc gathered everyone together and they met at my bedside. Claire was conspicuously absent.

"Where is she?" I asked Naomi.

She shrugged. "She's been poring over the Book of Fate."

"We need to find Wren and get that bead back," Talbot said.

"She's our best bet," Ambrose said. "But what makes you think Hecate doesn't already have it?"

"Hecate wouldn't want to carry all of her elements of power with her," I said. I turned to Naomi and made a vague waving motion. "Can't you just make it happen?"

"This isn't an episode of *Bewitched*," she said dryly. "I can't wiggle my nose and poof it for you."

"Wren is taking everything she learned about the Fates, Claire and Naomi," I said, "and using it against us."

"You think she's been planning this all along?" Talbot asked.

"I think it's time we do the same thing," I replied. "Claire was in the underworld long enough to learn a few secrets. I think Talbot's right. We need to find Hecate's Eye."

"Do you know what to do with it once we find it?" he asked.

"Not exactly."

"Naomi, dear girl, perhaps you learned something in your training?" Ambrose asked.

She shook her head. "Honestly, I feel like they didn't tell half of what they knew."

"Convenient," I muttered, but she heard me and glared.

"I suppose your mother taught you everything she knew."

"Don't talk about my mother," I said.

"Children, quit quarreling," Ambrose said.

"It's settled, then," I said. "I'll find Wren and get back Hecate's Eye."

"What are you going to do with it once you get it back?" Rebecca asked.

"Destroy it."

Destroy the bead. Destroy Hecate. Save the world.

Chapter Thirty-One

The only good news was that Hecate had retreated when I'd killed her Cyclops and had abandoned the trapped flesh eaters. There was a still a chance to save them. Talbot and Ambrose had been feeding them entrails and guts while Alex and Doc worked on the cure.

I was recuperating from the amputation but, even worse, I was drying out. No matter what I did, in the back of my mind, there was always the urge to reach for a bottle.

Doc had been going back and forth from our headquarters to Elizabeth's lake house. I was still in bed when he came to check on me.

"It's almost dinnertime," he said. "Why are you still in bed?"

So much for the solicitous parent. "I'm not sleeping that well." It was an understatement. My body ached for sleep, but it wouldn't come. And when it did, it brought only nightmares. The screams of those who'd stood with the House of Fates still rang in my ears. My sleep was filled with visions of blood and pain. I'd wake up dripping sweat, screaming.

"The pain from your arm will disappear in time," he replied. "I can give you some pain pills."

"It's not that," I said. "I thought I'd try the sober thing for a while."

"That sounds like an excellent idea," he said. He nearly smiled, but settled for a slight upturn of his lips.

"How is Elizabeth?" I asked.

"Don't worry," Doc replied. "She's safe. I have wards on that house that Zeus himself couldn't break."

"I want to see her," I said.

"No way, Nyx," he replied. "It's better if you stay away. At least until we find the cure."

"You're sure she's safe?" I wasn't in love with Elizabeth, but I still cared about her. She'd stumbled into the middle of my aunts' machinations and paid the price for it. I wanted her away from Minneapolis, for good this time.

"I should have never called Alex," I muttered.

Doc cleared his throat. "Elizabeth did mention something that concerned me."

"About what? Her safety?"

"She said you wanted to die," Doc said. "Tell me why."

"Nobody's ever asked me that before," I said.

"I'm curious."

"I just got sick of it," I told my father. "How have you managed all this time?"

He gave me a wry look. "I'd hardly say I managed, at least not very well. I screwed things up rather badly with Fortuna."

His voice always softened when he said her name.

"Love trumps hate every time," he said.

"Is that why you didn't kill Deci?"

"She was the mother of my child," he said. "Even though

I didn't love her, I could never hurt her." He rubbed his scar. "But she didn't feel the same way about me."

I had no trouble believing that my aunt would be that ruthless.

Ambrose came into the room. "We've finally heard from Fitch. You have to leave now. You're meeting him at the same location as before."

"Him? What about Ruth?" We were screwed if anything had happened to the fortune-teller.

Ambrose shrugged. "Didn't say. But the message did say to hurry."

I floored the Caddy on the way to the bus station.

Fitch waited for me on a metal bench inside the station. He was reading a newspaper, but his eyes weren't on the page. He scanned the crowd while he pretended to read.

Our eyes met, but he didn't show any recognition. I didn't see Ruth anywhere.

I circled around a few times and scanned the station for demons. I still needed time to get used to my missing limb. Even walking was different. I'd never noticed how much I swung my arms when I moved until one of them was missing.

There were a family of mortals waiting to board and a couple of homeless kids panhandling by the entrance, but I didn't sense any demons.

I sidled up to Fitch. "Where's Ruth?"

He didn't even look up from his paper. "She'll be along. There was something else I wanted to talk to you about first."

"What happened to you?"

"We were waylaid by a couple of demons," he replied. "That's what I wanted to tell you. They were waiting for us outside Ruth's store."

"Did they hurt you?"

"Roughed us up some," he said. "But that's not what I wanted to talk to you about. Someone knew we were meeting you."

"Nobody knew except…" My voice trailed off. Luke was Fitch's brother. He wouldn't set demons on his own brother, would he?

"Except who?" Fitch asked.

I answered reluctantly. "I saw Luke on my way out. He asked what I was doing there."

"What did you tell him?"

"I lied."

"Did he believe you?"

"I thought so at the time, but now I'm not so sure."

Fitch started to say something, but his attention was caught by a tourist. "There's my lovely lady now."

Ruth wore a wide-brimmed hat, Bermuda shorts with a bright orange shirt, and Birkenstocks. "Tony, my dear boy," she said loudly. "It's so good to see you." She hugged me.

"Tony?" I whispered to Fitch.

"She thinks you look like a Tony," he whispered back.

"I think I'm offended." Tony was such a prosaic name.

I kissed Ruth's cheek. "Hello, Aunt Edna," I said. She led me to a bench.

She smiled, but her eyes were serious. "Give me your hand."

I did as she asked. "Now concentrate on the item you are seeking."

I tried to imagine what the silver harpy feather would look like.

"It is very close to someone you loved," she said.

There were only a few people in this world I loved, and most of them were dead. Was it in a graveyard? "Where?"

"Red," she said. "I can't see anything but red."

"Anything else?"

"I'm sorry, but there's nothing."

"It's something," I said. "I'll think about it." I kissed her cheek. "I've got to go, but thank you."

"Be careful, Nyx," Ruth said.

I nodded and left. I was almost at the front door when I sensed demons. I turned back. Fitch's newspaper was on the bench, but he'd gone.

I ran through the depot, searching for him. Two demons held Fitch by each elbow, dangling him in the air. There was no sign of Ruth.

They threw him in front of an oncoming bus. The Greyhound screeched to a stop inches from Fitch's face.

I grabbed Fitch's hand and helped him up. "Where's Ruth?"

"She left before they showed. Pretty sure she got away."

"Go! Now."

He did as I asked. I faced the demons, who stopped snickering when I pulled the hoodie off my face.

"You want me, not him."

"He'll do." One of the demons started after Fitch, who moved pretty quickly for an old guy with a bad leg.

"What's the matter? Too scared to take me on?" I taunted. The demon forgot about Fitch and came after me. His buddy came up behind me and somehow managed to pin my arm back. A perfect target for his buddy's fist. Fighting one-handed was harder than I'd thought.

Ruth smashed a suitcase over his head. The demon crumpled, but his pal clawed at Ruth. He was quickly dispatched with Fitch's cane. Black blood spurted as Fitch bashed the demon's brains in.

"Thanks, Fitch," I said. "But I thought you were Switzerland."

He winked at me. "I am," he said. "But those two were in need of mediation."

We shook hands and went our separate ways.

Chapter Thirty-Two

I puzzled over Ruth's clue as I drove back to the fort. Red? Red had been my mother's favorite color. There was a painting of her dressed in red hanging in Morta's apartment.

I was halfway to Morta's before I swung the Caddy around and went to pick up Claire. I couldn't go without her.

Claire and Naomi were bunking in the nicest room in the hospital. Carlos, the mesmer, was sleeping there, too, but I couldn't complain. He'd been caring for the wounded and we needed all the help we could get.

Emmett was on watch and I nodded at him as I went by.

I knocked on their door softly and waited, but there was no answer. I knocked again and heard someone stumbling around before Naomi yanked open the door. She had a baseball bat in her hand.

"It's me," I said, before she decided to take a swing at me in the dark. "I need to talk to Claire."

"She's not here," Naomi said, yawning. She waved me into the room and sat on her cot.

"Where is she?"

"With Carlos."

"Doing what?" I asked.

"Jesus, Nyx, what do you think?" she replied. "It's three a.m. What do you think they're doing? Stop being so suspicious."

"Which room is his?"

"You can't go after her right now."

"Why not?"

At my blank look, she elaborated, "They're hooking up."

In my defense, I hadn't had time to pay attention to my cousin's romantic escapades. It made sense, though. Carlos was a good-looking guy.

"I can't wait until morning," I said. "I need to talk to her now."

There was a creak of a floorboard and I stilled, hand on my athame, but the creak was followed by a giggle and a man's low voice.

I opened the door. In the hallway, Carlos and Claire were kissing passionately. She was leaning against the wall near a poorly executed spray-painted dragon.

I cleared my throat. They pulled apart.

"Nyx, what are you doing here?" Claire asked.

I gave Carlos a severe look. "Hope you haven't been Mesmerizing my cousin."

"What are you talking about?" Claire asked. "Wait, Carlos is a mesmer?"

He nodded. "But I swear I've never used it on you."

She gave him a smile. "You didn't have to."

I cleared my throat. "Excuse us, Carlos. Family business to discuss."

"Later," Carlos said. He winked at Claire.

"Yeah, later, Carlos." What my cousin did with her free time wasn't my business.

I waited for Carlos to tiptoe away before I said, "I need you to come with me. Now."

She followed me to the Caddy and slid into the passenger seat seconds before I gunned it.

"What's your hurry?"

"I know where Morta hid the harpy feather," I told her.

She grinned at me. "And you came back for me?"

"Stop smiling like that," I said. "It's no big deal. I needed someone to watch my back."

"And you picked me?" she said. "I guess that means you don't think I'm Hecate's spy anymore."

I sobered quickly. "We do have a spy, you know."

She nodded. "It's not Carlos. Or Johnny."

"How do you know?"

"Rebecca and I are Wyrds," she said. "We gave each of them a test. They passed."

"Then who do you think is the spy?"

She shrugged. "I thought it might be Willow."

"She was possessed by Hecate," I said. "There's no way it was Willow."

"Do you have any theories?"

"Luke Seren," I finally said.

She thought about it. "It's possible. I wouldn't put it past him."

We were silent the rest of the way. I hadn't been to Morta's since the tornado. Was the building still standing?

I parked the Caddy in front of the building.

A strange smell was in the air. It was an odor I was familiar with.

"We might have a problem," I said.

"Don't worry," Claire said. "It's still there. I checked."

"Not that," I said. I pointed at Morta's building.

"It's empty," Claire said. "Except for a few mortals who don't know any better."

"No, it's not," I said. I couldn't see them, but I knew they were there. The smell of dark magic mingled with blood filled the air. "Wraiths. They're everywhere."

"How long until sunup?" she asked.

"Too long," I replied. The wraiths had already noticed us. They streamed out of the building.

"We should go," Claire said.

"I'm not leaving without that harpy feather."

"Then I guess we stay and fight," she replied.

"The last time I faced wraiths, Deci controlled them," I said.

"Is that why you killed her?"

"It was either that or get chewed to pieces," I said. I met her eyes. "I wouldn't have died, either."

She nodded to let me know she understood. "Then we find the witch who is controlling them and we kill her."

"You think it's Wren."

"Who else could it be?" Claire replied. "She's powerful, Hecate's daughter, and pissed off at the Wyrd family."

A flash of red caught my eye. Someone in a red Tria Prima robe stood near the entrance, watching us. A hood concealed the identity of the watcher.

"I'll try to keep the wraiths busy," Claire said. "You get the feather."

I pointed to the figure. "I say we have a little chat with Little Red Riding Hood over there."

"Does that make you the big bad wolf?" Claire asked.

The first of the wraiths reached us. Claire took out a woven sling and a pellet of some kind. "Old school," I commented.

She smiled right before she launched it. "I've made a few modifications."

The pellet landed in the middle of the wraiths. There was a beat and then an explosion. Wraith parts went everywhere. The wraiths who weren't blown to smithereens scattered.

The watching figure saw us coming and ran. Claire lobbed another one of her pellets and it landed feet from the robed watcher. The wide sleeve of the Tria Prima robe caught fire, but the watcher managed to put it out before vanishing.

Claire tugged on my arm. "Let's get the feather and get out of here."

Morta lived on the top floor with a fabulous view of the city. The elevator wasn't working, so we had to take the stairs. We were winded by the time we made it up to the top.

I hesitated before opening the door. There were signs that someone had tampered with the wards on Morta's door, but there'd been a lot of looting in the city, even by the sorcerers and wizards who liked to think they were above stealing.

"Do you think Hecate knows?" Claire asked.

"If she'd found it, we'd already be dead. She suspects it might be here. Or maybe she likes owning something of the Fates."

"She'll never own us," Claire said.

I opened the door. The apartment was empty. My mother's portrait hung in its place of honor above the fireplace.

"Hurry, Nyx," Claire said. "I hear something on the stairs." I yanked the painting from the wall and we ran. Wraiths chased us, but I held the painting tightly with my hand.

We reached the Caddy with a dozen wraiths not far behind. I threw the painting in the backseat and peeled out before Claire had the passenger door shut. A wraith clung to the open door, but Claire kicked at its hands until it dropped to the pavement. There was a wet squishing sound as it hit.

I drove in circles until I was sure we'd lost them. It was dawn when we made it back to the Dead House. I set the portrait on the folding table we'd scavenged.

"Are you sure it's there?" Claire asked.

"It better be," I said.

"Should we wake the others?" she asked.

"No," I said. "I don't want to get their hopes up. What if we're wrong?"

"We're not wrong," she replied. "The harpy feather is hidden in the painting. I can feel it."

We'd kept the windows boarded up, so it was dark in the room. Claire lit a lantern and brought it over to the painting.

"Careful!"

She stared down at the painting. "Your mother really was beautiful."

The painting was the only likeness I had of my mother. I wasn't looking forward to marring it, but maybe I wouldn't have to.

If my theory was correct, my silver harpy feather was hidden somewhere in the painting. I flipped it over, but the canvas back looked untouched. "It's not there." I flipped it back over.

"My mother did love her, you know," Claire said. "Even if she never showed it. We're alike in that. I have trouble expressing my feelings."

"You don't seem to have any problem with Carlos," I said absently, my attention still on the painting.

She giggled and punched me on my remaining arm.

I scanned the painting. Was one of the charms on my mother's necklace slightly askew?

"Can you see that?"

"There's something underneath the horseshoe," Claire said.

"Do you have a nail file or tweezers?"

She rifled through the bag where she kept her sling and came up with a pair of tweezers.

There was a good chance Morta had safeguarded the painting. I looked at again. She'd bespelled it.

"Only a magic word will unlock it," Claire said.

"But what word?" I thought and then said, "Fortuna."

The spell disintegrated, but the feather didn't appear. The painting didn't explode or dump acid on our heads, either. Despite the lack of results, I was certain we were on the right track.

Morta had been a wily one. I was sure she'd hidden the feather in the painting. I gently peeled the paint away from the horseshoe and a hint of silver gleamed through.

Claire inhaled. "We have it."

I used the tweezers to pry the feather away and held it up. It was barely bigger than my little finger, but stretched and grew to the size of a large hunting knife. To my relief, the paint reformed. In seconds, it looked like nothing had been removed.

"Your mother was a smart woman," I said. Claire and I exchanged grins. With the harpy feather, we stood a fighting chance against Hecate.

"How do you use it?" Claire asked.

"I have no idea," I said. "Still nothing in the Book of Fates?"

"I'll look. It's in my room." She left and returned a few minutes later.

She laid the book on the table in front of me. "Maybe you can see something I missed. There's a section about the three items of power, but no mention of what they do."

I read silently as Claire peered over my shoulder. "I found something," I finally said. "Here, look at this sketch. There's no mention of a harpy feather, but what does that look like?" The sketch depicted a sorcerer stabbing a figure.

"A knife?"

"It's a harpy feather," I said. "And he's using it to kill a god."

I knew what I had to do. It wasn't going to be enough to trap Hecate in the underworld this time. I was going to have to kill her.

"What should we do now?"

"Now we need to find the last item of power," I said. "And then we need to use them to stop Hecate."

Chapter Thirty-Three

Claire and I took turns poring over the Book of Fates, but it provided no other clues. There were other urgent issues demanding my attention. I needed to talk to Willow about Trey.

Without my left arm, it was difficult to create spells, but I was learning to work with my right arm. To go after Wren and the bead, I'd need to re-master a few spells. And then I'd go after Wren and make everything right again. Or as close to it as I could, considering the number of deaths I'd caused by my rash actions.

Trey Marin had managed to hang on, but it was by sheer will. He hadn't morphed into a flesh eater, but he was no longer in control, either. His eyes had a feral look and he watched us like he was choosing which steak he would barbeque. He was in an isolated area of the hospital. Emmett had volunteered to keep watch over him, but Trey was hours away from trying to eat someone.

Two days passed without any progress on the cure. We were sweating in the summer heat and the mosquitos ate us alive. It was getting harder and harder to find food for the flesh eaters Hecate had created. They were hungry.

There were two buckets of zombie chow left. Talbot and I had feeding duty. I grabbed a bucket and he did the same and we headed to the pit.

"What are we going to do with them if Doc and Alex don't find a cure?" I asked Talbot.

He gave me a somber look. "There's only one thing we can do."

"It's not going to come to that." The thought of slaughtering them was grim, but we couldn't let them loose on society.

We'd finished feeding time when Doc arrived. "I have good news," he said. He reached into the ratty trench coat he always wore and pulled out several vials. "The cure."

"You did it?"

"Alex did it," he said.

"Where is he?" I said. "I want to say thank you."

"They're already gone," he said. "They left this morning."

"But I wanted to say good-bye," I said. Elizabeth had been in Minneapolis all this time and I'd spent little more than an hour with her.

"It's better this way, Nyx," he said. "We have work to do."

I wanted to argue, but I knew he was right. "Let's get started," I said.

"There's only one problem," Doc said. "It won't work on the host."

"You mean Baxter won't be cured?" Talbot asked. "Who is going to tell him?" The flesh eater had been staying in a room on the far side of the fort. Unlike Hecate's creations, once his hunger was sated, he regained his civility.

"I will," I said. "But we should treat Trey first."

"Already done," Doc said. "He was my test subject. That's how I know it works."

"What about the others?"

"I need a bucket of blood to distribute the cure to the flesh eaters," he said. "Pig's blood should work."

I sent Emmett to a slaughterhouse north of the city. "It's about an hour drive," I said.

After he left, I went to talk to Baxter. He had a bottle of absinthe (mine), which he was chugging enthusiastically. It wouldn't hurt to wait until Emmett returned to break the news.

But Emmett didn't return until three hours later. He had a broken nose, but carried a bucket of blood and guts. Talbot took it from him and went to feed the flesh eaters. Their shrieks of hunger had been getting on everyone's nerves.

"What happened?" Doc asked.

"A couple of demons in cop clothes stopped me," Emmett said. "They caught me by surprise. But I fought them off."

"How did they know where to find you?" I asked.

He shrugged. "I don't know. I was careful leaving the fort."

Talbot and I exchanged glances.

"At least none of the blood spilled," Emmett said. It was his polite way of reminding us that we had zombies to cure.

I held up the vials. "Are you sure this is enough for all of them?" I asked Doc.

He looked offended. "Do you doubt my medical ability?"

"Of course not," I said. "I don't doubt you at all."

A strange expression crossed his face. I realized it was the closest thing Doc had to a smile.

We mixed the cure with the pig's blood. "We just fed them a few hours ago," I said.

Grunts and wails came from the pit. "From the sound of things, they're still hungry," Talbot said.

He lowered the bucket on a rope. There was the sound of frenzied slurping.

"How do we know everyone got a taste?" I asked.

"The ones who don't try to eat you are cured," Doc said wryly.

"How long does it take?" Talbot asked, peering into the pit.

"It took about twenty minutes for Trey," he said. "But the more flesh they eat, the worse it is."

A few hours later, we were hauling out bewildered magicians, satyrs, and naiads.

"You're free now," Doc said. "Go home to your families."

"What happened to us?" a tall satyr with dreadlocks asked.

"We'll explain later," Talbot said soothingly. "Let's get you cleaned up."

Baxter came rushing out. "You did it! You found a cure?" The hope in his voice made my heart hurt.

"Baxter, I'm afraid I have some bad news," Doc said.

Baxter's excitement faded. "What is it?"

"I don't think it will work on the host," Doc replied.

"The host? I don't understand."

"You're the host, Baxter," I said.

"Let me try," he said desperately. "Please."

Doc reluctantly handed him a vial.

Baxter gulped it down. "Now what?"

"We wait," Doc said. "The longer you've been exposed, the longer the cure will take."

"Then we have a very long wait indeed," Baxter replied.

We waited with him in silence, but four hours later, there was no change, except that Baxter's stomach was growling.

"There's still a chance," he said. "I'll work on it, see if I can find a way to cure you. But for now…"

"I'm stuck," Baxter said dully. "Back to being a flesh eater. A creature of the night. One of the unclean."

He stalked off. I started to follow him, but Doc shook his head. "Give him some time, Nyx," he said. "It's hard to have hope snatched away like that."

"'The thing with feathers,'" I quoted Emily Dickinson. "'That perches in the soul, and sings the tune without the words, and never stops at all.'"

From the look on Baxter's face, though, we'd taken the last bit of hope away from him.

Chapter Thirty-Four

My magical abilities had changed since the loss of my arm. I'd finally worked my way back up to a compulsion spell. I was ready to find the bead, whether or not Wren was ready to give it to me.

"No time like the present," I said. I'd need to be able to sustain a concealment spell as well, if I had any chance of sneaking up on Wren. I managed to hold the spell long enough to test it out on Talbot, who was in the hospital stockroom, organizing the supplies.

He didn't notice me until I knocked over a stack of bandages. He swore and looked around.

"Reveal," he said.

The spell held. "It's me," I said.

"Nyx, I should have guessed," he said. He addressed the air about twenty feet away from me. "I thought I saw your shadow."

The effort of holding the spell was making me sweat, so I released it.

"There you are," Talbot said. "Practicing?"

"I'm off to find Wren," I said. "And get Hecate's Eye back."

"Want me to come with?" Talbot asked.

"No, I just wanted someone to know in case I don't come back."

"You'll be back. Like a bad penny," he said.

I grinned at his tone, which held equal parts affection and annoyance.

I'd learned a few things from the Fates' Tracker. People were afraid to talk about Hecate's daughter, but at the end of the day, I finally caught a break.

It took too much energy to maintain the concealment spell. Besides, I was hungry. I grabbed a taco at Midtown Market. The place was full, mostly mortals there for happy hour, but I finally spotted three sprites sitting at a table, a pitcher of margaritas in front of them.

"Good day, ladies," I said. "Have you seen this woman?" I held up a picture of Wren.

"Yes, I've seen her," a wood sprite whispered. "In the woods."

"That doesn't exactly narrow it down for me," I said. "There are trees everywhere in Minneapolis."

The two other sprites giggled.

"She goes to the place where she was born," she replied.

The place where she was born? The place Sawyer had shown me. "Many thanks."

I picked up the Caddy and headed back to the wildlife reserve. I found my way to the cave. I would try to keep my promise to Sawyer, but it wouldn't be easy. Wren wouldn't make it easy.

There were dozens of candles burning inside the cave. It still smelled mossy and damp and there was a steady drip somewhere, probably coming from an underground stream.

Wren wore topside clothes—jeans, an Eternity Road T-shirt I'd given her, and boots. The caves were cold at night, even in summer.

"There's no place like home," I said.

"Hello, Nyx," Wren said. "I wondered when I'd see you again."

"Hello, Wren," I replied. "Give me the bead and nobody has to get hurt." My heart beat loudly in my chest. Despite everything that had happened, I didn't want to hurt Wren.

"You are my first visitor," she said, ignoring my demand. "Would you like some tea?"

"Is it hemlock tea? I'll pass."

I didn't see a red Tria Prima robe and her soft skin was free of any burns. If she hadn't been the watcher at Morta's apartment, who was it?

"I'm hurt," she said. "I did save your life, after all."

"You mean you slit my throat and left me to bleed out," I replied. I took a seat on a boulder. "And because of your mother, I'm missing something."

Her eyes went to the empty sleeve of my jacket.

"What makes you think I have the bead?" she asked.

"You need an insurance policy," I said. "You liked your taste of freedom, and keeping the bead is your way of keeping your independence."

Her pseudo-pleasant demeanor disappeared. "That's right," she snarled. "If I won't give it to my mother, what makes you think I'll give it to you?"

"This," I said. The compulsion spell flowed from my fingers. "Give me the bead."

"You disappoint me, son of Fortuna," she said. "Using a necromancer's trick. That won't work with me."

"No, but this will," I said. I used a concealment spell and disappeared.

"Reveal yourself, son of Fortuna," she cried. Wren was the daughter of a goddess, but I had Hades and Lady Fortuna on my side.

And I was sneakier. I'd spotted the chain around her neck when I first got there. While Wren was distracted by my disappearance, I slipped a finger under the necklace and yanked.

Her arm came out to block me, but the crimson eye bead appeared, rising from Wren's creamy cleavage. I stuffed it into my pocket and left. Wren's curses followed me, but I ignored her. I had what I wanted. I couldn't help but feel sorry for Wren. She was alone. Had Hecate abandoned her?

Part of me wanted to go back and fold her into a comforting embrace, but then I remembered how she'd viciously attacked Rebecca. Wren was her mother's daughter and I couldn't afford to show her any tenderness.

When I returned to the Upper Post, Trey had been moved to a room near the rest of us. I went to visit him. I had the bead, but I didn't know what to do with it.

"How are you feeling?" I asked.

"Like I'm ready to get out of this bed," he said.

I laughed.

"I'm grateful, Nyx Fortuna," he said. "The House of Poseidon is in your debt. We will stand with you." He held out his hand.

"We could use allies," I admitted. I clasped his hand.

"Maybe there's something I can do," he suggested. "I want to help," he added when he saw the protest written on my face.

"The best thing you can do is rest," I said. "It's not over.

FORTUNE'S FAVORS

Hecate will attack again. And next time, we might not have advance notice."

"Quarreling isn't going to get us anywhere," he said, seeming to concede.

"What do you remember about getting bit?" I asked him.

"Nothing," he said.

But somehow I didn't believe him.

Ambrose strode into the room. "Do you feel like a visitor, Trey?"

"It's always a pleasure to see you, Ambrose," Trey replied.

Ambrose smiled broadly. "Thank you, Trey, but it's not me. Luke Seren is at the gate and would like to see you."

"Luke is here?" Trey's expression was unreadable.

"I can tell him you're too tired for visitors," Ambrose offered.

"No, send him in," Trey said.

Ambrose left and returned a few minutes later with Luke in tow.

"Trey, so good to see you," Luke said.

"Is it?"

A tense silence fell. Ambrose and I exchanged glances.

"Nyx, let's give them some privacy," Ambrose said.

I looked at Trey, who gave me a short nod.

Shortly after Luke left, I looked in on Trey. He was already sleeping soundly. When I went to check on him a couple of hours later, Trey was gone.

231

Chapter Thirty-Five

We sent out a search party, but there was no sign of Trey. Willow was frantic. "He's dead," she said.

"You don't know that," Naomi said.

For the first time, Willow seemed to notice my cousin. "I do."

"We'll check his house. We'll find him, I promise," I told her.

We took the Caddy. I snuck glances at her as I drove, but Willow kept her gaze on a distant point outside her window. Naomi tried to talk to her, but eventually gave up when her efforts were met with silence.

Trey's house was empty, but I refused to give up. "Where else would he go?"

"To the water," Willow said.

That didn't narrow it down much in Minneapolis. The city was full of lakes.

"Does he have a favorite place?"

She nodded. "The river where he was born."

Trey was born in the Minnesota River, which wasn't far from the abandoned fort. Willow and I took the Caddy, but when we arrived, naiads had already gathered near the Mendota Bridge.

The naiads began to weep even before we found Trey floating facedown in the river, but Willow remained stonefaced.

It took two of us to pull his body out of the water. From the marks around his neck, he'd been strangled. I bent and took a closer look. There were fingerprints around Trey's neck, but there were only nine of them.

"Who would want to kill Trey?"

"Seren," I said. "He wants to consolidate his power."

"Why do you think it's Seren?" Naomi asked.

"Know anybody else missing his right ring finger?" I pointed to Trey's neck.

"He has to pay," one of the naiads muttered.

Willow's head whipped around. "Leave him to me," she said. And for a moment, I caught a glimpse of the rage she felt.

I drew her aside. "If there's one thing I've learned, it's that vengeance will eat you alive from the inside. Let it go."

"That is not the way of my people," she said.

"Maybe those ways should change," I said.

She pulled away from me. "Says the man who came to Minneapolis seeking vengeance."

"And look how that turned out," I said.

"Do not meddle in my affairs," Willow told me. "It is time we return my uncle to the water."

It was a naiad funeral tradition. No outsiders. I'd been to one, though, when my mother and I had lived with a colony of naiads on the island of Capri. They weighted the body down with stones and sang as the current carried it away and it sank.

*　　*　　*

Luke Seren had taken over the House of Poseidon and the House of Hades. He had been the one who betrayed us. I was sure he'd killed Trey, too. He'd been stupid enough to think that Hecate would protect him. He'd made his move and I'd been two steps behind the entire time.

Danvers's death had allowed him to take over the House of Hades. He was arrogant enough to think she'd keep her word. Sounded uncomfortably familiar. But that hadn't been enough for him. He'd killed Trey for more power.

I paced up and down outside the Dead House. It was stifling hot and the weather only increased my rage.

"Johnny Asari is on the run," Talbot said.

"He's welcome here if he shows up," I said.

"Thanks, Nyx," Rebecca said.

"I'm surprised he survived the takeover." Maybe there was more to him than what I'd seen. Or maybe that was what he had wanted me to see: an aging frat boy whose biggest goals were to party and get laid.

Talbot nodded. "He took out six demons before he escaped. Luke wasn't expecting a fight; otherwise, Johnny wouldn't have stood a chance."

I wasn't so sure about that.

Johnny showed up around sunset. "You've got to get out of here," he said. "Luke has been spying on you for Hecate." His face was battered and swollen and one of his arms was stuck at an odd angle.

"We already know," Rebecca told him. He swept her into his arms and kissed her. She resisted for a second before returning his kiss.

I cleared my throat and they broke apart. My sister blushed.

"I hate to break up the happy reunion," I said, "but, Johnny, is there anything you can tell us about Luke's plans?"

Rebecca blushed even more.

"He wants to run all four Houses," Johnny said. "Hecate doesn't care. She's been tearing Minneapolis apart looking for something."

Claire and I exchanged glances. "Any idea what?" I asked.

"No clue," Johnny said. "But she's pretty pissed at her daughter. Banished her."

I held out my hand. "Thanks, Johnny," I said. "Rebecca will show you where to sleep." The last part made my sister blush even more.

"Get the word out that if anyone spots him, they're to leave Luke Seren to me," I said.

"He should be easy enough to find," Johnny said mildly. "Hecate gave him Danvers's old house on Magician's Row."

"That house belongs to Willow," I snapped.

"What would a naiad want with a house like that?" Talbot asked.

"Doesn't matter if she wants to turn it into kindling. It's hers," I said. "Hecate took enough from her."

Despite their protests, I headed to Magician's Row alone. Luke must have expected that I'd be coming for him because the place was on lockdown. It had been triple-warded and booby-trapped with some very nasty spells.

I was patient, though. He'd have to come out eventually, and I'd be waiting.

Luke finally exited the house, but not before sending out a few demons to sniff the air first. I dragged them to the side yard and dispatched them quickly. I didn't want any black demon blood to get on the front sidewalk and alert Luke I was there.

He came out flanked by two more demons. "Goshay, get the car."

I had my athame at Luke's throat before the demons took two steps. I was tempted to slit his throat, but wanted to find out what he'd told Hecate.

"You're coming with me," I said. I pressed the knife into his flesh until a drop of blood welled. "Or I can slit your throat before these two have time to blink."

The bigger demon growled, but Luke made a curt gesture and the demon subsided.

"You've got a lot of nerve, Fortuna," he said through gritted teeth.

"Fortune favors the bold," I replied. "Now let's go."

I shoved him into the Caddy on the driver's side and slid in beside him.

"They'll kill you before you reach the fort," Luke sneered.

I laughed, but it was a hard sound. "What you don't realize is that you're expendable to her," I said.

That shut him up until we reached the fort. I yanked him out of the car and shoved him in front of me. "Walk."

Talbot saw me coming. "Nyx, what's going on?"

"Later, Talbot," I said. "Right now, Luke and I need to have a little chat."

I shut the door to the Dead House and locked it. He hadn't tried to fight back, but I expected that to change soon.

The attack came as soon as I turned my back. He tried to send a curse my way, but I deflected it. I slammed a spell back at him that left him unable to move. I tied him up anyway. The effects of the spell were only temporary.

"You're a better politician than you are a magician," I told him.

"And you're better dead than you are alive," he said.

"You took down the wards, didn't you? That's what you and Trey argued about. So you killed him."

He sneered at me. "It was easy. Trey barely even fought back."

"I'm going to kill you," I said.

"You won't kill me," he said. "You don't have the balls."

"You're right," I said. "I won't kill you, but it's not because I don't have the cojones."

"Indulge my curiosity," he said. "If it's not cowardice, what is it?"

I gave him my most unpleasant smile. "You're about to find out."

I didn't relish violence, but for Luke, I'd make an exception. I took out my athame.

"I want to know how to release the power in the bead," I said.

Either he was a good actor, or he wasn't faking his perplexed look. "I don't know anything about the bead," he said. "I thought you were looking for the harpy feather."

I took a closer look at his hands. One of his wrists had a burn mark on it.

"You were the person I saw in the Tria Prima robes," I said. "You set the wraiths on us."

"Dark magic isn't as hard as it sounds," he said. "And it gets easier every time."

"So I've heard," I said. I gave him a wide smile. "But I'm not looking for the harpy feather anymore."

I'd managed to wipe the smug smile from his face. "Why not?"

"Because I already found it."

"You couldn't have," he said. "No, you're lying." His face had gone pale.

I leaned in closer. "Afraid the boss isn't going to be happy? It's not Hecate you should be afraid of, it's me."

Something in my eyes seemed to convince him, because he cringed.

Doc interrupted. "Nyx, I hate to bother you in the middle of an interrogation, but I have news."

"I'll be right out," I said. To Luke, I said, "Don't go anywhere."

He glared. "Very funny. I'm tied to this chair."

"And you'd better still be here when I get back," I replied.

Doc paced outside. "What is it?" I asked him.

"Hecate's been spotted," he said. "She killed five people from the House of Zeus and strung them up on the Third Avenue Bridge."

"Damn it," I said. "I'm trying to get something out of Luke."

At my father's look, I added, "Without using a compulsion spell. I'm using good old-fashioned threats of dire pain."

"Good," he said.

When I went back inside to continue the interrogation, Luke was still there. But he was dead.

He'd managed to swallow something. Or maybe someone else had gotten to him.

"Doc, come here," I shouted.

Doc entered the room in his usual twitchy way, but stopped when he saw the body. "What happened?" The question sounded like an accusation.

I searched the area, but there was nobody else there.

Chapter Thirty-Six

"Luke Seren's dead." I broke the news to everyone at dinner. We were gathered around a makeshift fire pit. Ambrose had managed to buy a couple of steaks and some vegetables and Talbot cooked over an open fire.

Rebecca gasped. "Nyx, what did you do?"

"Thanks a lot," I told her. "I didn't do anything. I left the room and when I came back, he was dead."

Naomi was quiet. There were purple smudges under her eyes. She'd been the one to cut his thread of Fate. Even though she wasn't the one who had killed him, it was hard on her. I hoped it didn't get any easier. No wonder Morta had been as icy as a glacier by the time she'd died.

"Probably a wraith," Doc said. "Or maybe he had some poison on hand just in case."

"Either way, I didn't get anything out of him before he died," I said.

"You could try talking to him," Talbot said. "You know, postlife conversation."

"Maybe later," I said. "I need to figure out the Fates' secrets first."

Rebecca turned to Claire. "You're sure there's no mention of it in the Book of Fates?"

"Mentions, yes," she replied. "But nothing on how to activate its magic."

Talbot and I exchanged glances. Naomi caught us and kicked both of us under the table.

"What was that for?" I asked.

"You know," she said. "Quit with the conspiracy theories. It's not in the book. You're going to have to figure it out yourself."

We'd just finished dinner, or supper, as Talbot liked to call it, when Doc made an announcement. "It's time I went back to my life," he said.

"You're leaving? Before we defeat Hecate?" I asked.

"I can't stay, Nyx." His hands were shaking, so I didn't press it. My father was deserting me. Again. The thought filled me with rage, but there was nothing I could do about it.

I held out my hand. "Good-bye, Doc."

He clutched my hand tightly. "Why don't you come with me? Hecate will kill your friends and family in front of you."

That didn't make her that different from the Fates. "I'm not going to leave," I said. "I'd rather die with my friends than run."

"She will burn the city to the ground," he said grimly.

"I have to make sure that doesn't happen," I said.

"Hecate can't be defeated," he said.

"How do you know?"

"Because I've tried."

"Try again," I said. "Running is a cowardly thing to do."

"I am a coward," he replied.

"Stay and fight with us," I said. The rest of the table went silent.

"I can't," he said. "But I can give you one last lesson before I go." I couldn't really blame my father for wanting to run. I'd spent a life doing it.

"I do want to know something," I said. "Hecate killed Morta with my blood. Do you know anything about that?"

"You are the son of Hades, Nyx," he said. "Your blood is powerful."

He wasn't telling me the whole truth. "Fine," I said. "Teach me everything I can do one-handed." The sarcasm in my voice was not lost upon my father.

"The first thing I can teach you is that bitterness doesn't help."

"Neither does fear," I said. "You're not bitter?"

He shook his head. "I have regrets," he said. We excused ourselves and went to have a final father-son moment.

I cleared my throat. "Why can't I summon my mother?" I asked Doc.

"I don't know," he replied. "Maybe you're afraid of the pain that comes from the loss of something you loved."

"Can you see her?"

"Yes." The sadness in his voice convinced me.

"What good are my powers if I can't even talk to my mother?" I said. "Just once."

"Maybe it will happen when you don't expect it," he said.

"Or maybe I'll never see her again," I replied.

He put a hand on my shoulder. "I want to show you something."

"That one last thing before you go?" The sarcasm in my voice made him wince.

"This is the spell that Hecate used on me," he said. "It's called a Prometheus spell."

"What does it do?"

"It sucks the soul right out of you," he said. "And whoever you use it on is cursed to wander until he or she regains the lost soul."

"Did you regain yours?"

"Yes," he said. "But not without effort. And sacrifice." Doc had been through a lot in his long life. No wonder he wanted to hang out in Asphodel and be left in peace.

"Why are you showing me this?"

"Because Hecate will try to use it on you. It's what she used on Morta."

"Using my blood?" The thought sickened me.

He nodded. "She used my own blood on me once. I want you to be able to defend yourself," he replied.

We practiced the spell until Doc thought I had the hang of it. It left me wrung out and dazed.

"Does anything else work?" I said. "Say, Medusa's mirror?"

"Medusa's mirror has been lost for centuries," he said. "But, yes, if you could find it, the mirror would work to deflect the spell. But since we don't have it, this will have to suffice."

I started to tell him that I had the mirror, but decided against it. I wanted to tell him a lot of things, including that I'd miss him, but it was no use. He'd already made up his mind to leave.

Afterward, he gave me a brief hug and disappeared.

Chapter Thirty-Seven

I was trying to sleep, but not having any luck. I grabbed a flashlight and took the bead from its hiding place. I held it up to the light to examine it. Deci had loved fire. She'd been the one to guard Hecate's Eye. Fire had to be the answer.

On occasions reserved for dark winter nights when we were cold and hungry, my mother had told me stories of wondrous creatures, magic, and ancient battles. One of her stories was about how the Byzantines had used something called Greek fire in naval battles. It burned even on water. The secret recipe had been lost through time, but I had a good idea where it might be. Deci had been the Custos: Everything she knew was in the Book of Fate. I was betting that she had known plenty about fire in all of its forms.

I slipped out of the Dead House and headed for Claire's room. She had the Book of Fates, so if the secret to Greek fire was written down anywhere, it would be in that book.

She opened the door before I had the chance to knock.

"Expecting someone?"

"Not you, that's for sure," she replied. "What's up?"

"I need you to look for something in the Book of Fates. Anything about Greek fire."

"Right now?"

"Yes, right now," I said. At her look, I softened my tone. "It's important, or I wouldn't ask."

She nodded. "Give me a few minutes." I waited in the hallway and stared at the dragon.

I was half-asleep by the time Claire returned. "I found a list of ingredients," she said. "But I'm not sure you want to use it."

"Why not?"

"It could blow this entire base sky-high," she said. She handed me a scrap of paper with a list scribbled on it.

"I'll have to take that chance," I said.

"I don't know where you'll find the scale of a dragon," she said.

"I do." There'd been one in the display case at Eternity Road for ages, just gathering dust.

I scanned the list, which included a few more prosaic items, such as quicklime.

I waited until first light before heading to Eternity Road. I had no doubt that Hecate had a few of her demon goons stationed there just in case I showed up.

I took the Caddy, which was loaded with enough wards to stop a tank. I parked a few blocks from the store and observed Eternity Road from a nearby building. Someone had spray-painted a pro-Hecate slogan across it as well as Tria Prima symbols. The windows had been broken during the storm, so it was possible that anything worth taking had already been stolen.

It made me angry to see Eternity Road in such bad shape.

I finally made my move. The two drunken homeless guys pretending to be passed out on the sidewalk were really demons, but I wasn't worried about them. I was worried that someone had already beaten me to the dragon's scale.

I didn't want to fight them, not unless I had to, so I tried an obscura spell. It might work to conceal my identity if they were low-juice demons without a lot of powers. Or stupid. I was hoping for both.

I got lucky. The demons didn't notice me, or if they did, they saw me as just another looter. I slipped inside the store without incident.

It made me sick as I looked at the devastation. Everything worth taking, at least in most people's eyes, had been stolen, the display cases smashed, but the enormous stuffed bear lay in one corner.

Ambrose had managed to take several of the more valuable magical items, but there was one display case no one had touched. It had been heavily warded, so the casual observer would see mostly junk.

Still, judging from the scratches on the lock, someone had tried to break into it. The dragon scale was still there, tucked away in a corner, forgotten.

In my haste to obtain the scale, I touched the display case lock without first removing the ward. The protective spell propelled me backward and I slammed into the opposite wall.

"Damn it!" I swore. After I picked myself up, I tried again. This time I remembered to remove the ward before I unlocked the case.

The dragon scale glittered in my hand.

"What you got there?" a gravelly voice asked.

I turned and faced the demon. "None of your business."

"Look who we have here," he said. "Nyx Fortuna himself."

He knew who I was, which meant I had about thirty

seconds before he tried to kill me. It was harder to fight with one hand. I slid the dragon scale into my pocket, and then grabbed my athame. My throwing skills weren't as good with my other hand, but I wasn't my mother's son if I couldn't take on a demon or two, even missing an arm.

I threw my athame and it hit the demon, but it was a sloppy throw. Instead of a dead shot, it wounded him enough that he was just pissed off instead of permanently disabled. He pulled the knife from his side like it was a sliver and held it up. Black demon blood dripped from the blade.

Two of his friends appeared behind him. I scanned the display case, looking for anything to even up the odds.

They were almost upon me. I grabbed as many amulets as I could carry and muttered a quick concealment spell.

It seemed like nothing happened. I held my breath. "Now would be a good time to work," I muttered.

"Where'd he go?" one of the demons asked.

"Shut up," the one I wounded replied. "He's a frickin' necromancer. They're tricky."

I didn't bother correcting him. Instead, I slid my athame from his grasp and ran. I was usually up for a fight, any fight, but my newfound mortality had left me feeling strangely vulnerable. And I had work to do.

I mixed the Greek fire at the empty officer's quarters. It was farthest from the others, and if I set myself on fire, there was a good chance nobody else would get hurt. There was an unused fireplace there. I gathered logs and started a fire, then gave it a little magical goose to bring it to a roaring blaze.

There were still faded curtains hanging in the living room. I hoped they would block the glow of the fire from any curious passersby.

I dug it out of my pocket and held it up to the light. The little red bead on a chain was the source of Hecate's power. If I could tap into it, I could defeat her.

"Release the power within," I said.

I tossed the bead into the flames, but at first, nothing happened. There was a loud crack as the fire heated the bead. It glowed, first red, then blue, and finally silver before it turned black.

The spell was quenched. I fished the bead from the fire with a pair of tongs. The bead hissed as it cooled, but its secrets remained intact. Nothing happened.

I'd been sure that fire was the secret to releasing the magic.

Frustrated, I threw the bead against the wall. It shattered into tiny pieces. I crushed them under my heel.

"I'm missing something," I said.

I realized what I'd missed. Magic wanted one of three things: sex, blood, or sacrifice.

I got out my athame and sliced it across my thumb. I dripped the blood over the shards, and the magic was released. A shudder went through my body as it absorbed Hecate's power. All the magic she'd stolen, all the power she'd killed for, flowed into me.

The magic pulsed under my skin, glowing blue and green. The glow faded, but the buzz didn't. My skin strained to contain the magic. My face contorted, flattened, and then settled into what I hoped was its normal shape.

I watched as the fire turned to embers. The magic inside me strained to get out, but I held it in. The magic was changing me, molding me, turning me into something else entirely. Not a god, not a human, but something different, something new. I collapsed under the weight of the new me.

Hours later, I finally stirred myself. When I looked down, my missing arm had been replaced. Instead of an arm of flesh and blood, my limb was made of [0]a black stone that somehow managed to be pliable. The replacement arm was heavy and stiff, but I could move, touch, and feel with it.

I stuck my hands in the pockets of my leather jacket. My fingers touched Alex's note. I'd been carrying it around, trying to figure out what to do with it.

I took it out and examined it. The secret to eternal life was in my hands, literally. I wadded up the paper and threw it into the embers. The paper turned to ash. The people who had discovered the secret to immortality were all dead: Gaston, Sawyer, Deci, Morta, and Nona.

I still had to deal with Wren. She was still out there somewhere, hiding.

"You can't kill Wren." Sawyer's voice sounded in my ear.

"Spying on me, Sawyer?" I said. "I can't let her go, either."

"Remember, she's Naomi's sister," was his parting shot.

On a hunch, I took the Caddy and drove to the wildlife reserve.

The waterfall had slowed to a trickle in the late summer heat, but when I entered the cave where she was born, the cold hit me like a slap.

Everything was quiet, still, but I sensed her presence.

"Wren, come out. It's me."

She came out from behind a mossy outgrowth. Her dark red hair was wet and she wore a simple brown robe.

"Wren," was all I said.

Her eyes were rimmed with red. "Can't you leave me alone?"

"I came here to ask you to join us," I said. "Naomi is your sister. Can't you forget your mother's plan for revenge and join us?"

"Join the Fates?" she said. "I'd rather die." She gave a little shake of her head, emphasizing her rejection of my offer.

"You're a fool," I told her.

"And what are you?" Wren's lower lip trembled and my resolve weakened. She was so young and, as Sawyer so helpfully pointed out, she was Naomi's sister.

"I am your friend," I replied. "Whether you want that friendship is up to you."

"Poor Nyx," she scoffed. "For once your charm won't work. Not on me."

What was I going to do with her? Naomi would never forgive me if I killed her. I wouldn't forgive myself. There was a part of Wren that I loved, the part that reminded me of Sawyer and Naomi and the good things in my life. But the other part had slit my throat on her mother's orders, had attacked Rebecca without provocation, and had refused my offer of a truce.

"Do you hate us that much?"

"The only good Fate is a dead Fate," she said.

"I'm not a Fate."

"You are," she said. "You're one of them, through and through. The Wyrd family sticks together. There's no room for me. As much as you deny it, you belong to the House of Fates."

"What difference does it make?" I asked her. "House of Fates or House of Hades? My father is Hades, so you could say I belong to the House of Hades. My mother was Lady Fortuna, the fourth and forgotten Fate. For a long time, I thought I belonged to the House of Fortune, but I am my own man."

"We can never be friends," she said.

"Please, Wren." We'd had a hell of a breakup, but the thought of what I was going to have to do still hurt.

She shook her head. "I am Hecate's daughter."

"The only reason you aren't dead already is that I promised Naomi," I finally said. "You remember Naomi, don't you? Your sister?"

"I don't have a sister," she said coolly. She was a lost cause.

"You *wish* you didn't," I said. "What's the matter, Wren? You wanted Daddy all to yourself? You couldn't take it that Sawyer chose Nona over your mother. That's why you hate the Fates."

I'd goaded her, but I was still surprised when her arm came out and she sent a spell my way.

"*Revibro*," I said. The spell bounced back at Wren.

She smiled at me, thinking it hadn't worked, but the smile turned to panic as her limbs thickened and hardened.

I watched as Wren was frozen, turned to stone. Her eyes still moved, though, so I knew she was still in there somewhere. It was a terrible punishment, but I couldn't bring myself to kill her. It was the fate she'd intended for me.

"Sorry, Sawyer," I whispered. "I tried."

I wasn't expecting an answer, but I got one anyway. "Thank you, Nyx."

I stayed with Wren through the night. When the sun rose, I kissed her cold lips and then left her there, in the place where she was born, as frozen as her heart. Outside, I took a breath of the sweet, warm air. I'd made it through, not unscathed, but stronger. Sunrise shimmered on the horizon by the time I left.

Hecate was desperate, but she was a goddess. I couldn't count her out yet.

The question was, where would she go to regain her strength and plan her next attack? I needed to strike before anyone else died. I gathered up my athame and Medusa's mirror and went to kill a goddess.

Chapter Thirty-Eight

I stopped at the Dead House to gather my weapons. I'd been home less than five minutes when Hecate's forces attacked. Demons probed the wards I'd set. Talbot and I had been reinforcing the salt trails as well. I was almost sure our defenses would hold. Almost.

I let out a piercing whistle.

Within minutes, everyone in the camp was outside, ready to fight.

"Whatever you do, don't let them in!" I shouted. But it was too late. The gate had been forced open and demons streamed through.

Hecate was in the distance, watching the battle with pleasure on her face. She laughed in delight when her two demons grabbed a young wizard and pulled him apart like he was the wishbone after Thanksgiving dinner.

Johnny charged the two demons who still held the bloody remains of the young wizard. He inhaled and sucked the demons' blood from their bodies without even touching them. Seeing him in action, I readily believed he was related to the Egyptian god of the dead.

As Hecate's army closed in, I fought to get close enough to her to use the harpy feather, but the demons formed a solid wall around her.

Her bodyguards had fallen. I drew closer. More demons streamed in, blocking my way.

There was a scream. It sounded like Rebecca. Johnny sprinted toward the sound. A demon held Rebecca's arm on either side.

Johnny Asari's face turned into a death mask. Even some of the older magicians, who thought they'd seen everything, cringed when they saw him. He charged the two demons, who dropped her as soon as they saw him coming.

Rebecca pivoted and stabbed one of them in the chest. She held an athame. "Little present from dear old dad," she said. Johnny sucked the life from the other one. He said something to Rebecca, who nodded. Johnny charged back into the fray.

The next half hour was a blur: the smell of demon blood, the sound of a wraith's scream, and throughout it all, Hecate's laughter. I lost sight of Naomi, but Claire's sling bombarded our enemies with exploding pellets.

The ground was slippery with black demon blood, but they kept coming, more demons than I'd ever seen. It was the wraiths that had people running scared. I knew from experience that I had to kill the one who commanded the wraiths before they returned to their graves. If I fell, I would die. My good arm hurt from the repeated motion of jabbing with my athame. I switched and used the stone arm as a club.

Naomi walked among us, but she wasn't fighting. Her

golden scissors flew as she cut threads of fate. Tears trickled from her eyes, but she continued the task.

"Sawyer, are you there?" But there was no answer. I closed my eyes and called to the dead. I called to those I'd loved and those I'd hated and their voices started as only a whisper. I called to them and they came. The dead were all around us.

"Let the dead be heard," I said. The whispers turned to a deafening roar. Demons all around me fell to their knees and covered their ears.

"Necromancer!" Hecate shrieked. "Your tricks won't work here."

Slowly, we gained ground, but I lost sight of the goddess. "Where did Hecate go?"

She had Naomi pinned, surrounded by wraiths. Before I could reach her, Hecate wrapped her hands around Naomi's neck and squeezed. My cousin's golden scissors fell to the ground. I raced to her side.

Hecate had killed my aunts, almost killed Naomi. I couldn't let Hecate live. If I did, she'd come back and try again. Despite my father's warnings about dark magic, I knew what I had to do. The thought of taking someone's soul made me hesitate, but I had to use the Prometheus spell my father had taught me.

I cut my right arm and coated the blade of my athame with my blood, then stabbed Hecate in the stomach. It didn't kill Hecate, but she was bleeding badly. I whispered the words of the Prometheus spell my father had taught me and watched as the dark magic started to work.

She ran. I ran after her. Her demons were being quickly dispatched by the ghosts I'd summoned, we had her items of power, and she was injured. The deck was stacked against her, but I couldn't let her live.

"Control the magic," Sawyer said. "Or it will control you." His presence was stronger here on the battlefield. I could almost see his ghost walking next to me.

There was a soft rush of air near me, like he'd nodded.

I ran after Hecate, branches snagged my clothing as I went. A branch whipped back and hit me like a slap, but I followed her.

As I ran, an almost unbearable feeling of sadness came over me. A strong smell of sulfur wafted through the air. I followed the drops of blood. The wound in her stomach made it easy for me to track her.

She had fallen only feet from the lake. Her hair was lank, her skin a sickly green, but she maintained her regal air as she rose to address me, one hand on her stomach to stem the blood flow.

"It looks like your goons have deserted you, Hecate," I said.

She ignored my comment. "You took something of mine, son of Fortuna," she said. "My daughter."

I gestured to my new stone arm. "You took something of mine, too," I said. "Seems like it's only fair that I have something of yours."

"You are as arrogant as your father," she said. "Are you as stupid?"

"He's a better person than you'll ever be," I replied.

"It matters not. I'll bathe in your blood," she said. "And your precious father cannot stop me." Her attack was swift and deadly, but my father's warning had prepared me. She sent a Prometheus spell my way. It was about a thousand times worse than the curse I'd used on Danvers.

I had the Medusa's mirror in my hand and put it up to deflect her. The spell bounced back and hit her. Hecate was

Mesmerized by whatever she saw in its reflection, but it didn't kill her. It only held her spellbound. It was like watching someone engrossed in a play. The temptation was strong to look into the mirror. What was she seeing? What would I see?

I took out the silver harpy feather. It felt heavy in my hand. Why had Hecate been so desperate to find the harpy feather?

I had only had seconds to decide. I grabbed the silver feather and drove it into Hecate's heart. Or where her heart would be if she had one.

At first, nothing happened. Hecate smiled at me. Why hadn't it worked? I was sure the feather was the key to killing a goddess.

In the distance, I heard screams. It sounded like Naomi.

Hecate laughed. "Your friends are dead. My wraiths are eating their hearts as we speak."

Enraged, I pulled the feather from Hecate's chest and then stabbed her again. She made a choking sound and slumped over. She raised her hand to strike, but the feather had done its work. Black blood, thick as any demon's, oozed from the wound. It poured from her mouth, her eyes, and her ears until finally she was drenched in her own blood. She screamed as the blood began to dissolve her skin, tissue, and bones.

It took only minutes before Hecate was gone and only a thick gooey ooze remained.

I wiped her blood from the feather. "I wish you were smaller," I said. It obediently shrank to the size of a charm.

I hadn't known it could do that. I'd have to be careful what I said. I put it on my mother's necklace among the other charms. It was over.

The prophecy had been both right and wrong. The Fates

had fallen, but so had Hecate. A new generation of Fates would rise up, but Hecate was gone for good.

A long time later, I walked back to the fort. The demons had been defeated and the wraiths were in a puddle at our feet.

Johnny's face had returned to normal, but he was breathing hard from the fight. "Jesus, Johnny," I said. "I had no idea you could do that."

"Normally, I'm a lover, not a fighter," he said. "But no one lays a hand on my girl." His fists clenched.

"We might not have made it through without you," I said.

"I met your dad," he said. "He kicks ass."

"*My* dad?"

"Yeah, Lord of Bones, King of the Underworld, Hades," he said. "He goes by Doc when he's topside. He's your dad, right?"

"Right." Doc had come back?

"He was right in the middle of it," Johnny enthused. "Tore off this demon's head and ate it."

"Er, yay?"

"Don't tell me you're squeamish," Johnny replied. "I saw you take on a dozen wraiths just now."

"It doesn't mean I enjoy killing," I said. I had a suspicion that Johnny did enjoy it, very much, but without him, we wouldn't have won.

Doc stumbled into the room. His arms were stained with black demon blood up to his elbows. I knew from experience that demon blood burned.

His eyes were wild, his face splattered with body matter and demon blood. His trench coat was covered in more blood and guts.

"Doc, I heard you took on a legion of demons," I said. He didn't answer. His gaze was unfocused and the tremor in his hand was back. In fact, his whole body shook. I eased the coat off to check for injuries. He seemed unharmed, but it was hard to tell because of all the blood.

"Let's get you cleaned up," I said.

I wet a towel and washed away the blood. I was relieved to see that except for a couple of small cuts on his arm, he was unharmed.

I made him a cup of tea using the small camp stove and offered him a chair. The cup clattered in the saucer as he drank it, but the shaking in his hands gradually stilled.

"I thought you'd left Minneapolis," I said.

He nodded. "I came back. I couldn't turn my back on you. Not again."

"We needed your help," I said. "Thank you."

"Did you ... ?"

I nodded. "Hecate is dead. It's over."

We spent the rest of the day burying the dead and healing the living, but something nagged at me. I'd told my father that it was over, but that was a lie. It was *almost* over.

Chapter Thirty-Nine

Hecate had been defeated, her army of demons was dead or in hiding, and her allies were gone. Ambrose was at a meeting, so Talbot and I spent the morning cleaning up Eternity Road. The store was a mess. Tria Prima symbols were sprayed all over the outside of the building, the windows were shattered, and most of the stock was gone. They'd emptied the cash register, but left it. It was probably too heavy to move.

Harvey the bear still stood in the corner. He was bedraggled and smelled like wet bear, but was otherwise untouched.

"The store wouldn't be the same without Harvey," I said. I took a hair dryer and brush to the bear's fur. "Much better."

Talbot handed me a pointy wizard hat embellished with stars.

I put it on Harvey and then stepped back to survey my handiwork.

Talbot looked around the store. "Almost like it never happened."

"Almost," I replied. I looked at my watch. "I'm sorry, but I have to go. I'm late for the meeting."

I pulled up in front of Hell's Belles, which sported a fresh coat of paint and new windows. Bernie had reopened for breakfast the day after Hecate was defeated.

Since Parsi Enterprise's assets consisted of a destroyed corporate office and Hell's Belles, we held our first corporate meeting in my favorite booth at the restaurant.

I was late for lunch. My family was already huddled in a booth. Naomi had an untouched salad in front of her, Rebecca sipped her tea contemplatively, and Claire doodled something in the Book of Fates.

Naomi scooted over to make room for me in the booth. Bernie slid a pot of coffee in front of me. I poured a cup and chugged it, ignoring how it scalded my throat on the way down.

"How's it going, Bernie?" I asked.

"Better, son of Fortuna," she replied. "Much better." There was almost a smile in her sad basset hound eyes.

"Rough night?" Rebecca asked.

"The roughest," I replied. "I watched a chick flick with Talbot and Naomi."

"What happened with Wren?" Naomi asked. "Did you let her go?" I hadn't had time to tell her what I'd done before we'd been attacked.

I shook my head.

"But I didn't cut her thread," Naomi said.

"You didn't have to." I hadn't even thought of that possibility. I was doubly glad I'd let Wren live.

"So she's alive?" Claire asked. I gave her a sharp look. She and Wren had spent months together in the underworld, but she seemed disappointed that Wren wasn't dead.

"It's done," I said. "She won't bother us anymore." At least I hoped not. Sometimes, even kindness had a cost.

My sister gave me a round of applause, but Naomi wiped away a tear. "I know it had to happen," she said. "There's no chance she'll break free?"

I shook my head. Wren was alive but frozen. Hecate was dead. There was no one left who would free her, not even her own sister, especially if I didn't tell Naomi where she was.

"What now?" Claire asked.

We'd been so busy fighting for our lives that none of us had given any thought to the future. Probably because we didn't think there would be one.

"It can't be like before," I burst out. "The Fates thought they knew better."

"It won't be," Naomi promised. "We'll make sure of it."

"We need to figure out if the job of Atropos can be reassigned," I said firmly.

"I'll do it," Rebecca said.

Everyone stared at her.

"I'm the daughter of Hades, after all," she said. "And Johnny said he'd help me."

"You'd do that for me?" Naomi asked. Her eyes filled with tears.

"Don't get all teary-eyed," Rebecca replied. "We haven't even figured out how to make it happen. Or if it can happen."

"It'll happen," I said. "We'll make sure of it."

"Promise me one thing," Naomi said gravely.

"What?"

"That we'll do better than they did."

"We can try," Claire said.

"We can succeed," Rebecca corrected her.

"When I first came to Minneapolis, I was alone." My mother's face came to my mind, but instead of the image of her as she lay dying, I saw a picture of her smiling and at peace.

"And now?"

"Now I have a family," I said. "I am truly fortunate. Together, we can change the way the Fates operate."

We sat at the booth and made new rules. After all, we were a new generation of Fates. It was time to do things differently. It was time to do it our way.

Chapter Forty

Doc came by Eternity Road, which was up and running thanks to Fitch and his magical elves. Ambrose and Talbot were bringing up stock from the basement, which had been overlooked during the looting. A few magicians had even, shamefacedly, brought back a few items, telling me that they'd "found" them.

Minneapolis, the mortal and the magical, gradually returned to normal. Crews painted over the Tria Prima symbols with heavy white paint, erasing the signs of Hecate until from the outside, no one would have known she'd even been there.

Talbot and his dad had refused to move the store to a new location. The graffiti had been painted over, the windows repaired, and the store completely restored. There were scars, but the city rejoiced when Eternity Road announced the grand reopening.

Rebecca and I were tidying up for the event when Doc walked in. His trench coat was gone. Instead, he wore a black suit, white shirt, and a red tie patterned with tiny white flowers. His shoes had been ferociously polished.

"Hello, Daddy," she said. I snickered and she punched me on the shoulder.

"Rebecca, it's good to see you getting along with your brother."

He made it sound like we were squabbling teenagers, but maybe to him, we were.

"What's up, Doc?" I'd been dying to say that since I met him. He looked blank when Rebecca chuckled.

"I'm leaving Minneapolis," he said.

"You're not staying for the reopening?" Rebecca asked.

"Where will you go?"

My father put a hand on my shoulder. His hand was steady. "Where I belong. I'm going to take back my kingdom of the dead. There will always be a place for you in the underworld. For both of you."

"Thank you, but I belong here." I stuck out my good hand, but instead, he folded me into a brief hug.

He embraced Rebecca, who looked like she didn't know whether to kick him or kiss him. She settled for a kiss on the cheek. Doc slipped out of Eternity Road, his shoulders straight. We went to the window to watch him until he disappeared from sight.

"You know," Rebecca said thoughtfully, "he may have redeemed himself after all."

"Anything's possible," I said.

Talbot and I put out food and booze. My cousins and sister were supposed to be helping, but Claire had disappeared the minute Carlos arrived. Naomi sat in a comfy chair that Talbot had brought down from his apartment.

"Did we really need all these decorations?" I asked, hitting a balloon and sending it floating to the ceiling.

"Naomi, Claire, and Rebecca spent half the night decorating," Talbot said. "I wouldn't touch a streamer."

I smiled at him. "We have something to celebrate," I said.

"We do?" he replied. "I mean, I think so, but I'm surprised you do."

"Of course I do," I told him. "We survived."

Carlos and Claire came out from the stockroom, giggling madly. Rebecca was on the phone with Johnny. Talbot and Naomi were on opposite sides of the room, but he couldn't stop looking at her.

Everyone was paired up, in love. Except me. I thought about slipping away, jumping in the Caddy and driving wherever the road led, but then my sister slipped her arm in mine.

"You're not alone," Rebecca said.

"How did you know what I was thinking?"

"I've felt the same way. Many times," she said. "You can't leave. It has to be *four* Fates. Like it was before."

The door opened as our guests arrived. The store was soon filled with the magical community, all eager to tell us how grateful they were. Representatives from each of the Houses arrived for the ribbon-cutting.

"Where's Ambrose?" I asked. It was his big day. He was the new leader of the House of Zeus and he hadn't even needed to kill anyone to do it.

"Just getting the champagne," Ambrose said.

Willow had taken her uncle's place as the head of the House of Poseidon, and the House of Hades was represented by Johnny Asari. The House of Fates would lead as a foursome.

Ambrose popped a bottle of bubbly and we all cheered. He and Talbot filled up glasses and passed them out.

"Here's a glass for you," Talbot offered. I tried waving it

away, but he put it in my hand. "It's sparkling cider," he said. "No alcohol. You're on a roll. Let's keep it that way."

My heart lifted and then settled when Willow entered the store. A dozen or so naiads trailed behind her. Her dark hair had been styled into a crown of braids and she wore a simple green dress and sandals.

She was stopped by magicians who wanted to offer their condolences for her uncle's death. She was gracious, but brief. She finally made it to my side.

"This is Nyx Fortuna," Willow told one of her entourage. "He is the head of the House of Fates."

"The House of Fortune and Fates," I corrected her. "And I am only one of the leaders."

She smiled. "It is a fitting tribute to your mother," she said.

We watched silently as Ambrose used a pair of comically large scissors to cut the red ribbon wrapped around the display cases. After the ribbon was cut, the crowd burst into applause.

"Nyx, come take a photo with us," Claire called out from the other side of the room.

I gave Willow a smile. "Duty calls."

"It was good to see you, son of Fortuna," Willow said.

"It was good to see you, too," I said, "Lady of the Lake." I kissed her cheek before I left.

I joined my cousins and we linked arms as we posed for pictures. "Where's Johnny?" I asked Rebecca as the flashes went off.

She pointed to Johnny, who was holding court near Harvey the bear. "Doing the political thing. Glad-handing all those magicians who turned their backs on us."

"He'll do a good job as the head of the House of Hades," I said.

"He'd better," she said.

Eventually, the crowd's exuberance was too much for me, so I slipped into Ambrose's office for a moment of quiet.

I touched the charms around my neck. "I hope you're proud of me, Lady Fortuna," I said softly.

"I am." Her voice was a whisper.

"Mother?" I could almost see her face.

"Yes, it's me," she said. "I'm proud of you, Nyx."

"Proud?" I knew my mother loved me, but since I'd arrived in Minneapolis, I'd done many things that I was not proud of.

"You have managed to do what I could not. Reunite the House of Fates. That was your true destiny."

"House of Fortune and Fates," I corrected gently.

"Fortune and Fates," she repeated. "I like that."

"I have so much to tell you," I said. Silence. She was gone.

When I rejoined the celebration later, Naomi handed out more champagne. "I wanted to toast to the Fates who came before us," she said. "All four of them."

She popped the cork and poured glasses for everyone. I declined mine.

"I'll stick with the apple juice," I said.

"Here's to a new generation of Fates," Naomi said.

I lifted my juice glass and clinked it with the other Fates. "With Fortune's favor," I said, "we will succeed."

My sister, my cousins and I took our places and once again, there were four Fates. And fortune favored us.

extras

orbit

meet the author

Marlene Perez is the author of paranormal and urban fantasy books, including the bestselling Dead Is series for teens. The first book in the series, *Dead Is the New Black*, was named an ALA Quick Pick for Reluctant Young Adult Readers as well as an ALA Popular Paperback. *Dead Is Just a Rumor* was on VOYA's 2011 Best Science Fiction, Horror, & Fantasy List. Her novels have been featured in *Girls' Life*, *Seventeen*, and *Cosmopolitan*, and Disney Television has optioned the rights to the first three books in the Dead Is series.

Marlene grew up in Story City, Iowa, and is the youngest of twelve children. She lives in Orange County, California, with her husband and children. Visit Marlene at www.marleneperez.com or at the Welcome to Nightshade Facebook community page at: http://www.facebook.com/pages/Welcome-to-Nightshade-DEAD-IS/128231240528721.

Also by Marlene Perez

Dead Is

Dead Is the New Black

Dead Is a State of Mind

Dead Is So Last Year

Dead Is Just a Rumor

Dead Is Not an Option

Dead Is a Battlefield

Dead Is a Killer Tune

Dead Is Just a Dream

The Comeback

Love in the Corner Pocket

Nyx Fortuna

Strange Fates

Dark Descent

Fortune's Favors

introducing

If you enjoyed
FORTUNE'S FAVORS,
look out for

CHARMING

Pax Arcana: Book One

by Elliott James

John Charming isn't your average prince...

*He comes from a line of Charmings—an illustrious family
of dragon slayers, witch finders, and killers dating back to
before the fall of Rome. Trained by a modern-day version of
the Knights Templar, monster hunters who have updated their
methods from chain mail and crossbows to Kevlar and shotguns,
John Charming was one of the best—until a curse made him
one of the abominations the Knights were sworn to hunt.*

*That was a lifetime ago. Now, John tends bar under an
assumed name in rural Virginia and leads a peaceful, quiet life.
That is, until a vampire and a blonde walked into his bar...*

❧ 1 ❧

A BLONDE AND A VAMPIRE WALK INTO A BAR...

Once upon a time, she smelled wrong. Well, no, that's not exactly true. She smelled clean, like fresh snow and air after a lightning storm and something hard to identify, something like sex and butter pecan ice cream. Honestly, I think she was the best thing I'd ever smelled. I was inferring "wrongness" from the fact that she wasn't entirely human.

I later found out that her name was Sig.

Sig stood there in the doorway of the bar with the wind behind her, and there was something both earthy and unearthly about her. Standing at least six feet tall in running shoes, she had shoulders as broad as a professional swimmer's, sinewy arms, and well-rounded hips that were curvy and compact. All in all, she was as buxom, blonde, blue-eyed, and clear-skinned as any woman who had ever posed for a Swedish tourism ad.

And I wanted her out of the bar, fast.

You have to understand, Rigby's is not the kind of place where goddesses were meant to walk among mortals. It is a small, modest establishment eking out a fragile existence at the tail end of Clayburg's main street. The owner, David

Suggs, had wanted a quaint pub, but instead of decorating the place with dartboards or Scottish coats of arms or ceramic mugs, he had decided to celebrate southwest Virginia culture and covered the walls with rusty old railroad equipment and farming tools.

When I asked why a bar—excuse me, I mean *pub*—with a Celtic name didn't have a Celtic atmosphere, Dave said that he had named Rigby's after a Beatles song about lonely people needing a place to belong.

"Names have power," Dave had gone on to inform me, and I had listened gravely as if this were a revelation.

Speaking of names, "John Charming" is not what it reads on my current driver's license. In fact, about the only thing accurate on my current license is the part where it says that I'm black-haired and blue-eyed. I'm six foot one instead of six foot two and about seventy-five pounds lighter than the 250 pounds indicated on my identification. But I do kind of look the way the man pictured on my license might look if Trevor A. Barnes had lost that much weight and cut his hair short and shaved off his beard. Oh, and if he were still alive.

And no, I didn't kill the man whose identity I had assumed, in case you're wondering. Well, not the first time anyway.

Anyhow, I had recently been forced to leave Alaska and start a new life of my own, and in David Suggs I had found an employer who wasn't going to be too thorough with his background checks. My current goal was to work for Dave for at least one fiscal year and not draw any attention to myself.

Which was why I was not happy to see the blonde.

For her part, the blonde didn't seem too happy to see me either. Sig focused on me immediately. People always gave me a quick flickering glance when they walked into the bar—excuse me, the pub—but the first thing they really checked out was the clientele. Their eyes were sometimes predatory, sometimes cautious, sometimes hopeful, often tired, but they only returned to me after being disappointed. Sig's gaze, however, centered on me like the oncoming lights of a train—assuming train lights have slight bags underneath them and make you want to flex surreptitiously. Those same startlingly blue eyes widened, and her body went still for a moment.

Whatever had triggered her alarms, Sig hesitated, visibly debating whether to approach and talk to me. She didn't hesitate for long, though—I got the impression that she rarely hesitated for long—and chose to go find herself a table.

Now, it was a Thursday night in April, and Rigby's was not empty. Clayburg is host to a small private college named Stillwaters University, one of those places where parents pay more money than they should to get an education for children with mediocre high school records, and underachievers with upper-middle-class parents tend to do a lot of heavy drinking. This is why Rigby's manages to stay in business. Small bars with farming implements on the walls don't really draw huge college crowds, but the more popular bars tend to stay packed, and Rigby's does attract an odd combination of local rednecks and students with a sense of irony. So when a striking six-foot blonde who wasn't an obvious transvestite sat down in the middle of the bar, there were people around to notice.

Even Sandra, a nineteen-year-old waitress who considers customers an unwelcome distraction from covert texting, noticed the newcomer. She walked up to Sig promptly instead of making Renee, an older waitress and Rigby's de facto manager, chide her into action.

For the next hour I pretended to ignore the new arrival while focusing on her intently. I listened in—my hearing is as well developed as my sense of smell—while several patrons tried to introduce themselves. Sig seemed to have a knack for knowing how to discourage each would-be player as fast as possible.

She told suitors that she wanted to be up-front about her sex change operation because she was tired of having it cause problems when her lovers found out later, or she told them that she liked only black men, or young men, or older men who made more than seventy thousand dollars a year. She told them that what really turned her on was men who were willing to have sex with other men while she watched. She mentioned one man's wife by name, and when the weedy-looking grad student doing a John Lennon impersonation tried the sensitive-poet approach, she challenged him to an arm-wrestling contest. He stared at her, sitting there exuding athleticism, confidence, and health—three things he was noticeably lacking—and chose to be offended rather than take her up on it.

There was at least one woman who seemed interested in Sig as well, a cute sandy-haired college student who was tall and willowy, but when it comes to picking up strangers, women are generally less likely to go on a kamikaze mission than men. The young woman kept looking over at Sig's table, hoping to establish some kind of meaningful eye contact, but Sig wasn't making any.

Sig wasn't looking at me either, but she held herself at an angle that kept me in her peripheral vision at all times.

For my part, I spent the time between drink orders trying to figure out exactly what Sig was. She definitely wasn't undead. She wasn't a half-blood Fae either, though her scent wasn't entirely dissimilar. Elf smell isn't something you forget, sweet and decadent, with a hint of honey blossom and distant ocean. There aren't any full-blooded Fae left, of course—they packed their bags and went back to Fairyland a long time ago—but don't mention that to any of the mixed human descendants that the elves left behind. Elvish half-breeds tend to be somewhat sensitive on that particular subject. They can be real bastards about being bastards.

I would have been tempted to think that Sig was an angel, except that I've never heard of anyone I'd trust ever actually seeing a real angel. God is as much an article of faith in my world as he, she, we, they, or it is in yours.

Stumped, I tried to approach the problem by figuring out what Sig was doing there. She didn't seem to enjoy the ginger ale she had ordered—didn't seem to notice it at all, just sipped from it perfunctorily. There was something wary and expectant about her body language, and she had positioned herself so that she was in full view of the front door. She could have just been meeting someone, but I had a feeling that she was looking for someone or something specific by using herself as bait…but as to what and why and to what end, I had no idea. Sex, food, or revenge seemed the most likely choices.

I was still mulling that over when the vampire walked in.

VISIT THE ORBIT BLOG AT

www.orbitbooks.net

FEATURING

BREAKING NEWS
FORTHCOMING RELEASES
LINKS TO AUTHOR SITES
EXCLUSIVE INTERVIEWS
EARLY EXTRACTS

AND COMMENTARY FROM OUR EDITORS

WITH REGULAR UPDATES FROM OUR TEAM,
ORBITBOOKS.NET IS YOUR SOURCE
FOR ALL THINGS ORBITAL.

WHILE YOU'RE THERE, JOIN OUR E-MAIL LIST
TO RECEIVE INFORMATION ON SPECIAL OFFERS,
GIVEAWAYS, AND MORE.

imagine. explore. engage.